"BEFORE THE GAMES BEGIN, THERE IS ONE BIT OF BUSINESS THAT MUST BE COMPLETED."

■ ■ ■ ■ ■ ■ ■ ■ ■ ■ ■ ■ ■ ■ ■ ■

The regal voice intruded on Braldt's thoughts, speaking in imperious tones through the silver disc fastened to his skull. "As you will notice, each team consists of five members. Your first task will be the elimination of one member of your team. That choice we leave up to you..."

A loud outcry rose from the armed gathering while others brandished their weapons.

"You will choose the member to be eliminated, or we will make the choice for you," the speaker said, his voice growing harsh and cold.

Randi moved to Braldt's side, pressing her lithe form against him. Allo and Septua drew in as well, until the four of them stood back to back in a tight formation. Marin was the odd man out.

"Marin, we do not have to do as they say," said Braldt. "Let us fight together. They cannot make us fight each other if we refuse."

Marin was crouching low, trident jabbing forward like a tongue of a striking snake, nearly touching Braldt's chest. In his other hand his net swirled slowly. If he heard Braldt's words, he gave no sign...

■ ■ ■ ■ ■ ■ ■ ■ ■ ■ ■ ■

ALSO BY ROSE ESTES

THE HUNTER

THE HUNTER ON ARENA

BY ROSE ESTES

WARNER BOOKS

A Time Warner Company

WARNER BOOKS EDITION

Questar is a registered trademark of Warner Books, Inc.

Cover illustration by Clyde Caldwell
Cover design by Don Puckey

Warner Books, Inc.
666 Fifth Avenue
New York, N.Y. 10103

A Time Warner Company

Printed in the United States of America

First Printing: May, 1991

10 9 8 7 6 5 4 3 2 1

1

Falling. It was not unlike the sudden, frightening sensation of falling that sometimes comes with sleep, followed by the immediate jerk of wakening. This time, however, there was no salvation to be found in wakening or at the end of the dream, for the endless drop persisted, accompanied by strange, flashing lights and a roaring blur of vision and sound that so confused Braldt he was unable to tell whether he was sleeping or awake.

He tried desperately to grab onto something, to catch hold, to stop the awful whirling that sickened his senses, but his hands caught nothing but air. He closed his eyes, trying to steady himself, to take stock. Where was he and what was happening? Slowly his senses cleared, and with an intense concentration of effort, knowing it was vitally important, he recalled the strange series of events which had brought him to this point.

He was Braldt the Hunter, warrior protector of the Duroni, chosen to follow Auslic as High Chief. But Auslic had fallen ill, and Braldt and his adopted brother Carn had been instructed to enter the Forbidden Lands to acquire a medicine which would heal Auslic. This command had been given to them by the high priest and was

1

very unusual in that no one, not even the warrior protectors, had ever been allowed to enter the Forbidden Lands.

Their directive was strange enough, but many things had been peculiar in recent days. The God Lights, the bright display of colors that had always leaped and danced in the night skies over the Forbidden Lands, had mysteriously ceased, revealing a view of stars never before glimpsed.

There was also the matter of the karks, a lowly and unintelligent race of beast creatures who had begun to invade Duroni lands, leaving violence and death in their wake.

Shortly after entering the Forbidden Lands, Carn and his sister Keri (who had joined them on their journey) were captured by karks. Braldt and Beast, a half-tamed lupebeast pup who was Braldt's loyal companion, had to join forces with Sytha Trubal, a kark princess, in an attempt to save Carn and Keri from death.

Compromises were reached with the karks who referred to themselves as Madrelli and were far from the savages the Duroni priests had led Braldt and the others to believe. Theirs was an amazing story, for they claimed that they were visitors from another world. They had been the minions of a race they called "the Masters," who had manipulated their genetics, raising them from semi-intelligent, dextrous animals to reasoning, thinking beings.

But still, they were controlled by the Masters, their every move overseen by machine-like beings known as the hard ones who controlled them through the administration of a pill which maintained their level of intelligence, without which they would lapse into an animalistic state. But their most vulnerable points were their ears which contained fragile, delicate implants which were surgically linked directly into the pain receptors of the Madrelli's brains. Should they offend or disobey their rulers, punishment by means of hideous pain was their instant reward.

Shortly before Braldt's arrival, the Madrelli had been told that their mining efforts were no longer cost effective, and that the planet was to be abandoned and destroyed so that the mineral the Masters sought could be more easily extracted from its ruins.

The Madrelli had other plans, however, for they had found a shrub on the planet which duplicated the chemical which was so necessary to their survival. They had come to love the planet and to hate their Masters who regarded them as little more than valued slaves. Seeking an alliance with the Duroni, their efforts had been met with violence and death. It was decided that the only way to prevent the Masters from carrying out their plan was to sabotage the mechanism that allowed their ships to come and go unseen by the Duroni and other tribes that roamed the planet. These were the Duroni's "God Lights," actually no more than an electrical aurora that masked the coming and going of the great space vessels.

Braldt and Keri were shaken by the Madrelli's words, disturbed by the realization that their own lives had been manipulated as well, for it seemed apparent that there was some collusion between their priests and the Masters. Their entire religion, based on the cycles of the moon, was called into doubt and it seemed that many of their beliefs and taboos were conveniently meshed with the needs of the Masters.

Carn alone had disagreed, maintaining that the en-

tire tale was a devious kark trick. Braldt and Keri had
begged the Madrelli to help them find the medicine that
would save their chieftain's life, but the Madrelli were
reluctant to do so, for the medicine was to be found in
the very chamber that controlled the arrival and departure
of the Masters. And it was that very lever that created
the masking aurora that Braldt had been commanded by
the priests to pull. The conflict was obvious.

In the end, the Madrelli won their alliance, and it
was agreed that a Madrelli known as Batta Flor would
accompany them into the mountain. They would make
their way to the heart of the mountain, and if such a thing
was possible, they would retrieve the medicine kit, but
not pull the lever.

The journey had been long and difficult and danger
had dogged their heels. Carn had become separated from
them, and after being severely traumatized, had experienced
a religious vision wherein he imagined that Mother Moon
had spoken to him directly, commanding him to serve her.

Braldt and Keri had survived, and had discovered
the depth of their feelings for one another along the way.
Batta Flor had not been so fortunate. The Madrelli's
sabotage had blocked the flow of a subterranean river
which now seeped into the heart of the volcano, causing
a tremendous build-up of pressure which threatened to
destroy the mountain. Quakes had become a constant
danger and Batta Flor was seriously injured when his ear
was nearly severed by a falling panel. This was far more
than a cosmetic injury, for the delicate tubes in the
Madrelli ears controlled their balance, equilibrium, intelligence, and even the ability to feel pain and procreate.

Batta Flor, who had hoped to win Sytha Trubal after the completion of the mission, had been strangely calm in the wake of the accident and had brushed aside their concerns, determined to press ahead. They had honored his wishes and found their way to the flooded control chamber. Braldt and the lupebeast had gained access to the chamber, and through the use of explosives had diverted the flow of the underground river.

Their joy was shortlived, however, for even as they gained the precious medicine which would restore Auslic's health, a crazed Carn had appeared, and despite their horrified cries had pulled the lever.

The streaming blur of lights, the dizzying sense of falling, the roar of heavens in his ears . . . it was no dream, but the result of Carn's pulling the lever. What did it mean? Was he dead and on his way to take his place with the gods? No, one could not be nauseous and dead at the same time. And if the Madrelli were right, the gods of his youth were but figments of another's imagination. Who were these Masters and what reason could they have for inventing a religion?

Braldt fought off the taste of sickness that threatened to overcome him and felt for his weapons. If and when the journey came to an end, he would not be taken unaware. His short sword was gone, the scabbard empty, but his knife was still in its sheath and he gripped the handle tightly. He wondered what had become of Beast and Batta Flor and more importantly, Keri. He tried to look around, but any movement only seemed to make matters worse, sending him careening off balance, head over heels, spinning round and round until he lost momentum and bobbed to a halt like a twig in a stream. He had seen enough to know that he was alone. The thought should have comforted him, but instead he was swept by an incredible feeling of loss. Where was he? What was happening to him and would he ever again see those whom he loved?

The turn had revealed a long, dark tunnel, black as the darkest of nights, stretching out behind him. This darkness was surrounded by a corona of bright lights, bright as stars interspersed with wisps of color, the rosy pink of sunrise, the pale, pale blue of a freshly washed sky and the palest yellow of delicate, mountain flowers. And nowhere had there been any hint of solidity or end.

And then it seemed to him that he was falling even faster, the sensation even more intense than it had been. Pressure began to build inside his head and chest and he wondered if he were about to die. His eyes were all but closed against the fierce pull, and through watering lids he perceived the darkness before him grow smaller as though he were hurtling through space into an opening too small to receive him.

Fear fought with rage and nausea and he gripped the hilt of his blade even more tightly, wishing that if he must die, he could do so fighting an opponent of flesh and substance rather than an enemy that could not be seen or felt.

The roaring grew louder as the lights flashed past, searing his eyes and ears with a blaze of brilliant sound. *The music of the stars*, he thought, as consciousness left his body and darkness exploded inside his mind.

2

The end of the dream state came swiftly and without warning. One minute Braldt was falling, surrounded by the circle of bright lights and the loud roaring, and in the next, abruptly and without transition, it was over. There was a hard, bone-jarring thump that stunned him and emptied the breath from his body. When he shook the dizziness from his head and the ringing in his ears diminished, Braldt found that he was sprawled on a hard, metallic floor that mirrored his ungainly posture in the silvery shine of its gleaming surface.

Still dazed by the disconcerting turn of events, Braldt nonetheless took note of the unusual floor. He stroked the cold material, appraising and admiring its apparent strength, surely stronger than the bronze blades to which he was accustomed, but such contemplation had to be put aside until other, more important questions had been answered. Such as where he was, what had happened to him, and where were Batta Flor, Keri, and Carn, as well as the lupebeast pup whose loyal presence he sorely missed. Gripping his knife firmly, he rose to a crouch and looked around him, searching for some of the answers to his questions.

There was little to be seen. He was in a chamber no

more than twelve feet square with bare walls constructed of a firm, ungiving, non-metal material. Braldt withdrew his fingers and wiped them on his cloak, grimacing with distaste at the feel of the substance, disliking the Master's choice of building materials. Other than a doorway set in one wall, there was nothing else to be seen or learned from the room.

Although it was not to his liking, the appearance of the room was strangely reassuring, for it was not unlike other chambers that he and his companions had discovered in the endless labyrinth of passages beneath the mountain. Perplexed by the question of how he had come to be there, Braldt hurried to the doorway, calling out Keri's name, hoping to hear her voice, to find her somewhere nearby.

Braldt's heart was pounding and his mouth was dry, and he realized how desperately he wanted to see Keri, to hold her against him and know that she was all right. Disappointment struck hard as he reached the door and looked out, seeing nothing but another stretch of empty corridor, unbroken by doors or the sight of any living creature.

Despair broke over him in waves and the feeling of hope retreated. Where were the others? Braldt made his way down the corridor, determined to find them. Eyes fixed forward, he took no notice of the rows of tiny lights implanted in the walls at waist level, nor comprehended the ramifications as he moved through the seemingly innocent lines of light, interrupting the flow of their all but invisible beams.

*   *   *

Other eyes, however, had no difficulty noticing and correctly interpreting the message. "He is in the passage," intoned a voice that resonated oddly as cleverly replicated metal fingers made delicate adjustments to a knob. A large screen crackled and leaped to life, and Braldt appeared on the face of the monitor, totally unaware that his every move was being observed.

A hand, completely human in appearance, wearing a large, signet ring set with a deep, green stone came to rest on the shoulder of the robotic figure seated before the console. There was the deep release of a sigh, the sound of relief, perhaps even satisfaction of a worrisome thing reaching a satisfactory conclusion. The hand tightened on the robot's shoulder and gave it a tiny shake. "Good. It is done. And now, let the trials begin."

Braldt was troubled. There was no answer to his calls. Either Keri and Carn and Batta Flor had somehow been injured when the lever was thrown, or he had fallen farther than he had first thought. But Beast's hearing was acute, and if he were anywhere within hearing range, the pup would find him.

But there was another matter that troubled Braldt even more. The corridor did not resemble any passage they had traveled in their search for the flooded chamber. Furthermore, it was undamaged, with no sign of flooding or violent, seismic activity which had been their fearful companion for so long.

Troubling as these thoughts were, Braldt was forced to put them aside, for a new, more immediate danger had presented itself. The floor was becoming hot.

At first it had been barely noticeable, a mere hint of warmth, certainly not unpleasant. But the temperature had increased steadily until it could be felt even through the thick layers of hardened leather from which the soles of his sandals had been fashioned. Furthermore, the smooth walls that lined the corridor had given way to stone. Small, rounded stones, immense boulders, and craggy blocks rose from the metallic floor to the ceiling, which now held the tiny lights which cast a dim light, scarcely brighter than stars, in the night sky.

The floor had not changed in appearance in any way, but there was no doubt that it was radiating heat and would soon be too hot to stand on. Braldt could see no doors, no exit anywhere; the corridor stretched on indefinitely until it faded into darkness at the edge of his vision. He had no reason to believe that the room from which he had emerged would offer any sort of sanctuary; there would be no help from that quarter. The walls were at arm's length on either side. The floor was now painfully hot and wisps of steam were rising from the edges.

Braldt's first thought was to cling to the wall and make his way from rock to rock, but this ploy proved impossible, for many of the rocks were too smooth or set flush against the wall and offered no purchase. But there was no more time for puzzling the matter through—it had become mandatory for him to get off the floor immediately, for the heat had grown far too intense; he could feel the soles of his sandals cracking and breaking apart.

Without conscious thought or decision, Braldt stepped up onto a small outcrop that was barely large enough to hold one of his feet while bracing himself against the far wall with his hands. Slowly, carefully, he scraped the disintegrating sandals from his feet, and with his feet free to find their own holds, crept up the wall, hands on one side, feet on the other, until he was safely braced four feet above the floor which now glowed a dull, cherry red.

It was a difficult but not impossible position to maintain, one that he had used in the past while rock climbing in the mountains. So long as the distance between the walls remained constant and he had the strength to support himself, he would be safe.

The journey, such as it was, continued for an interminable period of time, measured only by the degree of his exhaustion. For even though Braldt was in prime physical condition, the activity he was engaged in was most unusual, putting an unfamiliar strain upon his muscles as he scuttled sideways—hand, foot, hand, foot—resting only when the occasional large stone provided adequate support. The instant relief which resulted was followed by an involuntary trembling of overstressed, aching muscles. Then, far too soon, the journey resumed, for to stop too long was to risk exhausted muscles locking up, stiffening, refusing to function. And beneath him, the floor grew hotter still, now a bright, fiery crimson from which rolled wave after wave of blast-furnace heat.

It was after one such brief rest that it happened. A sense of dizziness came over him and he braced himself hard against the stones on either side, fearing that he was about to fall. However, the whirling sensation was not a trick of his mind, but reality. The fiery floor suddenly appeared above him, and he shrank back despite himself, fearing that it was about to fall on top of him. In doing so, he lost his hold; his fingers, raw and bleeding from the constant abrasion of the rough rock, were unable to support his weight.

He fell, twisting in mid-air, throwing out his arms to catch himself, expecting to land on what had been the ceiling only seconds before, the little lights shining up through the darkness below him, but then, an instant before he landed, the lights and the ceiling fell away and once again he found himself falling into nothingness.

Despair fought with confusion as well as anger, although against whom or what he could not have said, but it was then that he first began to suspect that someone or something was purposely manipulating him, and a resolve grew within him to fight back, not to give in, or to allow them to win, to defeat him. He was Braldt the Hunter, a warrior protector of the Duroni. He would not be vanquished by unseen enemies who played upon his fears of the unknown. Somehow he would survive.

He had half expected to find himself surrounded once again by the whirling tunnel of bright lights, but such was not the case. Turning in mid-air, he suddenly found himself in yet another corridor. Startled, he barely had time to take a deep breath before he smacked face down in a roaring maelstrom of water which raced through the narrow channel formed by the metal walls. Instantly, he was seized by the turbulent water and flung headlong, only to be pulled beneath the surface by the foaming torrent. He surfaced briefly and sucked in a gasp of air, as well as a mouthful of water, before being dragged under yet again. The current was as fierce below as above, but lacked the violent turbulence which resulted from currents crashing into the walls and rebounding.

The walls were smooth, without purchase, and he began to grow desperate for it was all but impossible to take in air without swallowing equal amounts of water. Then his fingers found a seam, a narrow, raised edge of the wall, and he clung to it in desperation, meeting the flow of water head on so as to give himself the most leverage; to have turned the other way was to risk being washed away. It was not much, merely a fingerhold, but it was enough to allow him to raise high enough up out of the water to breathe. It also afforded him the first look at his surroundings.

Initially, it appeared to be no different than the first corridor, other than the race of water. Then, glancing up, he saw that the ceiling was crisscrossed with numerous, thin beams of light. None was even half as wide as his littlest finger, but all of them shone with an unnatural intensity. Above the lights, there appeared to be some sort of metal grid, almost ladderlike in design, perhaps a catwalk that would allow access to the flooded corridor from which he had first fallen.

His mind racing, Braldt was determined to pull himself from the water and reach the catwalk, although such a thing was surely not intended by whomever or whatever had constructed these unwelcome challenges. Then, perhaps he would have a few surprises of his own.

By some miracle he had not been parted from his cloak which was still draped over his shoulder, plastered against his body by the press of water. With some degree of difficulty, he was able to pull it free and hold it above the flood. This required that he retain his grip on the crevice with but a single hand. More than once he was nearly pulled away by the force of the water, but he was determined and fueled by anger, and in the end he was able to maintain his tenuous grip while balancing the sodden bundle of material in his hand. Steadying himself, he flung the cloak upward while holding onto the end. The cloak shot upward, but fell short of the ceiling and dropped back into the water, where once again the current did its best to pull it from his grasp.

Over and over he tried, but to no avail, and despite his resolve, found that he was losing strength. The water, while not actually cold, was chill, and by drawing off his body heat it was leaving him weak and shaking, barely able to cling to his position much less fling the heavy cloth upward. But he would not give up, for he suspected that to do so would spell his doom.

Braldt wondered if those who had fashioned this torture were watching, unseen. His teeth bared in a grimace of hatred at the thought and the flash of anger gave him the strength to fling the robe farther than before, and he saw that it would reach the ceiling. With luck it would wrap around! . . . Zooks, what was this! As the robe rose upward it crossed the path of one of the bright, shining lights and the light lanced through it, shearing the robe as cleanly as a knife stroke! The robe dropped into the water and was carried away instantly before Braldt's stunned eyes. The uppermost bit of cloth fell back through the grid of lights and was sliced apart by the crisscross beams, the remaining bits fluttering down to the water like damaged butterflies to be instantly swallowed by the maelstrom.

The lights . . . slicing the robe. Braldt swallowed hard. It could just as easily have been flesh instead of fabric. He looked up at the web of lights, noticing for the first time how there was no space large enough for his body to pass through the grid of bright beams, realizing, if not understanding, that the lights were weapons more dangerous than any blade he had ever known.

How could he win against such an adversary? "Come out!" he screamed. "Show yourself! How can I fight what I cannot see? Come out and fight me fairly like a man and I will kill you!"

The water swelled around him, flowing with an even greater force than before, and as his fingers lost their tenuous grip on the tiny edge and he was swept away by the torrent, it seemed to him that he heard a chuckle of laughter.

3

Water poured down Braldt's throat and seeped into his nostrils. He choked and coughed, gasping for air, and the powerful current seized its advantage and flung him headlong into the wall. Stunned, he slid into the depths and found almost by accident that here the current ran slower, with none of the surface violence. With luck, he found another crevice which allowed him to rise and fill his lungs with air, then descend to the more peaceful depths and make his way to the next handhold. In this odd manner, Braldt was able to progress, swimming along with the flow of the water, rising whenever possible to search for a way out. No such option presented itself nor did the bright grid of lights diminish.

After a time, it seemed that the rate of the flow was growing more swift and it became increasingly difficult to maintain his grip when he surfaced for air. Braldt grew worried and he wondered what new torment would be thrust upon him and how he would find the strength to fight it. Then, before his exhausted mind could conjure up any new horrors, the current suddenly plunged downward, wrapping him firmly in its grip and carrying him with it, helpless to resist.

He felt as though the life was being sucked out of

him. The pressure was intense, squeezing him on all sides, immobilizing the rise and fall of his chest. Blackness and pain were everywhere, shot through with lines of crimson. He wondered if he were dying and an image of Keri came to him. The thought of her gave him new strength, for he was unwilling to die now that he realized the depth of his love for her.

The weight of the water was like a giant fist closing around his chest, holding him tightly, suffocating him. He yearned for the cold, sharp sting of air, and then, as though his prayers had been answered, he felt himself released, shooting upward, carried along by a great outwelling of water rushing toward the surface. He caroomed out of the water, sucking precious air down into his starved lungs, gasping and choking as he fell back into the water, limbs flailing, unwilling to be swallowed up again.

Gradually his panic diminished as he realized that the water was calm and placid and no longer appeared to offer a threat. Floating atop the still waters, he saw by the dim light that filled the chamber that he was in the center of a large pool of water contained by naturally formed rock walls. He swam to the edge of the pool and hoisted himself out onto a rough ledge with the last of his strength and lay there, studying his surroundings while regaining his strength.

There were no bright beams of light crisscrossing the chamber, nor was there any other sign of danger. Braldt was not fooled into relaxing his guard. Whatever this place was, it was no haven of safety.

The water eddied gently as it lapped against the

edge of the pool, then slowly slid along to the right. Following the current with his eyes, Braldt could see that there appeared to be a stream of water flowing out of the chamber; it was from this exit that the diffuse light emerged. Chilled by his long immersion in the water, Braldt could feel his muscles tightening, growing stiff, and he knew that despite his exhaustion, he had to move now or soon he would be unable to rise.

Creeping along the edge of the chamber, he made his way toward the stream of water as it flowed out. Now he could see that the water ran between two steep banks and then passed through a narrow aperture. It was from this opening that the light came.

It was a perfect trap. If there was danger waiting for him, it would be found on the other side of the narrow channel, but it appeared to be the only way out of the chamber other than the way he had arrived. From the ache in his muscles, Braldt realized that he did not have the necessary strength to fight the current, had he wished to do so. He could not stay in the cave; it would serve no purpose, and the longer he worried about what might be on the other side, the harder it would be to act.

Braldt tested the stream and found that it flowed deep between the ledges that contained it. The ledges were broad, broad enough to walk along or cling to as one crawled through the opening out of the darkness of the chamber and into the bright light streaming from the other side. The light would be blinding after the darkness of the cave. Braldt had no way of knowing for certain that an enemy waited on the other side of the wall, but all his senses and his training told him that it was so.

The only thing to do was the last thing that was expected. Taking a deep breath to fill his lungs with air, Braldt submerged and dove for the bottom, allowing the current to guide him as he passed through the narrow channel into the light beyond. He did not surface then, but swam along the bottom until his lungs were screaming for air. Only then did he reach for handholds to pull himself slowly to the top, permitting only his nostrils to break water. Once his lungs had ceased burning, he lowered himself and swam along the bottom until his outstretched fingers bumped into a solid wall and he could go no further.

Quick, cautious trips to the surface allowed him to spy out the situation. Once again he was in a chamber fashioned of rough boulders. The stream flowed through the center of the chamber; from a wide, circular disturbance on the far side, it appeared to exit through some underground device. Braldt had no desire to explore this avenue; he was more than ready to leave the water. This cavern, with its broad, flat, hard-packed earth lying on either side of the stream, was larger than the room he had left.

But it was neither the whirlpool nor the earthen floor that attracted his attention. He had not been wrong to sense a trap, for poised at the edge of the water flow, far enough back so that its shadow would not announce its presence, was a creature such as Braldt had never seen before—a creature straight out of a nightmare.

It was tall and broad, taller than Braldt by a full head, and its shoulde were half again as wide. Its arms were long and muscular and its chest corded with sinew.

It had no skin, but was covered with dark, green scales, and a ridged crest of some hard, horny substance ran from the top of its narrow skull to a point midway down its back. Its hands and feet were webbed and the digits tipped with long, sharp, ivory-colored claws. It wore no clothes other than a sword belt strapped crossways about its chest; a long knife hung from this belt. The sword was gripped in its hands, cleaving fashion, above the watery opening. The hideous creature was bathed in a pale, glowing light that followed its every move. Braldt traced the light to its source and found that it had its origin high up on the rough, rock walls, emerging from a perfectly round aperture.

Braldt was tired. He had no wish to fight the creature, but it appeared that there was no way to escape it. He pulled himself up out of the water slowly and crept toward the enemy, searching for a weapon, for even his knife had been lost to the raging current. There was nothing, other than the occasional rock, and he picked up several, although what possible effect they would have against this armored monster, he could not have said. His only advantage was surprise. And then, as though growing restless, still unaware of his presence, the hideous creature lowered its head and peered into the water, probing the depths with its blade. It was too great an advantage to miss. Braldt rushed forward, abandoning all pretense of stealth, catching the beast off guard and more importantly, off balance. As it turned its head, startled at the sound behind it, Braldt hit it at chest level. It was like running into a stone wall, but his impetus and the element of surprise combined were enough to throw the creature off balance and slowly, waving its arms futilely, it toppled into the water.

Braldt wasted no time. Before the monster could regain its balance or its senses, Braldt wrested the sword from its grasp and plunged it into its body. Then, to his astonishment, the creature vanished! It did not writhe in agony or collapse amid gouts of blood as might be expected, it simply vanished! One moment it was there and the next it was gone, leaving Braldt standing there holding a sword and feeling extremely befuddled. For a moment, he wondered if he had imagined the whole thing, but there was the sword in his hands, reassuringly heavy, gleaming brightly along the honed edges, solid evidence that he had not dreamed the monster. Even as he stood looking down at the sword, he heard a low, rumbling growl behind him. Cold dread filled his chest, and gripping the blade, he turned. There, standing no more than six paces behind him, was yet another horrific apparition. Even as he wondered how it could have approached without being heard, the thing began to move toward him.

Braldt backed away slowly, edging the stream, his feet sliding along the smooth surface of the rock ledge as he gauged this new threat. It resembled a lupebeast in that it was wolf-like with double rows of jagged fangs set in its elongated muzzle. Its coarse fur was mottled black and gray and brown, and it sported a long, whip-like tail that curled up beneath its belly. As with lupebeasts, the thing was able to walk on hind legs and its head was even with Braldt's. But unlike a lupebeast, the creature clasped a double-edged sword in its paws and from the manner in which it swung the blade in great scything motions, there was no doubt that the beast knew how to use it. Its eyes glittered darkly with intelligence and hatred as it advanced steadily. The first monster had been dispatched with relative ease. Braldt feared this one would be more difficult.

The contest began and it was as Braldt thought; his every move was matched by the hideous creature, in a classic, precise technique that mirrored his own training. In fact, the creature matched him blow for blow, wearing him down while itself exhibiting no signs of weariness.

Already tired from battling the fierce currents, Braldt knew he could not continue the battle for long. Swordplay, while looking graceful and light to the casual observer, was hard work that quickly exhausted the participants as they wielded the heavy blades. And yet, despite his determination, Braldt could seize no advantage; it was as though the creature knew his every move before he made it.

Braldt began to wonder how it was that the thing knew how to fight him so precisely. There were many different forms of swordplay and no two masters followed the same technique. It was almost as though this creature had trained under Braldt's master...or...a startling thought came to him. Perhaps it was exactly that, a mirror image of his own efforts. He feinted to the right. The creature feinted as well. He swung his blade overhead only to be matched by an identical move by his opponent and the two blades clanged off each other with a bright flash of sparks.

Braldt circled out of his opponent's reach while his

questing eyes sought and found what he suspected he would find—a pale aura of light bathing the creature. Tracing the light to its source, Braldt saw that it originated as a narrow beam from a tiny opening set between two boulders high on the rocky wall of the chamber.

Anger burst over him in a fiery rush, and ignoring the sword-bearing wolfthing, he turned and ran toward the beam of light, smashing at the tiny opening with the hilt of his sword. There was the sound of breakage, a gratifying tinkling, and the feel of something shattering beneath the force of his blows. He heard the creature grunt and growl behind him, felt its paw close upon his shoulder, felt its hot slaver drool down upon his back, and then the light blinked out and there was nothing. Nothing at all. Braldt turned and found that he was alone. The monster was gone, vanished as though it had never existed. And his hands were empty; the sword was gone as well.

Braldt slumped against the wall, exhausted, allowing his eyes to close, admitting the bone-deep fatigue that filled his body. Thoughts cartwheeled through his head, filling him with confusion. Where was he and what was happening? He was being manipulated, that much was clear, but by whom or what—that was the question. Weariness seeped into his limbs, weighing them down, and his eyes closed as though of their own accord, even though he knew that the danger had not been eliminated with the destruction of the mirror beasts. His breathing slowed and Braldt fell into a deep and bottomless sleep.

It seemed to him that he dreamed, but it was an odd dream, like nothing he had ever experienced before. It seemed that he was floating bodiless, hovering just below the rough ceiling of the cave, looking down on himself as he slept. As he watched, the walls seemed to open behind his somnolent body and a host of monsters crept forth. He counted sixteen in all, each more hideous than the last. The wolfthing and crested lizard were there as well.

Strangely, there was no feeling of danger, rather, one of gentle concern, almost pity. He knew in some vague way that his amorphous self had no way of communicating with his slumbering body, to warn it of danger, to urge it to waken, but somehow, there was no feeling of need. As he watched, the creatures lifted his unresisting form between them and carried it away. As they vanished, his vision dimmed and he knew no more.

4

Consciousness returned with a sudden, swift rush. Braldt found that he was being carried down a long, brightly lit corridor constructed of the same smooth, shiny, metallic substance as the room he had first entered in this gauntlet of dangers. He studied his captors from beneath his lids while still feigning sleep. He could feel a number of hands or paws supporting his body, yet he could see only the two creatures who carried his legs; he dared not open his eyes further for he did not wish to reveal that he had wakened.

Neither of those who gripped his legs were human. The thing on the left was squat and blocky with rough, warty skin the color of ochre mud. Its head sat on its broad, muscular shoulders like a boulder. It had a brief, sloping forehead, tiny, round eyes, and no chin to speak of. The entire front of its face was squeezed into a snout that ended in soft, flexible flanges of flesh that probed the air restlessly. The pig-like creature wore two broad, leather straps crisscrossed over its chest and shoulders, and narrow, leather bands held a variety of swords and knives which glinted sharply under the bright lights. The handles were smooth and well worn with use. The creature wore nothing on its ruddy body other than a small, leather loincloth, and its rust-colored flesh rippled with the play of muscles beneath the thick, lumpy skin.

The creature to its right was little better. This was another lizard-type being, but shorter and tougher looking than Braldt's first opponent. This one was dark brown in color; the horny, segmented plates that defined its various body parts were burnished a deep mahogany as though the creature spent hours oiling and polishing itself. Its head was broad and flat, its eyes placed on either side of the flat muzzle and hooded by layers of armored scales. The scaly muzzle was edged with sharp, triangular fangs both top and bottom, and the jaws were held slightly agape, revealing a slit tongue that flickered in and out with every breath. Its back was covered with the same heavy, ridged scales and bore a complex pattern ranging from a delicate shade of cream to darkest brown. The mottled complexity of the shadowy pattern deceived the eye and Braldt guessed that it was designed as protective camouflage for the creature's natural habitat. It wore no clothing, and so far as Braldt could see, carried no weapon. But its digits, all eight of them, were tipped with long, curved, sharp claws that could rip a man from chin to belly as easily as it might gut a fish. Further, the top of its flat head, the length of its spine and broad tail, the crest of its shoulders, and the backs of its hands all bore a prominent ridge of sharp spikes as sharp and dangerous as any knife. The creature had no need for armament, its body provided all it would ever require.

Braldt could not see who belonged to any of the other hands that gripped him, but from the murmur of voices around him, he knew that his initial count of sixteen was not far from the mark.

The voices told him nothing and revealed no new information, for they were a babble of unfamiliar sounds that made absolutely no sense to him. He wondered how it was that they were able to understand each other, for no two of them seemed to utter the same sorts of sounds. It was then, as the two creatures holding his legs turned to speak to each other, gesturing ahead, that Braldt saw, for the first time, the tiny, silver circles embedded in the flesh between their eyes. It startled him so that he jerked violently, and the swift movement of their passage faltered as his captors turned to stare at him with suspicion, while reaching for their various weapons. Braldt sighed and allowed himself to go limp, pretending that his action had been but an involuntary sleep motion. He could feel the weight of their gaze resting on him speculatively and he prayed they would believe the ruse, for the odds were greatly against him.

They spoke among themselves and one of them laughed, a harsh, braying sound with no humor. Reassured, they continued on, jogging along the narrow corridor, bearing him toward he knew not what. A short time later they stopped, and Braldt could feel an air of nervousness, palpable in the small enclosure, rising from their bodies like the stink of fear. There was a shuffling of feet, and then the armored beast banged upon the wall with his spiked fist. Bright light streamed outward as a door slid open, words were exchanged, and they entered, all talk silenced, and Braldt could feel their tension through their grip. He gathered himself, alarmed by their fear, ready to act if the need arose.

Then, abruptly, in response to another guttural command, he was deposited on a long, cold, metal slab with bright lights beating down on him from the ceiling, and abandoned. The multitude of voices faded away, leaving him alone and unguarded, and strangely, rather than relief, he felt a cold shiver of fear trace itself down his backbone. The beasts had meant him no real harm; they were neutral parties in whatever game was being played, perhaps even unwilling pawns themselves. With their departure, Braldt felt even more alone than before.

He calmed his mind and forced himself to empty it of fear, allowing his senses to probe the room. There was a soft, continuous murmur, not human, not alive. There was the susurration of breathing, some hoarse and shallow, some soft and deep. Occasionally, there was a thump, then a deep hum followed by a circulating of fresh air. There was no hint of movement. Puzzled by the strange sequence of events, Braldt sighed deeply, then sprawled to one side as though stirred by a dream, allowing his forearm to come to rest along his cheek. With his face thus hidden from view, he opened his eyes and blinked against the bright light flooding the room.

When his vision cleared, he saw that he was lying on a silvery, metal table in the middle of a large room filled with numerous identical tables. Lying atop many of the surfaces were a multitude of forms. It was a startling sight, one he could barely comprehend, for while some of the figures were human, or at least humanlike, he could not identify any of them. They were unlike any tribe he knew. Others, however, were definitely not human. At first he thought they were all dead, but then as his mind grew accustomed to the sight, he realized that they were not dead, merely sleeping or unconscious.

A low moan rose from the table next to his and his eyes were drawn to the tall, slender figure of the woman who lay upon the cold surface. She stirred restlessly; her body, clad in some strange, silvery material that fit her like a shadow, heaved with agitation as she fought her way back to wakefulness. Her dark hair was long and thick, and as she turned on the hard table it escaped its bindings and flowed over the edge, nearly brushing the floor. A delicate hand, the fingers long and tapered, the nails neatly shaped into ovals, relaxed, opening like a flower, exposing the fragile wrist with a heartbreaking vulnerability. Braldt found himself drawn to this unknown woman, affected by this unconscious display of helplessness and wishing to protect her.

She stirred again as though rousing under his gaze, and a low moan escaped her narrow, well-drawn lips. There was the sound of footsteps, and then much to Braldt's astonishment, two of the hated hard ones, those mechanized men who were the tools of the "Masters," appeared, laying their metallic hands on the woman, pressing her down against the table as full consciousness returned.

One of the inhuman creatures began to draw a set of straps across the woman's body while his companion pressed down on her chest, pinning her against the cold metal. So great was the pressure of this single hand that she could do nothing but curse and beat upon its hard body with her fists. Braldt knew from bitter experience just how futile such actions were. The bodies of the hard ones were far too tough to be intimidated by the blows of soft, human flesh.

Braldt considered the wisdom of action for a brief moment, knowing that caution was probably the wisest course, lying low and watching to see what became of the woman. But so great was his hatred of the hard ones that he was unable to control his emotions, and wisdom was replaced by the need to act. He leaped from the table without further thought and flung himself on the back of the hard one closest to him, bearing it to the floor with the unexpected burden of his weight. The metallic figure struck the table as it fell, causing the table to roll several feet, and Braldt realized belatedly that all the tables were on wheels.

The movement disturbed the second hard one's balance and it stumbled, momentarily losing its hold on the woman. She seized the opportunity instantly, leaping from the table with an agility that startled Braldt as much as the animal-like roar of fury that burst from those same shapely lips he had so recently admired. The woman was a blur of motion as she seized the only weapon at hand, the cart she had so recently rested upon, and began battering it into her opponent. It was not much of a weapon, but she was aided by the element of surprise and she took the hard one off guard as well as off balance and never allowed him to regain the upper hand.

Braldt would have liked to have watched the woman. He had never heard of a woman warrior, and her technique was unusual to say the least, but his own opponent gave him no opportunity for such a leisure activity, as it was already rising to its knees.

Imitating the woman's plan of attack, Braldt hurled himself on the hard one's back, driving it to the floor once again with his knees planted between its shoulders. He seized the smooth roundness that was its head and twisted 'til it turned at an angle that would have broken a man's neck. There was no welcome crack of vertebrae, instead, a thin, human voice trickled out of a round, silver plate set in the metallic head, shocking Braldt with the unexpected sounds so that he nearly lost his hold.

The voice was imperious, commanding, and speaking in a language he could understand. "Cease your attack! Stand back and no harm will come to you. Do as you are told, immediately!"

Braldt was accustomed to obeying Auslic, the chief and leader of his tribe. He was also accustomed to doing the bidding of his commander, but he felt no such allegiance to the disembodied voice. It only served to anger him further, for this must be the voice of the "Masters," those who contrived to destroy his world to satisfy their own selfish needs. Locking the creature's head between arm and body, he pried at the silver disc until it came free, trailing the multicolored entrails which Batta Flor had called wires, behind it. Braldt wrapped them in his fist and yanked them free. The voice squawked a single protest, then fell silent. Braldt banged the metallic head against the floor, maintaining and increasing the awkward angle until at last some critical connection separated and the head flopped forward. Limbs constricted, fingers clutched, and its metal heels beat a staccato tattoo upon the floor as it shivered its way toward death.

Braldt looked upon his work with satisfaction as the thing slowly died. Fingers closed upon his arm and he jumped back, thinking that more of the metal men had joined the battle, but it was only the woman, staring at him with impatient eyes, her mouth stretched taut into a grim line of anxiety. Looking around the room with alarm, she beckoned for him to follow as she turned and ran toward a door set in the far wall.

Braldt followed her without hesitation, for as the heat of battle faded from his mind he realized the folly of remaining. The Masters knew that something was wrong, it would only be a matter of time before they were pursued.

If only he could find Batta Flor and Keri!

As they made their way across the room, they heard the pounding of steps in the corridor at the other end of the room. The woman seized his wrist tightly, banged her fist twice upon a silver plate set into the wall at head level, and pulled him through the door as it hissed open. Once through, she turned and pounded once on an identical plate set in the wall on the opposite side. The door hissed closed. A small, metal object no higher than knee height, stood a short distance away. The woman grabbed it, broke off the dish that was attached to the slender column, and began to pry at the edge of the plate that operated the door. Angry cries could be heard approaching on the far side.

The silver plate was attached to the wall with four small screws which had not been designed to resist attack. They gave way easily, revealing their own set of coiling wires. The woman smiled and ripped them from the dark opening, setting off a shower of sparks that cascaded harmlessly to the floor. Heavy hands pounded on the far side of the door, but it did not respond to their demands.

The woman leaned against the door and looked at Braldt. Her dark eyes, sparkling with intelligence, tilted up at the corners. She grinned at him, a crooked, lopsided grin that was somehow self-mocking as though she did not take her own efforts too seriously. Her face was narrow and foxlike, with high, rounded cheekbones and a delicately pointed chin. They gazed at each other for a moment longer, the woman not bothering to hide the fact that she was as curious about Braldt as he was about her. Evidently what she saw was to her liking, for after a moment she nodded. She spoke to him urgently, and with a sinking heart, Braldt heard words and sounds like none he had ever heard before. They were musical sounds, pleasant to the ear, a combination of trills and clicks and soft sibilants completely unknown to him. He shook his head.

The woman stared at him impatiently as though wondering at his lack of comprehension. She uttered another sequence of sounds, this time obviously a question, and tilted her head as she waited for a reply.

"I do not understand you," Braldt said gently. "Do you not speak the language of the Duroni?" The woman stared at him blankly. Braldt then tried the language spoken by the traders, a bastardized idiom widely used among the various tribes that populated the world. The woman did not respond. In despair, she, too, attempted another language, speaking slowly and carefully. It was incomprehensible gibberish. The two of them stared at each other in dismay, realizing that while they had formed a desperate alliance against the enemy, they could not understand anything that the other said.

The woman made an impatient gesture with her hand, then seized Braldt's wrist and began dragging him down the corridor. Looking up, she stopped abruptly as she saw the now-familiar clear circles of light set in the walls at regular intervals. Her lips drew back in a grimace, revealing tiny, white teeth. She spat a curse, then swung the metal column which she still held, shattering the brittle, transparent covering. Instantly, the beam of light winked out. Smiling with satisfaction, the woman proceeded down the corridor, destroying each of the tiny windows of light.

Surprisingly, there was no sound of pursuit. The door behind them remained sealed, although Braldt had expected to see it pried open at any moment. Ahead of them, they could see that the corridor was intersected. Beyond, there was a heavy door, unlike any of the others they had encountered, and Braldt sensed that this door would lead outside. He yearned to breathe crisp, fresh air again, rather than the dead air of the corridors. The need was great in him to see something green and alive instead of mile after mile of dead, unnatural, unfeeling substances composed of strange materials that had never known life. He moved ahead impatiently.

The woman put out a slender arm, her hand resting lightly on his chest, stopping him. She put a finger to her lips, then pointed to the corners of the intersection, her bright eyes conveying a silent, urgent message.

Braldt knuckled his forehead, berating himself inwardly for ten kinds of stupidity. He should not have needed the woman's warning to alert him to the fact that the intersection was a logical place to expect an ambush. He nodded his understanding and the two of them crept forward silently. The woman looked up at the unblinking circles and made a moue of distaste, for there was no way she could disarm them without announcing their presence to whomever might be waiting for them.

They stopped just short of the passageway, and although nothing and no one could be seen, an unknown presence was palpable in the air. They divided—Braldt on the left, the woman on the right—and edged forward until they reached a point where stealth would no longer protect them from those who might watch and wait. Their eyes sought each other and there was a sense of companionship even though they had no words to express themselves. The woman nodded, and brandishing her silver column, rushed ahead, screming the astounding barrage of sound that had so startled Braldt.

Braldt was no more than a step behind her, although he had no weapon other than his strength and determination to remain free.

They had guessed correctly. As they approached the meeting of the corridors, six humans stepped forth to meet them, three on either side. They were human, that much was clear, but what tribe or race of men could not be told, for they were clad in an unfamiliar type of armor that obscured much of their features.

They stood quietly, not the least concerned, waiting for Braldt and the woman to reach them, and it was their air of confident calm, more than the swords they held, that gave Braldt his first twinge of doubt.

The woman slowed as well, and it was obvious that she shared his concern. Without speaking, they moved closer until their shoulders brushed against one another. The waiting warriors made no move toward them, nor raised their swords in readiness, but merely watched as they approached.

They were clad in metal-edged, leather armor. Their heads were covered in form-fitting helms that extended over their ears and down the nape of the neck, leaving nothing exposed. A spine of metal sheathed the crest of the skull and ran down between the eyes and the length of the nose. The shiny metal reflected the light into their eyes, an effective weapon in itself. Their chests and backs were covered with heavy, leather plates fixed together with a free-moving mesh of fine, chain links and held together at the sides; this extended the full length of the body, ending just above the knees. Their arms and legs were also sheathed by bands of leather and metal, leaving little flesh vulnerable to attack. Braldt could but admire the cleverness of the armor while seeking some little advantage, but even if he had been armed, there appeared to be no chink in the protective gear, unless the weight of it could be used against those who wore it.

Strangely, the warriors made no move to attack them as they edged ever closer. As they drew even with the silent warriors, the men moved aside, allowing them to pass. Braldt exchanged a brief, puzzled glance with the woman, but there was no answer to the unspoken question. Nor could they stop to wonder why if their freedom was to be gained. Back to back, facing their gauntlet of armed watchers, they made their way to the door.

The warriors closed ranks behind them. Strangely, it seemed that they were barring the way behind them as though there was some reason they would want to return! The door was within reach now. Without taking her eyes from the armed guard, the woman reached up with her fist and pounded twice upon the silver square fixed to the wall. There was a moment of heart-stopping panic when it seemed that nothing would happen, then there was a low hum and the door swung smoothly open. Sweet, warm air flooded into the chamber, surrounding them with its fragrance. Birds could be heard twittering in the distance and they could hear the wind soughing through the branches of unseen trees.

Braldt was overwhelmed by the desire to turn and run, to embrace the world after the long, enforced confinement in the strange, unnatural surroundings. His heart began to race at the thought that soon he would find Batta Flor and Keri, and be able to return to his tribe and tell Auslic all that had transpired, and seek wisdom in understanding the strange events. And then there was the woman. A way must be found to communicate with her to reassure her. But most importantly, there was the matter of the strange beings who had somehow infiltrated their world—a way must be found to deal with them. They . . .

As the door slid closed, cutting them off from the silent guard, Braldt became aware that something was wrong. The woman was lowering her arm, the silver staff dangling useless at her side as she looked around in bewilderment. Braldt looked up to see what it was that troubled her and was stricken with a sense of numbing horror. The sky above was scarlet red, lit from behind low, crimson clouds by dual orbs that rode heavily above an unfamiliar horizon.

Braldt and the woman turned to each other in horror. A low hissing filled their ears, and as their senses dimmed and they collapsed onto the blood-red earth, they knew without a doubt that wherever they were, it was not a world they had ever known before.

5

Consciousness returned slowly, filtering through the heavy darkness as though he was rising from the webs of a dream. Braldt clung to the illusion, for the reality of wakefulness was far worse than any imagined nightmare. Shutting out the waiting world, he went over the sequence of events in his mind, beginning with the sterile room that had begun the gauntlet of horrors.

One thing had become increasingly clear. He was no longer on his own world. Somehow, the act of throwing the lever that had prevented the Masters from traveling between worlds undetected, had transported him off his world and into theirs. His mind told him that this was true—there was no other explanation for the events that had transpired—but stubbornly, his heart resisted accepting this fact. Would he ever see Keri again or hold her in his arms? The sense of loss was overwhelming and his chest hurt as though he had suffered a mortal wound.

His entire body throbbed with a dull, feverish ache, and as full consciousness returned, he realized that he was experiencing actual pain. Concentrating, he shook off the last, foggy vestiges of the drugged sleep and took stock of his body. His head was radiating the pain outward in waves.

He raised a hand and gingerly touched his skull with fingers that felt as thick and sensitive as rope cables.

He found no evidence of a wound and that was reassuring. The worst of the pain seemed to be focused behind his right ear. His gesturing fingers reached and found a circlet of hard metal lying flat against his skull! A current of fear lanced through his body and he sat upright, even though the movement set off ripples of nausea.

His vision was blurred and a sea of red dots obscured his sight. His fingers sought the object again and felt along the edges. There could be no doubt—whatever it was was firmly embedded in his skin. He dug into his flesh, trying to remove the disc, but it did not move and the effort caused him such severe pain that he nearly retched. He collapsed, his head swimming, tears running from the corners of his eyes, gagging as the pain slowly ebbed away.

"The pain is not good, but it will pass," said a low voice coupled with a wry chuckle that contained no humor.

Braldt turned slowly toward the sound of the voice, breathing deeply to quell the pain and nausea, trying to clear his vision. Slowly things took shape around him. He was lying on a hard mat, similar to those he had once trained on.

Next to him, head resting on the palm of its hand, reclining leisurely on an identical mat, was a manthing, clearly not human, but not animal either. It was taller than Braldt, but possessed the same body structure. There, however, the similarity ended, for the being was covered with a dense shag of orange fur from the top of its squarish head to its claw-toed feet. Its eyes were large and bright with intelligence, its nose (no nose in the sense that Braldt was accustomed to) was a series of flanged openings spread across the center of its face that opened and shut in random sequence as it breathed. Its mouth was quite human in shape and quirked up at one corner in a wry, mocking grin. The orange fur that cloaked its face was neatly parted below the multiple nostrils and swept down like two giant moustaches on either side of the mouth. It re-formed at the chin to form a sharply pointed beard which the creature stroked reflectively with a clawed hand. A bright silver disc had been implanted in the being's forehead, the fur neatly trimmed along the edges. Other than a tight-fitting, silver, metallic collar that extended in a downward point nearly to the center of its furry chest, the creature wore no clothing.

"I know it hurts," the manthing said sympathetically, "but it'll pass soon enough. Lie still and breathe deep; moving just seems to make it worse."

"Who—who are you?" Braldt asked, his tongue moving sluggishly, the words emerging thickly.

"I am Allo," replied the furred one as he sat up and placed a large hand with immense curved claws on Braldt's chest. "Be still. I am not your enemy. You have nothing to fear from me."

"The woman . . . my companion," Braldt said, struggling to rise, but helpless against the pressure of the creature's hand and the weakness that filled his limbs.

"She is here beside me, as are two others," said Allo. "They are stirring and will waken soon. We must help them to accept what has happened."

"And what exactly is it that has happened?" Braldt asked, shoving the creature's hand aside and sitting up despite the dizziness that filled his head.

The furred being fixed Braldt with a calm eye. "The tone in your voice says that you believe me to be an enemy or to have played some role in our present circumstance. I assure you that neither assumption is correct. I am as much an unwilling victim as are you and your companion. I know little or nothing about this place and what has occurred. I *do* know that this is no longer the world that I have always known and that we have been taken as captives, although by whom or what or for what purpose, I cannot say.

"Whatever I am, sir, it is not your enemy, and I can only assume that we are here by force to serve some other's purpose. If we are to survive, we must become friends and rely upon each other, for surely we are alone, and without help, other than each other, and our own wits."

Braldt studied the furred one who regarded him with a level gaze. There was no sign of duplicity or falsehood in the dark, brown eyes. He sighed deeply and felt the anger ebb away.

"My apologies, Allo. I am taking my anger and frustration out on you. You speak the truth—none of us asked to be here and it is those who brought us, the ones known as the Masters, who deserve our hatred." He touched the silver disc and grimaced as pain lanced through his head. "Do you know what these are and what purpose they serve?"

"There was another here before you," Allo said. "It was a Galurian, a lizard-man from a portion of my world that is nought but swamp and water. These Galurians are ignorant, wild beasts with a language unknowable by any save their own kind. Yet this beast and I were able to speak—communicate so far as its limited thoughts were able to form—clearly and easily in the same tongue. It was taken away soon after I wakened, but long enough for us to speak. I have been pondering the meaning since its departure. Now, you arrive, the four of you, all quite dissimilar. It is plain that all of you have been gathered from different places of origin, yet despite our different backgrounds, I suspect that we will be able to converse with ease. I believe that these discs are translators of some sort, enabling us to speak to one another despite our various points of origin."

Braldt rubbed his forehead. Allo's words made sense, but still there was a sense of rage, of violation, and he wondered if he would ever get to face the unknown Masters who had so manipulated his world and his life.

The woman stirred and moaned. Allo turned toward her. There was the sound of violent retching, and at the far edge of the room a man held his head and keened in wordless anguish. Braldt leaped to his feet and would have gone to the woman's side, but a voice rang out inside his head, causing him to pause.

"Welcome and congratulations, Marin of Un 7, Septua of Valhalla, Randi of Earth, Allo of 2x71, and Braldt of K7. By your cunning, dexterity, and will to survive, you have passed the trials set before you. As a result you will be spared from slavery and given the opportunity to earn glory."

The man at the far edge of the room scrambled to

his feet and shouted, "Who are you and where are my companions?"

The voice replied smoothly. "You must earn that answer and any others that you might wish to know. From this day forward you must cease to think of yourselves as individuals and forget your own petty dreams. You must become a team with but one brain and thought—that of survival—or you will surely perish. Welcome to Arena, and now . . . let the games begin!"

As the ominous words concluded, the wall before them slid aside, drawing back smoothly and silently. Instantly, their eyes were dazzled by the brilliant, scarlet light that filled this world's atmosphere. Braldt shielded his eyes against the blood-red glare and staggered forward. He felt a slender hand clutch his wrist and slipped his arm around the waist of the woman known as Randi, oddly comforted by her presence. Slowly, his eyes adjusted to the hideous light and he took several steps forward, anxious, yet fearful of what he would find.

There was a harsh intake of breath and the woman uttered a cry of dismay. Braldt blinked and narrowed his eyes against the bright light of the two suns now hanging at the edge of the horizon. Randi's hand tightened on his wrist, her nails pressing into his flesh, and he saw what had caused her such alarm. The parting of the doors had revealed an arena fashioned of red, marbled stone, rising in tiers on all four sides and reaching high into the bloody sky. At the center, directly opposite them, the stone on the first tier had been carved into graceful arches and pleasant pavilions which trailed gossamer cloth in pale, pastel colors. Plump cushions could be seen piled atop the hard, stone risers; clearly this was where the royalty would be seated.

The floor of the arena was composed of crushed, red stone and sand, the sand shifting perilously underfoot, offering little purchase. Braldt scanned the arena as he and his companions slowly stepped onto the playing field. Circling the arena below the first level of seats were a number of arched doorways, closed off and tightly barred with no hint of what might lie behind them. As they made their way into the center of the arena, they heard a smooth rumble and the doors to the chamber where they had wakened slid shut behind them, sealing them onto the playing field.

They turned to face one another for the first time, studying each other, taking each other's measure, for if the anonymous voice had spoken truly, their very lives would depend upon each other.

Randi stood at Braldt's side, defiant and proud, and from what little he had seen of her, he knew that she was resourceful and quick, a steady ally. The being named Allo stood to Randi's left, taller than Braldt by at least two heads. He was broad in the chest and shoulders and his long arms hung nearly to his knees, ending in two curved digits tipped with sickle-like claws as long as the digits themselves and thicker than any claws Braldt had ever seen. They would be fearsome weapons. Allo's feet were similarly constructed with an additional spur rising off the heel.

The fourth member of their party was a manthing, the one called Marin who had challenged the voice, who was built like a boulder. His skin was black as night and rippled and shone as though it were polished rock or oiled metal; the muscles stood out in strange relief in unfamiliar patterns. Although he had a man-like form, with the appropriate number of appendages, there was something about him that was not right. His eyes were small and bright and burned with a dark rage. His head was smooth and devoid of hair and eyebrows which gave him a cold, threatening look. The bright, silver disc, positioned directly between his eyes made him appear even less than human. "What the fuck you lookin' at?" snarled Marin, his mouth stretching into an unpleasant grimace revealing black, metallic teeth serrated along the edges.

"Come, Marin, we are not the enemy," Allo said gently. "We must take care not to set upon each other for surely our only chance for survival lies with one another."

Marin's eyes seemed to glow for a moment, and then without even replying he swept his arm outward as though throwing a disc, and slammed it into Allo's unprotected abdomen before any of them realized what he was going to do. Allo crumpled with the force of the blow and fell to the ground, groaning.

Braldt would have flung himself on Marin, but Randi placed herself before him and put both of her hands on his chest. "No," she said quietly, but with force. "There is no percentage in fighting among ourselves. It is what they would want. What chance will we have if the two of you kill or disable each other? Think about it."

The fifth and final member of their group, unnoticed until now, bustled forward, and Braldt saw with a shock that he was quite small and possibly deformed, built like a man but shortened and condensed, with all of his features squeezed into a fourth the space he should have taken. He was smaller than a child of five summers, but squat and compact as though four others had been squeezed into the same amount of space with him.

He bustled across the arena with an odd, jerky swagger as though his various limbs were not accustomed to working with one another; he winked broadly at Randi and stroked her thigh as he passed. Taken aback by the unexpected gesture, uncertain whether to take offense, Randi did no more than blink before the dwarf was past her and advancing on the gentle Allo.

" 'ere, 'ere, Allo, lemme give you a hand up. I'm sure there weren't no 'ard feelin's intended. Just a misunderstandin', like. We all be friends 'ere, right?"

He addressed this statement to Marin, who stood poised, ready to strike again, even as he slid a small, muscular arm beneath Allo and helped him to his feet. Surprisingly, Marin made no comment, but merely blinked and growled at the little man who continued to chatter as he urged the stunned Allo to his feet.

Together—Randi and Braldt in the lead with Septua and Allo following close behind and Marin bringing up the rear—they circled the arena, seeking out whatever they could learn about this new world where they were held captive.

6

Keri wakened.

She did not open her eyes, dreading what she would find, putting off until the last possible moment the deep, silent darkness that she knew would be there. It had been like that since the moment Carn pulled the lever, the lever that would save Auslic's life and prevent the Masters from destroying their world. Pulling the lever was to have solved all their problems, according to the priest who had sent them on their mission, but instead it had only made them worse. Carn had drawn the lever down, and a spiraling band of light filled with bright, shimmering particles surrounded Braldt, whirling around him and enveloping him from head to foot. When it faded, he was gone. The place where he had stood was empty; it was as though he had never existed.

She had screamed then and rushed toward the spot where he had stood. There was a slight tingling on her skin and the air seemed thicker, almost viscous and hard to breathe, slowing her passage. But when she reached the lever, her senses confirmed what her eyes had seen, Braldt was gone.

The lupebeast pup who had been Braldt's constant companion growled and bared his teeth as he sniffed the air, and Batta Flor, the Mandrelli who had led them to the chamber despite the dangers, gripped her arms and pulled her gently to his furry chest, uttering soft, meaningless words of comfort.

In time her screams stopped and the tears slowed, and together they explored the ruined chamber for some clue, some explanation of what had become of Braldt but they had found no answer. Keri had wanted to throw the lever, reversing Carn's actions in the hope that it would undo whatever he had done and return Braldt to them. But Batta Flor had pinned her wrists together in one of his huge hands, restraining her gently but firmly.

"Think about what you are doing," he said. "To do this will affect everyone on our world, undo what the three of us struggled so hard to achieve. If the lever is reversed, the Masters will once more be able to come and go freely between their world and ours. They will be free to destroy us as they had planned. The safety of our world depends upon keeping them at bay and there is no assurance that Braldt will be returned to us if you reverse the process."

She had looked into his eyes then and saw nothing but sorrow and compassion and knew that his grief was as real as her own. Beast whined then and pawed at the lever, sliding his muzzle along its edge, perhaps scenting the human who had won his loyalty and love. They moved to the pup's side, their hands outstretched to comfort him and then it happened—the whirling, the bright spiral of multicolored lights that fragmented their world and drew them down into nothingness.

Keri knew that she screamed, she could feel her

mouth open and close, but there was no sound. She saw Beast turning head over heels in the air before her, his body breaking up in tiny dots, drifting away like amorphous threads of storm-torn clouds. She reached for him to draw him back, and to her horror she saw her own hand and arm disintegrating as well. She turned toward Batta Flor and saw him being sucked down into the rapidly swirling vortex. He grimaced. His lips moved but she heard no sound. The visual whirlwind bombarded her, beating upon her skin, passing through her flesh with tiny spears of light, separating her from herself painlessly until she hung suspended, an essence rather than a corporeal body of flesh and bone and blood and then she was caught up in the whirling maelstrom and borne away, down, down, down into black nothingness, and she was no more.

When she opened her eyes again, it was to that same vision of darkness, a total absence of light. She had felt a moment of utter terror as she relived the memory of her body separating and she wondered if she were dead. Her hands rose to her face and she felt cheekbones and nose, mouth and chin positioned exactly where they were supposed to be. The rest of her seemed to be intact as well. Then she was not dead, but where was she? She cried aloud, calling Batta Flor's name and Beast's as well, but there was no reply, only a hollow echo that mocked her efforts. Then had come the long waiting, the fears, and finally, the anger which had sustained her.

She was in a chamber constructed of some smooth material that was neither metal nor wood. It had no seams of any sort at the juncture of wall and floor or anywhere else that her questing fingers could find, and she had been over every inch of the room a hundred times since her first awakening.

The room was no more than ten paces in any direction and round in shape. It was neither cold nor hot but perfectly balanced to her own temperature so that it almost felt as though she were enclosed in some giant womb. A steady rhythmic pulsing throbbed through the walls of the chamber, intensifying the sensation, and she soon identified it as a duplication of her own heartbeat which increased with her fears and slowed in sleep.

Food and drink arrived almost magically, although by what means she had yet to discover, for it was always beside her when she wakened. She had tried to remain awake in order to discover who or what brought the meals, but she had been unable to do so, her eyes growing heavy despite her resolve. She had tried to feign sleep as well, but all in vain. Her wastes were disposed of in a deep depression in the center of the chamber and a bone button torn from her shirt brought no sound of bottom. As the depression was no wider than her arm and would provide no possible route of escape, she ceased to consider it.

And then the nightmares began.

They were always the same, bright, blinding lights that she could not escape shining into her eyes, her body unable to answer the most simple commands. She could not even blink. There were questions, or rather the reverberating memory of questions, that hung in the air like angry bees. Nor could she remember their content when she wakened. She was not alone in these nightmares; the presence of others was tangible and she could see their blurred forms bending over her but she was unable to make out their features. They wanted something from her, she knew that much, but she did not know what.

Slowly, Keri became aware of the presence of another. She could not have said what it was that alerted her, but somehow, she knew it to be true. The hair prickled on the back of her arms and neck and she opened her eyes, willing herself to see through the impenetrable darkness. But to her amazement, the familiar darkness, pressing down on her like a heavy weight, was gone. The chamber was filled with a soft, gray twilight, almost too bright for her stunned senses to comprehend.

There was a soft groaning exhalation of breath. Keri turned quickly, and there, sprawled on the floor behind her, was Batta Flor and beside him, legs spread awkwardly, tongue lolling between his teeth, was the beast pup.

Keri bent over the Madrelli, fearful that he was dead. He was alive and showed no sign of injury, but fixed in the middle of his forehead, flush with the tangled, furry skin, was a bright, silver object punctured with a regular pattern of holes each barely larger than a pinprick. Keri reached out with trembling fingers and touched it. Batta Flor moaned and turned his head aside, and Keri darted back, terrified that she had caused him pain.

Even as she stared at the Madrelli in dismay, she became aware of a dull, persistent throbbing above her own left ear. She raised her hand and probed gently, fearfully, afraid as she had never been afraid before.

It was there. She was filled with nausea. A sickness rose in her throat all but overwhelming her with a sense of defilement. She fell to her knees, overcome with the desire to retch, and then as she swayed there, her hair sweeping forward to cover her shame, another emotion began to grow. It was a tiny thing at first, no more than a tendril winding in among the clouds of horror, but it grew steadily like a winter storm that sometimes swept in off the plains blotting out the sky from heaven to horizon. Her anger fed on her sense of betrayal, her shame, and her outrage until it burned steadily, a bright fury against those who had used her body for their own purposes.

She turned her attention to Batta Flor and the lupebeast, contenting herself that they had not been harmed. The beast, while unconscious, did not appear to wear the metallic implant. Keri sat back on her heels and waited for them to waken. While she waited, she laid her plans. They had been taken captive and were at the mercy of unknown others, but they were not helpless, passive creatures to do another's bidding. They would watch and wait and learn. The three of them had faced the odds before and survived. They would do so again.

Suddenly there was a soft rumbling sound and a section of the wall began to slide smoothly aside. Brilliant light tinged with red flooded the small chamber. Her eyes were unprepared for such a vivid display and she put her hand up to block the light. As she did so, three figures appeared before her, silhouetted against the bright backdrop, a corona of jewel-like rays outlining their bodies. There was something familiar about the form that halted the scream that rose in Keri's throat. They paused, and then as her eyes slowly became adjusted to the glare, the figures stepped forward. Keri's hand dropped from her eyes and came to rest on her throat, daring to hope, yet fearful and disbelieving. She could not believe what she was seeing; her brain and her heart warred with one another and the desire to believe won out over cold intellect. Dropping her hands to her sides, eyes shining, a smile trembling on her lips, she stepped forward, ready and willing to accept whatever would come.

7

Braldt had often observed the slavers on his own world as they plied their miserable trade between the various tribes, making certain that they did not enter the city nor attempt to abduct any of the Duroni. He had seen the unfortunate captives beaten and abused, and those deemed to be of little value deprived of their meager rations, dragging listlessly in their chains until they died or were ruthlessly killed. He had seen hideous wounds and grievous suffering during times of war and he had often seen death. But none of it had prepared him for the misery he found waiting for him in his new life.

Shortly after they completed their tour of the amphitheater, an arched door opened on the side of the ring and a small contingent of warriors dressed in heavy leather and metal armor marched toward them. They were led by a single man, so huge and thickly muscled that his armor creaked and groaned at his every step. It was immediately apparent from their posture and the way they held their weapons at the ready that the warriors meant to take them prisoner and were prepared to do battle if necessary.

Looking around the circular confines of the amphitheater, the small band of disparate comrades had sought

an avenue of escape, all thought of enmity gone as they
closed ranks against the common enemy. As though
anticipating their thoughts, the warriors had spread out at
a signal from their leader, surrounding them, swords and
shields held at battle height. Freedom, if such a thing
were possible, would be won at a heavy cost.

Rather than risk the loss of one of their members,
they had allowed themselves to be herded through the
dark opening of the stone arch, the cool shadows a
welcome relief after the heat of the unfamiliar suns.
Surrounded on all sides by the silent but watchful guards,
they had filed down a broad corridor lined with barred
and hobnailed doors set deeply in the thick, stone walls.

Furtive faces had peered out at them through small
openings tightly gridded with heavy, metal mesh. Fury
and rage burned in many of those eyes, but there was
also the dull, listless gaze of those who had ceased to
hope and the bright, burning light of the hopelessly
insane.

There was a cacophony of sounds as well; the rattle
of bars, the pounding of fists and feet against ungiving
wood, a litany of curses in a multitude of languages all of
which Braldt understood, the growls and demented screams
of those who had fallen over the edge of sanity, and
numerous, abusive comments upon each of the new
arrivals, gauging and wagering on the odds against their
survival. Above all there was a wild howling, growling,
roar of animals rising from somewhere in the bowels of
the earth.

The stench was indescribable, rank and fetid not
unlike the stink of a merebear's cave after its seasonal

hibernation. It was a combination of filthy unwashed bodies, fermenting bodily wastes, and the sweetish aroma of rotting flesh. The only way to endure the hideous odor was to close one's nostrils and breath through one's open mouth, mimicking the guards who marched along stolidly, ignoring the insults and curses which were hurled their way without so much as a sideways glance.

These guards were of varied races, barely half of them human in form, others were a multitude of furred or carapaced creatures with varying numbers of appendages, eyes and body openings in unusual places. The single common denominator was the silver circlet of metal affixed to some portion of their heads as well as the armor and weaponry which so clearly separated them from those they guarded.

Finally the corridor ended, terminating in a giant, oblong enclosure with bars running from floor to ceiling. The heavy door was unlocked and the guards stood to one side, hands gripping their weapons, eyes hard and watchful, clearly ready for any sign of resistance.

Braldt paused, knowing the odds were against him but wondering if they would ever have another chance. But before he could act, Allo placed his large, clawed paw on Braldt's shoulder and murmured into his ear, "Not now, my friend, there are too many of them and they are too ready for just such an attempt. Be patient, victory is patience's reward." Still Braldt hesitated, unwilling to calmly enter the cell like some sacrificial offering. The head guard shoved his men aside with the back of his hand and approached Braldt, barreling forward until they stood toe to toe, chests and chins nearly touching. Braldt fought down the need to step back, to reclaim his aura of space, and held his ground, meeting and matching the man's truculent stare. They stared into each other's eyes without flinching for a seemingly endless period of time. The noise of the prison seemed to vanish and Braldt was aware of the beat of his heart, the pulse of blood in his temples, and the collective tension emanating from his companions as well as the guards.

And then Randi was beside him, sliding her cool, slender hand into his. Startled, Braldt broke his concentration and glanced down at her for the merest fraction of an instant. That was all it took; the guard butted Braldt with his chest, knocking him through the door and into the cell. The others were quickly prodded through at swordpoint and the door swung shut behind them with a resounding clang.

The sound had barely finished echoing in the dark recesses before they became aware of the press of bodies closing in around them and hands reaching out, seizing on Marin's leather vest and Braldt's belt as well as Allo's thick pelt and the silvery fabric of Randi's close-fitting garment. There was a sudden outcry of pain and a body flew through the air, its arm bent at an angle nature had never fashioned. Marin growled and a space opened around him momentarily only to close in once again, shoved forward by those in the rear who were not in any immediate danger and had no compunction against offering up their comrades for sacrifice. Only by placing themselves back to back and presenting a united front against the wild mob that surrounded them, were Braldt and his companions able to gain a moment's respite.

The guards stood outside the cell and watched with obvious interest. Coins changed hands as they wagered among themselves how the newcomers would fare. Braldt had only a moment to observe their interest as well as to conclude that they could expect no help from that quarter no matter what the outcome before the mob closed in on them again.

This time the crowd was better prepared and brandished a variety of homemade weapons. Those without weapons protected themselves with filthy mattresses leaking lice-ridden straw and crudely fashioned chairs; the legs acting as both weapons and the advance guard.

They were an ugly group of beings, the dregs of humanity whose narrow brows, jutting jaws, and shambling gaits spoke eloquently of their low breeding and even lower intellect. But what they lacked in evolutionary advancement, they had learned to compensate for in survival techniques. In the blur of time that followed the first opening feint, Braldt and the others were forced to rely on every trick they knew just to stay alive.

Eventually, due to their superior physical condition and the years of training each of them had undergone, they defeated the mob and sent them whimpering and howling back to their corners nursing their aching heads and bruised and broken bones . . . but it was a hard-won victory for they themselves had been pummeled and struck hard and often, and bore numerous wounds of their own. Allo was the most severely injured, partially because of his size, for in sheer bulk, he was the largest among them and the slowest moving.

Despite his impressive build and the wicked-looking

claws, it was obvious that Allo lacked the vicious temperament that combined with his size would have made him a dangerous opponent. He had suffered a long, ragged gash across the upper back that had peeled back the thick pelt exposing the bands of muscle. He had also been cut above the left eye, and while the wound was not deep, it bled profusely, matting his fur together and dripping off the ends of his moustaches and beard.

Braldt, who was still taking stock of his own inventory of bruises, did what little he could for Allo, but other than requisitioning a half-filled pail of murky water that was meant to serve the entire cell, he had no means of cleaning and dressing the wounds. In the end, he could do no more than swab out the cuts and draw the edges closed by tying strands of Allo's own fur together tightly.

Randi had begged the guards for assistance, but they had ignored her request, even those few who had wagered on her and won. Evidently more than a few of them had been misled by Allo's appearance and had bet on him and lost heavily. Disgruntled over their loss, they did not bother to reply. Several of them showed their displeasure by spitting on the ground before walking away.

While they were tending to Allo's injuries, there was a clattering at the bars and once again the inhabitants of the cell surged forward. Braldt and his companions fell into defensive postures and only when derisive laughter broke out did they realize that food was the attraction and not a second attack.

By the time they realized their mistake, the single bucket which was meant to feed the entire cell had been scraped clean of the last scrap of food. Watchful eyes regarded them above closely guarded containers, and from the grim expressions in their eyes, Braldt knew that what had gone before was merely entertainment and that his cellmates would fight in earnest should any attempt be made to separate them from their rations.

An uneasy, guarded truce descended upon the cells as the inhabitants took stock of their injuries and pondered the strange turn of circumstances. The day passed slowly, the time made even longer by the unrelieved ache of their wounds and the discomfort and horror of their surroundings. The single tiny window set high on the wall was stained crimson with the light of the sinking suns when the denizens of the cells once more stirred to life. Seizing various cups and gourds, they pressed forward toward the barred door. Braldt and Marin worked their way forward, earning themselves the hiss of bared teeth and open hatred, but the pitiful collection of prisoners chose not to fight and Braldt edged his way to the entrance.

A creaking, wooden cart came into sight. It was little more than two large wheels, a small platform, and a ladderlike back supporting a large barrel dripping with moisture. The primitive device was propelled by an odd, lizardlike creature swathed from head to toe in a long cloak. Little could be seen of its features other than a single hooded eye and a long snout. It trudged along the corridor, pushing the heavy barrel before it, muttering to itself and seeming almost unaware of its surroundings. It seemed to carry on an angry, querulous dialogue with itself, all of its attention focused inward instead of on its duties. The cart rolled past a cell, unmindful of the extended arms which waved wildly in an attempt to catch the water carrier's attention. Nor did the harsh clatter of metal cups banged against the bars break into its sorrowful litany.

It appeared quite possible that the water bearer would pass them by as well, and Braldt's throat constricted, making him aware of his need for water. His arm shot out between the bars, and lunging hard against them, he succeeded in grabbing onto the water carrier's cloak. Twisting his fingers into the fabric, he jerked the lizard to an abrupt halt.

There was no noticeable difference in its demeanor. The creature did not appear angry at such a rude interruption; it made no hostile move, but merely swung about and trundled toward the cell where it filled the waiting containers with an absent-minded air, all the while muttering to itself. Braldt studied the water carrier with interest, noting that beneath the heavy cloak, it had but a single eye, almost covered by an opaque membrane; the other eye was missing entirely, with nothing but a scarred hump to show where it had once been. Its gray muzzle was crisscrossed with ridges and welts of horny scar tissue. He also noted with interest the heavy ring laden with keys that swung from a belt at the reptile's waist.

Braldt's action seemed to have lessened the hostility of his cellmates, for it was obvious to all that without Braldt's intervention, they would have gone without water. With little more than token hostility, he was able to fill the bucket and return to his comrades with Marin still at his side.

The lizard never once raised its single eye, mumbling to itself in a constant monotone as though arguing some ancient, unresolved grievance. Less than half the outstretched cups had been filled before the creature wandered off, wheeling the creaking cart back the way it had come, still reciting its litany of woes. Some of the prisoners beat on the bars and yelled at the retreating lizard, but it paid no attention and plodded stolidly out of sight.

Allo drank a little of the water, then lapsed into a feverish sleep. His large figure was racked with fits of chills and violent shivering as darkness filled the room. Torches were lit in the corridor but did little to alleviate the deep gloom of the cells. The prisoners seemed to grow more melancholy as darkness pervaded the cells and their cries and shrieks grated on the nerves. A pair of heavily armed guards patrolled the corridor at infrequent intervals, taking no notice of the prisoners' wails.

First Braldt and then Randi attempted to call attention to Allo's worsening condition, but the guards paid them no mind and it became obvious that no help would be forthcoming. It was equally obvious that Allo would die if nothing were done, even though the injury did not seem very serious. Marin had turned his broad back on them and was lost in his own surly thoughts. Randi and Braldt took turns trying to soothe Allo's restless stirrings. None of them even noticed when Septua crept backward and disappeared into the black shadows.

The cellblock was far from silent, echoing with moans and groans of pain and misery; somewhere close by a man was weeping in utter desolation. Therefore Braldt took no notice of the occasional cry or curse that rang out in their own cell. Only when Septua crept to his side and pressed a hard crust of bread into his hand and covered Allo with a coarse, stinking blanket did Braldt realize what the little man had done. The lamps flared briefly and the dwarf looked up from the bit of bone he was gnawing and winked at Braldt, a broad grin stretching across his face.

"What was it Allo said?" he whispered. "Patience rewards victory, right? Well, I were patient and when nothin' happened, I just thought I'd give it a 'and!"

Morning arrived after an eternity of the dark night. The guards returned in force, led by the same officer. Braldt and his companions were motioned out of the cell at swordpoint, the other inhabitants cringing back against the walls and making themselves as still as possible, obviously fearful of the soldiers.

But Braldt and the others stood by Allo's side and refused to move, although Marin had hesitated for a moment as though undecided. Braldt turned to him and said in a low tone, "Think, this could just as easily be you lying here." The big man nodded slowly, his small, dark eyes registering the thought, and without a word he turned toward the soldiers and crossed his arms over his chest, completing the unbroken front.

For a moment it appeared as though the officer would order his men to drag them out by force, then the point of his sword lowered and he spat on the filthy stone floor and gestured toward Allo. "Pick him up," he said in a guttural tone. "Bring him with. He will be of more interest alive than dead."

They did as they were ordered, and staggering under Allo's great weight, they retraced the steps they had taken the previous day, emerging into the hot glare of the rising suns which quickly burned away the damp chill of the prison. The officer gestured for several of his men to take Allo, but Braldt, distrusting the officer, refused to relinquish the body of his companion who shook beneath his hands with uncontrollable, feverish tremors. The gentle being had lost consciousness some time during the night without muttering a single word of complaint.

The officer stared into Braldt's eyes. "If I wanted him dead, I'd've stuck him back there or let him die on his own. It don't take much to kill offworlders; they don't have any resistance to foreign bugs. But it don't matter to me one way or the other; give him up or tend to him yourselves."

It was clear that Allo would die if he did not receive medical attention and equally obvious that they had no way of administering it themselves. They had no choice but to trust the man. Reluctantly, they stepped back and let the soldiers carry Allo away, although in the end, it took six of them to lift his furry bulk.

The rest of them were ushered across the red sand of the arena and led through an open arch which bustled with activity. Two forges were situated in the center of the huge room. Heavily muscled men, naked but for leather loincloths and dripping with sweat, beat upon bars of flaming metal with steady rhythm. A lizard creature and a half-man/half-cat being operated the bellows, keeping the coals glowing red. Others stood waiting their turns in long, patient lines, carrying a variety of broken weapons and pieces of armor, all in need of the smithy's attention.

They trailed past the waiting lines; curious and hostile eyes assessing them, sizing up their strengths and weaknesses as they made their way into the shadowy reaches under the stands of the coliseum. Leaving the smithy's chambers, they entered a broad, curved corridor carved from the solid earth, also bustling with activity. Humans, half-humans of all descriptions, and strange animal types that defied description, as well as multitudes of soldiers and hard ones traveled along the corridor in both directions.

No one took note of their passage as they joined the flow of traffic. By pokes, prods and guttural grunts, they were herded into a good-sized room that smelled sharply of astringent. A number of metal tables of differing sizes and heights were bolted to the stone floor. A line of windows lined the upper reaches of the walls allowing the hot, red suns to fill the room with stains of crimson despite the heavy bars across the glass.

Allo was stretched out on the largest of these tables; it was barely long enough for his immense form. A man wrapped from head to toe in a single, form-fitting garment with a large, glass lens strapped over his eyes, was bending over Allo, probing his injuries with gentle hands.

The rest of Braldt's group was examined less than gently by a man with a healer's touch, but lacking his caring concern. Their clothing was stripped from them and their bruises washed with foaming suds and rinsed with a stinging antiseptic. Their bodies were explored from head to toe, eyes, nostrils, mouths, ears, and other orifices clinically inspected despite their protests. Ever present were the guards with their swords and their watchful eyes, waiting for the slightest sign of rebellion. The officer remained by the door, discussing them with the primary healer, making notations in a small book.

When the ignominious inspection was over they were taken, still naked, to a much smaller room. The sight of his own body and those of Marin and Septua were of little concern to Braldt, but he could not help but notice that Randi's slender, muscular build in no way detracted from her attractiveness. Feeling his eyes upon her body, Randi blushed deeply, then raised her chin and glared at him defiantly.

Before he could speak, a tall and impossibly slender being that resembled nothing so much as a leaf-eating insect grown to gigantic proportions entered the room and began to measure them with a strange, silver square that emitted a thin, red beam and registered an ever-changing stream of figures on its face. Even though it bore the now-familiar silver implant, its voice and language were little more than a series of querulous chirps and clicks.

It seemed aggravated when they did not understand its commands to lift their arms or legs or turn as directed. It aided their comprehension with sharp pinches from its ratcheted pincers and flailed them with its whip-like antennae if they did not move quickly enough. The resulting bruises and stinging, red welts were painful as well as unexpected, and provided the guards with much cause for merriment. They quickly learned to anticipate the creature's demands, and with the exception of Septua to whom the bug-like being seemed to have taken a special dislike, they escaped without further injury.

But Septua was not entirely without means of his

own, and as they were about to leave the room, the little man leaped on the back of the unsuspecting insect, wrapped his thick, muscular legs around its chest and squeezed, bringing it to its double-jointed knees, gasping for breath. The guards sprang forward, then stopped, eyeing the rest of them nervously. It would be necessary to break through their ranks if they were to rescue the insectman. Perhaps he had caused them pain in the past, for after a quick glance among themselves, they stood their ground. They did not retreat, but neither did they go to the insect's aid.

Septua took advantage of their brief hesitation and his thick hands flew. When he sprang aside wearing a wide grin, releasing his prisoner, the unfortunate creature lay gasping on the ground, its delicate antennae tied in a series of complex knots, the fragile length forever broken and bent.

The soldiers grinned at Septua, all but slapping him on the back, and made no attempt to help the fallen insect as he lay there chirping in distress. Nor did they interfere as their prisoners put on their clothing; Septua's action seemed to have won them a small amount of approval.

Their next stop was an armory, and here they were let loose to wander among an impressive array of weapons, many of which were entirely unfamiliar to Braldt. He was immediately drawn to a rack filled with swords of every description, crafted of gleaming metal completely unlike the dull, bronze weapons he was accustomed to. These weapons were bright and shiny and bore a razor-keen edge that would deflect the hardest blow without sustaining damage. There were short swords and long swords, curved blades, tiny, wavy-edged daggers, and immense, two-handed swords that even Braldt with all his strength could not have lifted.

Randi showed no interest whatsoever in the swords, dismissing them with but a single glance and then hurrying toward a glass-fronted case displaying an odd assortment of dull, black objects whose use Braldt could not even guess at. She lifted the glass top and reverently took out one of the bulky objects, gripping it with her hand and inserting her index finger into a small hole. She hefted it appreciatively and sighted down its length, thumbing back a small protrusion on its upper surface and nodding happily.

Marin had made his way to a rack of lances, all tipped with wicked-looking metal points and barbs. He tried a number of them, dropping them on the ground with a growl when they failed to meet his approval. At last he found one that satisfied him, fashioned of dark wood, as dark as his own gleaming skin and longer than he himself by half a body length. It was tipped with a large, metal point and vicious-looking barbs were embedded in its sides for more than half its span; the base of the lance was sheathed in metal. Nor was the big man finished. He stalked the aisles of weapons and accessories, choosing a small, metal trident which he tucked into his belt like a dagger and a rope net weighted at the edges with heavy, metal discs.

Septua was sitting crosslegged on the floor crooning happily, sifting through a pile of objects like a child playing in a sandbox. He had accumulated a sling and a large sack filled with round, metal marbles, a wooden blowpipe, two boxes of sharp-tipped, feather-edged darts, an unusual dagger with a twisted corkscrew of a blade, and a handful of prickly, metal things, each no larger than a thumbnail that looked like sandburs with wicked hooks on each point. Chuckling to himself, the dwarf scooped up the strange items and poured them into a leather sack which he knotted and hung around his waist, with the exception of the dagger which he carefully sheathed and attached to his belt.

Braldt could not help but wonder what the purpose was of arming them with the weapons of their choice, for what was to prevent them from attacking the guards? But no sooner had the last of them made their choices than the guards moved in, surrounding them on all sides and relieving them of their weapons at swordpoint. Marin growled and raised his spear, but in an instant four swords pricked the skin of his throat.

Then the captain, with his sword at Marin's throat, said, "Do not throw your life away for nothing. The weapons will be given back to you in good time. It is nothing to me if you choose to die. If you want to make a fight of it, we will gladly spill your blood here and now."

Marin hesitated and then, a contemptuous sneer twisting his lips, he dropped the lance to the ground with a clatter. Brushing the swords aside, he swaggered toward the door, forcing the guards to hurry after him.

This proved to be the end of their outing and they were marched back to their cell following the curve of the passageway as well as a labyrinth of dark, twisting corridors. It was apparent that the arena and its surrounding environs consisted of a far larger area than any of them had realized.

Throughout the entire journey, there had been the rumble and shriek of wild animals, sometimes distant and at other times seeming quite close. Several times they had intersected corridors that sloped down, and the sounds were loudest of all at these junctures as was the stink of wet fur and offal.

"I don't understand," Braldt said to Randi as the door to the cell clanged shut behind them and they settled onto the cold, stone floor. In their absence, the water bucket and the flea-infested blanket had been reclaimed by the inhabitants of the cell.

"What don't you understand?" Septua asked, casually resting his hand on Randi's thigh.

"I don't understand why they took us through all that nonsense. What is it they have planned for us?" she replied with a frown, lifting the dwarf's hand off her thigh and placing it firmly in his lap.

"I think we are to fight, to provide entertainment for these so-called Masters," Braldt said slowly. "Remember what they said, we are to fight or perish."

Marin smiled, an unpleasant grimace with no hint of humor in it, and he cracked his knuckles as though wishing it were someone's neck. "I will fight for them gladly," he said, the points of his teeth visible behind his bared lips. "And maybe I will kill a few of them along the way."

Septua's mobile face brightened at the thought of reclaiming his deadly assortment of toys and he nodded his approval. "When we are armed, they cannot stand up to us, I think. After we kill a few of them, then we will escape!"

A shrill cackle interrupted their conversation. A small, withered figure wrapped in rags, its gender and even its race indeterminable, wiped its rheumy eyes as spittle drooled from its toothless mouth. "Escape you say? Why, you fools, don't you know that the only way you're likely to escape this place is feet first, if you still got any feet left when they be done with you?"

"What are you saying?" Marin demanded, seizing the ragged creature and shaking it violently. The old man's hand streaked inside its mantle of filthy rags and withdrew a homemade blade, slashing Marin across the wrist. Marin released the stinking bundle with a curse and clamped his hand on the wound which was already coursing with streams of bright blood.

"You are fools," the old one said bitterly as he scrambled backward out of Marin's reach. "No one gets out of here alive. No one. We exist only for the pleasure of the Masters. When you cease to amuse them you will die just like all the others. They will feed you and dress you and arm you and set you against each other. You will vow undying friendship and loyalty to one another, but in the end you will betray each other. Some few of you will remain loyal and those will die soonest. The others, those with the least amount of loyalty or trust, will live longer, but in the end, they will die, too. Death is the only escape from the arena."

8

"It cannot be true, nor would I believe it had I not seen him with my own eyes," the man said in a whisper as he turned from the narrow slit in the wall and sagged against it in despair.

His companion stepped forward and peered through the narrow crack, no more than a chink between the stones unless one knew what to look for. He wore a troubled expression on his lean face. "Perhaps we are mistaken. Maybe we are imagining it simply because we wish it to be so," he said in a low voice.

"Think what you are saying, Erte. Why would we wish to see Jocobe here in this place, a prisoner, fodder for the games? No one misses him more than I, but surely he is better off in exile, far better anywhere than here. To be here is death. And if it is Jocobe, where is Mirim? No, I think we are deceived. This is merely one who looks like Jocobe through some trick of fate."

"I have never known another race that looked like us," Erte said softly, laying a hand on his friend's shoulder. "We are unique in the universe as well you know, Brit. This is Jocobe; it can be no other. The question is, what shall we do about it?"

"We cannot let them put him into the arena," Brit

said despondently, sinking back against the wall. "Dare we risk rescuing him? How could he have fallen into their hands a second time? I thought he was safe from harm on that speck of a world. How does he come to be here?"

"It has been twenty years and more since we saw him last," said Erte. "Anything could have happened on that distant world. One of us had best attend a Council meeting; they cannot keep from gloating, and one of them will say something and tell us what we wish to know."

"They will not talk with us there," Brit said bitterly.

"No, Brit, you are wrong. That is precisely why they *will* talk," argued Erte. "They always suspected that we were sympathetic to Jocobe and Mirim's cause, even if they could not prove it. They will not miss this opportunity to let us know that he is in their grasp again."

"But how, Erte, how could it have happened? All these years, with all the defeats, at least I have been able to think that they were safe and well, living their lives in peace, that our efforts have not all been in vain. My little sister . . . and the child? What of the child?"

"Calm yourself, my friend. The years have not been entirely in their favor, we have had our victories too. Kiefer's way has not been entirely free of strife. Jocobe and Mirim will be proud to learn what we have accomplished. Nor are we alone or powerless in the Council these days. There are many who side with us and many more who would do so if only they dared. The day is fast approaching when we will be strong enough to challenge Kiefer openly rather than work from behind the scenes.''

"We cannot let them have Jocobe," Brit said resolutely. "Somehow we must rescue him. He is not a young man. He would not survive the arena. Somehow we must save him."

Erte opened his mouth to speak, to remind his friend of the difficulty and danger of such a task, but seeing the steely resolve in Brit's cold, blue eyes, he could only nod in silent agreement. She was right. Somehow it would be done.

9

Batta Flor wakened with a bad taste in his mouth. His tongue was coated with foulness as though a merebear had hibernated there. He opened his eyes slowly and groaned as a bright, red light struck him, driving shards of crimson sunlight into his brain. A shadow fell over him, dulling the light somewhat, and sounds echoed inside his head. He lifted a large hand and shaded his eyes, blinking against the light, trying to bring the figure into focus. Distantly, he took note of the absence of strength in his body, but somehow it failed to concern him. He squinted upward.

"Batta Flor, don't you recognize me?" The voice spoke, the lips opening and shutting in a comic manner, and then slowly, the words themselves filtered through and took shape inside his mind. He grunted and lay back, closing his eyes with a sigh. His hand thumped against the ground, too heavy to hold upright.

Small hands seized his shoulders and shook him; a flea trying to move a boulder. He ignored them and began to drift back into the comfortable, muzzy darkness that had held him for so long.

But the voice turned insistent, and the hands on his body refused to relinquish him to sleep, tugging and pulling, yanking him this way and that, forcing his head upright, even prying his eyelids open and yelling into his face. What did they want of him? Why would they not let him be?

The thing would not go away and now it was joined by a second creature who yapped and yipped in a most annoying manner. The sounds were muted, muffled as though they came from far away, but it was hard to ignore them, knowing they were there. The smaller creature seized hold of his hand, sinking its double rows of spiked teeth into his tough, dark skin and began to pull. Batta Flor could see the dots of blood welling between the beast's teeth. He could see the bright, red trickles of blood as they matted his thick fur and dripped onto the ground. Some part of his mind that was still functioning recoiled in anticipation of the pain, but there was none. He felt no pain. He felt nothing.

The ... girl, yes, that was what she was! His mind wrapped itself sluggishly around the word. The girl stared in horror at the blood and tried to pull the beast away without success. Tears began to course down her cheeks.

It was this that stirred him at last, the depth of the girl's distress. Somehow he had to let her know that it didn't matter, that he was not hurt.

He sat up slowly, and closing his fingers around the muzzle of the yapping creature, brought pressure to bear at the base of its jaws. A startled look filled the beast's eyes and its jaws popped open. Batta Flor extracted his hand and examined it casually, inspecting the damage calmly as though it had happened to someone else. Blood still dripped from the neat row of punctures, but his skin was quite thick, and as there was no pain, he felt no concern. He shrugged and tried to smile to reassure the girl, but she did not appear to be comforted at all. Instead, she cried all the harder and buried her face against his chest.

Batta Flor looked down at her, taking note of her neaving shoulders, feeling the warm moisture of her tears as they seeped through his fur and onto his chest. He knew that he should do something, the same portion of his brain that told him about the pain urged him to respond to the girl's distress. But he could not think of what it was that he was supposed to do and so he did nothing, merely let her cry until there were no tears left.

After a time, the girl sat down next to him. She tucked her hand into his and rested her head on his shoulder. "Don't worry, Batta Flor. We'll get out of here, wherever here is. I'll think of a way somehow and I'll get us home, the three of us. And I'll get your ear fixed, too. That must be what's wrong—why you're acting like this and why you don't feel the pain. Don't worry, I'll take care of us."

Batta Flor heard the words. They buzzed around inside his head like flocks of stingers. Some of them bore meaning, others were merely sounds. Worry? What was there to worry about? The girl droned on, speaking to him earnestly, reassuringly, patting his arm from time to time and looking up at him with worried eyes. After a while, Batta Flor lost interest in the girl and her words and stared ahead with empty eyes, thinking and feeling nothing.

10

Sweat poured off Braldt's body as the heat from the crimson suns beat down on his head and shoulders. The unfamiliar weight of the metal helm covering his head distracted him, as did the strip of metal that extended across the bridge of his brows and down the length of his nose, but he did his best to ignore it, grateful for what little protection it offered. Never taking his eyes from his opponent, he circled warily, feeling the red stone and sand crunch beneath his sturdy, leather sandals, shaking the salty, stinging sweat from his eyes. The metal-sheathed butt of the spear struck out suddenly and whistled past his head, missing him by a narrow margin. Marin chuckled mirthlessly, the suns glinting off his pointy, black teeth in a rainbow of light.

Braldt was accustomed to being the best in everything, especially in combat. Seldom if ever had any of his comrades been his equal in strength or skill. Others had surpassed him when he was younger, but as he grew to adulthood, none could match his abilities. He had always been the best.

Here, everything was different. In the days that had passed since their capture he had seen many who were as good as he, and not a few who were better. And those were merely the human types. Of those who were of unfamiliar races, there was no counting the variety of peculiar and very deadly skills they employed. There was a large, amorphous thing whose shape changed from moment to moment, flowing effortlessly from place to place as easily as the wind blows, who had no real skills as such, but possessed the ability to expel a cloud of noxious gas that killed anything unfortunate enough to pass within its range. Other creatures had multiple limbs capable of wielding a multitude of weapons.

The routine was always the same. They were led out of their dark, odiferous cell early each morning, long before the dual orbs crested the edge of the dark horizon, and led shivering to a cavernous hall where they filed past ranks of steaming kettles. These enormous cauldrons were overseen by a bent, reptilian crone most certainly blood-related to the water carrier of the dungeons. Here they received a thick, gluey dollop of cereal and a mug of hot brew, unidentifiable in content but welcome for the jolt of stimulus it imparted. The steaming cereal did more than fill the emptiness in their bellies, for it sustained them throughout the long and arduous morning that followed.

After the brief meal, they were given their weapons under the watchful eyes of the guards and led into the arena where they sparred and honed their skills against one another until the suns hung directly overhead and even their keepers showed the effects of the heat.

Marching back into the welcome shadows of the arches at the edge of the arena whose darkness imparted little or no relief from the rising temperatures, they collapsed on the hot sand and rested until the suns made their slow descent from the burnished sky. The reptilian water carrier, still muttering to itself, trundled up and down the line of sprawled, exhausted bodies, doling out lukewarm tots of moisture that did little to replace the fluid they had expended.

A second lizard followed in its wake, silent and uncommunicative, passing out fist-sized lumps that contained grains, nuts, shreds of meat, and strange, red pebbles of tart sweetness, perhaps a fruit, all bound together by a suety, clotted, white fat that left a disagreeable coating on the tongue and roof of one's mouth. But Braldt ate it and urged his companions to do the same, for he recognized that disgusting as it was, the lumps had been formulated to provide them with everything their bodies needed to remain in good condition.

It was becoming increasingly obvious to all of them that despite their circumstances, their captors had no particular wish to harm them or see them dead. At least not immediately. They were treated as though they were valuable herd animals, their physical needs scrupulously attended. Injuries were seen to immediately and their condition and ability assessed constantly by the prowling guards. Those who were seriously injured and those in the cells who failed to prove useful at the various menial chores, however, disappeared and were never seen again.

After the suns edged past the top of the arena, they were herded back into the amphitheater where they continued their competitions until nightfall.

Occasionally, early on, there were those who could not or would not fight. Clusters of guards gathered around these individuals and they were urged by word and metal-toed boot to resume their activities. A few did not need the warning. The first time this occurred, a pale, blond youth from Randi's home planet lay mewling on the ground, arms covering his head, weeping hysterically, refusing to move.

A dark figure emerged from the arches and came speeding across the loose, shifting sands. Braldt started, a surge of anger coursing through his body as he stared at the new arrival. It was a hard one, its legs replaced by a single, broad wheel centered below its waist. It conferred with the guards who maintained a careful, respectful distance, their eyes averted.

The guards spoke urgently to the youngster, prodding him with their feet and the butts of their spears, but the youth was too far gone to respond. And then, in obvious response to an order from the hard one, despite the crowd of onlookers, or perhaps because of them, one of the guards lifted his spear and plunged it into the body of the helpless boy, impaling him. Dark, red blood gushed out of the thrashing body and poured onto the coarse, red earth.

When the last of the boy's life had ebbed away, the guard withdrew his spear. The body was left to lie where it had fallen, and numb with shock and anger, the prisoners were forced to resume their battles, the pitiful corpse lying untended like a bit of cast-off garbage. Still, there were those who tried to defy the guards, but any and all resistance was dealt with swiftly and harshly. Those who remained did as they were bid, following the brusque regime, rising each morning for the brief bit of sustenance, fighting all day in the hot sun, then collapsing in the cold, damp dungeons, too exhausted, both mentally and physically, to even contemplate escape. For a few moments before sleep came, they may have pondered the reason for this new existence, wondered what the future might hold. But all too soon, they drifted into silent sleep, too exhausted to pursue their thoughts.

All except Braldt. No less exhausted than his companions, his mind refused to cease its constant ramblings. Who were these Masters and why had they been brought here to such a place? Was it possible that they had been assembled for no other reason than to fight for the amusement of these so-called Masters? The idea was preposterous, but by their own statement, it appeared to be so. They were being groomed for the arena—that much was obvious—and only the best would survive. If and when they won a match, they would be rewarded by the answer to a question, and by the gift of life itself.

But how long could any one of them hope to survive? Although the training was rigorous, the guards harder taskmasters than any Braldt had known before, his body was responding well. True, he was bruised and stiff and sported half a dozen minor wounds, but he had also attained a new level of proficiency and could already feel his muscles working past their complaints, sliding more smoothly, becoming more powerful.

There was joy in the heft of the new weapons, the blade better balanced, more keen than any he had known before. The guards did double duty as trainers and he was learning moves and ploys that had been unknown at home. Much of what he learned was unconventional and even underhanded, but if it meant his survival, honor was a luxury he could not afford.

Whenever he was able, he watched his companions, Septua, Marin, and Randi, as well as the others, all of whom had to be considered as opponents.

Marin constituted the greatest single threat, for even though they had been grouped together and were considered a team, he entertained no such thoughts, and for some unknown reason, singled Braldt out as his personal enemy and sought to fight him whenever there was an opportunity. Normally, they were paired with others not of their team for their daily matches. But Marin often overrode that arrangement, pushing aside Braldt's assigned opponent and substituting himself in the other's stead. At first, the guards had sought to intercede, but they were a cruel and indifferent bunch and were quick to see the humor in pitting the two teammates against one another.

Marin fought with spear, trident, and weighted net, as well as a dagger in his belt. Braldt himself fought with the more conventional weapons he had been accustomed to, a double-edged long sword, a more utilitarian short sword for close work, and a shield.

Fighting Marin was tricky business, for both of them depended on keeping their opponent at bay with sword, spear, and trident while seizing their moment to dart inside the other's guard and put an end to the battle with the smaller weapons. But Marin and Braldt were evenly matched in ability, neither of them being obviously superior. Marin was larger and heavier than Braldt, and had he been able to pin him, the contest would have been over. But his bulk also worked against him, for Braldt was far more agile and moved more swiftly, avoiding the larger man's moves with relative ease.

Nor did the deadly game cease when the day's activities drew to an end, for Marin fixed on Braldt with singleminded determination that did not waver. He wanted to kill him. While not unwilling to fight the black man, Braldt would have preferred to do so with a weapon in his hand, and as time passed, he found it wearying to watch his back against the possibility of an attack.

Randi and Septua had allied themselves with him, disliking and distrusting Marin, perhaps realizing that if Braldt were to die, they themselves would become his next victims. Their decision quickly earned them Marin's scorn and hatred. They kept as much space between themselves and the black man as possible, sleeping on the far side of the dungeon cell and allowing others to come between them in the food and water lines. There were no weapons outside the ring, but Marin needed no weapons. He could snap their necks between his fingers as easily as one broke a dry stick—if he could get close enough. They took care to see that he did not.

One morning, Braldt and his allies were overjoyed to see that Allo had been returned to the cell, his wounds healed. They greeted him gladly, for all had feared that the gentle Allo had perished. The other inhabitants of the cell, those who had caused his injuries, ignored him, less than happy at his presence, for he represented one more mouth to compete for the water and one more empty belly to fill.

While the morning meal was closely observed and

fairly apportioned, at least for those who were being readied for the ring, the evening meal was another matter. The reptilian crone delivered the kettles to the guards and its dispensation was left to them; the guards missed no opportunity to bully or humiliate those in their charge. On some nights, prisoners were paired against one another, both portions of food the incentive for the victor. If both refused to fight, neither was fed. At other times, the entire cell's worth of food was dumped onto the filthy floor and the guards stood back, safe behind the bars, laughing at the melee that followed.

Sickened at first by the indignity and not wishing to provide the guards with entertainment, Braldt had refused to fight, refused to become a part of the snarling mass that clawed and fought for a handful of food. But the pains in his belly, and more importantly, the resulting weakness in his limbs, soon convinced him that dignity would have to join honor; neither were affordable under the present circumstances.

For seven days they toiled in the arena and on the eighth day they rested, confined to their cells for the entire day and night. But even though they welcomed the respite, there was little or no rest, for on that eighth day the games were held.

Even though they themselves were far below ground and a fair distance from the gaming area, they had no difficulty hearing the musical fanfare that preceded each match or the roars and screams of the crowd. And even more ominously, the hideous shrieks and sudden silences.

There was little talk on the eighth day, the captives

silent, wrapped in their own unhappy thoughts. Nor did they respond to the guards' cruel banter and had little appetite for their evening rations.

As game day drew to an end, the crimson light streaming through the high windows staining them all the color of fresh blood, a single, drawn-out death cry pierced the air and hung there until it was suddenly choked off, all the more horrifying for its abrupt end. A heavy silence fell upon the dungeon and the captives eyed each other nervously. Their silence was broken by one of the guards, a one-eyed monster noted for his penchant for cruelty. He raised his scarred face to the bloody light as though savoring the echoes of that terrible cry, then looked at them with his single, glittering eye.

"Best start saying your prayers. It's your turn next."

His words brought instant consternation to the inhabitants of the cell. Some spoke bravely, boldly issuing challenges and admonishing their unknown competitors to bolster their own courage. A few wept, but most held their tongues, retreating into their thoughts, pondering the fragility of their lives and perhaps thinking of those they had left behind.

These thoughts were never far from Braldt's mind. He himself, while somewhat concerned about the prospect of the games, welcomed the opportunity for action and the possibility of learning the answers to the questions that troubled him most. Those questions and thoughts were always at the back of his mind, worrying away at his heart. His concern was not so much for himself but the need to know what had happened to the others in his absence.

Randi had proved herself to be a loyal companion and her combat skills were impressive. She had also indicated in subtle ways that she would not be adverse to a closer relationship. Braldt appreciated her handsome features and her quick wit, and was attracted by her lithe, trim body, but in the end he always retreated, for she was not Keri.

The memory of Keri filled his thoughts, waking and sleeping, and he worried about what had become of her. Did she think about him, too? Did she believe him to be dead? Would she forget him in time? These thoughts and others equally disturbing and unanswerable chased themselves round and round in his head as he lay waiting for sleep to come night after tormented night.

Batta Flor and Beast shared his thoughts, too, as well as concern for Auslic and Carn, his jealous and ambition-torn brother. What had become of them and how had his disappearance affected their lives? He would have given anything to know. If the Masters had told the truth, victory would earn him the answer to one of his questions. Braldt was not accustomed to taking lives except to protect his own, but if deathdealing were the cost of learning what had happened to those he loved, he had no choice but to steel himself for the task.

11

There were not many of them, all things considered, especially when one balanced the dangers and the risks involved, as well as the overwhelming numbers opposing them. But they represented some of their best and brightest minds, and they were determined to set right the wrong that was being done. The stakes were far larger than the cost of their lives.

To look at them was like looking into a multi-faceted glass that reflected multiple images of the same object. They were identical in all but the most minor of details. All were tall, men and women alike standing a hand's width over six feet, slender and willowy of build, with broad shoulders and narrow hips and waists. Their eyes were a bright, clear shade of cerulean blue, their cheekbones high, prominent, and slanted upward. Their hair was such a light shade of silvery blond as to nearly disappear in strong light. And while their eyes spoke of great intellect, their bodies spoke eloquently in their fragile delicacy of generation after generation of line breeding.

"Are you sure there can be no doubt?" a woman murmured, her long fingers twisting nervously in her lap. "After all, there are so many different permutations among them, perhaps he just looks . . . an accident, you know. . . ."

"No, Lomi, there is no mistake, no accident. He is one of us," Erte said gently.

"But how could he have survived in such a place after all these years?" asked another woman.

"More importantly, how could they have dared to bring him back?" stammered a third. "Can they be so reckless, so bold? Do they truly believe themselves to be above the law? Surely they realize the risk?"

"Yes, I think they do consider themselves above the law," the man said reflectively, pondering the woman's questions. "They certainly do not take us seriously, we have had ample evidence of that. But what do they have at risk? They have escaped detection for so long the risk is minimal, and unless we do something to help him, he will surely die. It's only a matter of time. No one can hold out forever in the ring. And once he is dead, they will feed his body to the beasts, and the risk, what little there was, will cease to exist."

"But what can we do?" asked one of the men as he fidgeted and rearranged the green gemstone on his shoulder which held his body cloth secure. "If what you say is true, this one is kin to me, the son of my sister, and I, more than any of you, have to try to save him. But we are so few; even if we were to attempt such a thing, how could we do it?

"Just think of the danger involved, not only from those of our own kind, but the gamers. How do we know what he has become over the years? What if he does not know who or what he is? Even worse, what if he hates us, blames us for deserting him?''

"What are you saying, Jorund? Are you saying that we should leave him where he is, let him take his chances in the ring?" challenged the first woman, her fingers twined stiffly among themselves.

"No," Jorund said heavily. "For the memory of my sister, if for no other reason, we must help him and pray that his heritage has sustained him on that barbaric planet. But by the stars, I pray that we are right."

"Pray to the stars all you wish, Jorund. Who knows, it may even help," Erte said dryly. "But I think it will be more useful to help us think of a plan that will get the job done."

There was an awkward silence as the two men stared at one another, then a woman cleared her throat and spoke. "Look here, what about this tunnel here . . ." The tension broken, there was a sudden babble of voices as the small group gathered around the woman and offered up their thoughts for consideration.

This day was different. They could feel it in the air, a sort of nervous tension that tingled along the skin and bristled hair in anticipation. Nothing was said, no sign was given, but everyone could feel it.

Braldt sipped his hot brew, forcing himself to swallow the steaming liquid. He knew he would need the energy for whatever was to come, but it was impossible to eat. The few bites he swallowed lay like lumps of stone in his belly and he knew that he would be sick if he forced himself further. He shoved his plate away and looked out across the vast hall, already half obscured by a miasma of steam from the kitchen fires and the rising stink of unwashed bodies.

The others shared his apprehension. All around him was the flash of frightened eyes and the babble of tongues loosened by terror. He could smell the fear on them, a brassy, metallic, sour stink. There had been no word, and yet they knew.

The guards broke the fearful reverie, moving in from the edges of the room and herding them out into the arena even though few among them had finished their meals. Utensils, half-filled bowls, and cups still trailing their pennants of steam, remained at their places, and Braldt could not help but wonder as he was driven toward the arena at spear point, how many of those cups would be lifted at the end of the day.

The suns had just crested the edge of the red stone walls and were already beating down full force on the sands of the arena though the last of the night's chill still hovered above the ground.

Without words, the guards divided up the groups and passed out their weapons. The guards seemed especially watchful and their numbers were nearly doubled, standing in pairs around the edge of the arena with swords drawn and shields raised.

When the last of the groups were armed, a trio of men appeared, framed by the narrow arches of the stone tiers. They were flanked by six hard ones, but it was the men themselves who earned Braldt's attention. He stared at them in disbelief. Despite the distance separating them, he could see quite clearly that they were so like him as to be mirror images! They were as tall as he, and as blond, and their bone structure was the same. He was not able to see their eyes but somehow knew without a doubt that the eyes would be the same bright shade of blue. Each of the men wore a white drape of cloth about their bodies, fastened at the shoulder with a silver ring. The rings flashed shards of green and red and blue in the sunlight, and unconsciously, Braldt's fingers rose to his own shoulder to stroke the ring that was no longer there. He had once owned such a ring! Who could these people be and what did it all mean?

Confusion tore at his mind, conflicting thoughts pinwheeling through his head as he stared at the men who were most probably his enemy yet looked enough like him to be brother or father or both. Then a voice intruded on his thoughts, speaking in imperious tones through the silver disc fastened to his skull. "Contestants, gladiators, the games are about to commence. The moment you have waited for will soon be here. We have followed your progress with interest and feel certain that the contests will be worthy of our efforts."

Those standing in the arena began to stir restlessly, eyes darting nervously in all directions. "Worth whose effort?" spat one of the reptilian men, his comment echoed by a score of his companions.

The regal voice continued on as though unaware of the murmur of discontent rising from the sands below. "As promised, at the close of each contest, the victors will be rewarded by the answer of a question. But before the games begin, there is one further bit of business that must be completed. As you will notice, each team consists of five members. Unfortunately, that is one too many. Your first task will be the elimination of one member of your team. That choice we leave up to you. . . .''

A loud outcry rose from the armed gathering. Team-mates stared at each other in distrust and dismay while others brandished their weapons at the speakers.

"You will choose the member to be eliminated, or we will make the choice for you," the speaker said, his voice growing harsh and cold. "There is nothing to be gained by procrastinating, for the outcome will be the same."

Beside Braldt, a small, furred creature with four arms whirled on its companions, those it had eaten, slept, and trained beside, and stabbed a smooth-skinned hunch-back between the eyes, pinning him to the ground and falling on his chest with his knees until the flailing limbs lay limp and unmoving in the red dust. The furred beast clung to his weapon and glared defiantly, baring his fangs in a growl at those who stared at him in shocked disbelief.

All around him there were mutters and the ring of steel being drawn from scabbards and sheathes. On the perimeter of the arena, the guards moved closer, closing the circle, weapons at the ready for the first sign of rebellion.

"This ain't right," complained a voice. "They can't make us kill each other, can they? I mean, it ain't like we're all cold blooded . . ." There was a sudden shriek and the voice ended abruptly.

Randi moved to Braldt's side, pressing her lithe

form against him, drawing the object that she had named a laser gun and thumbing it back to the stun setting. Allo and Septua drew in as well until the four of them stood back to back in a tight formation bristling with weaponry in all directions. Marin was the odd man out.

Still, Braldt had no wish to fight the black man, or see him die for that matter. If they must fight in competition, the black man would be a valuable fighter—he was strong and skillful and crafty in the art of deception. To sacrifice any of his companions was unthinkable.

"Marin, we do not have to do as they say," said Braldt, lowering his sword and speaking earnestly to the black man who had gone into a crouch, his trident extended before him, nearly touching Braldt's chest. "Let us put our differences aside and fight together; they cannot make us fight each other if we refuse."

The sounds of battle were all around him, steel ringing against steel, the thunder of small explosions, the screams of men dying. Marin's eyes were shuttered against the rising suns. His blue-black lips were drawn back in a mirthless grin that exposed his filed, pointed teeth. He was crouching low, his trident jabbing forward like the tongue of a striking snake. In his other hand the net swirled slowly, the weights sighing through the air with a low moan. If he heard Braldt's words, he gave no sign, but advanced steadily, his small, dark eyes never leaving Braldt's face.

"He means to fight," Randi said tensely. "I'll throw a jolt into him, knock him out until we can talk some reason into him." She pointed the stubby weapon at

Marin who did not even spare her a glance, but Allo pressed his huge, shaggy hand down upon her wrist gently.

"No," he said softly. "If it does not happen now, it will merely postpone the inevitable. Marin is determined to fight Braldt. He has been seeking such a confrontation. We cannot stop it."

"But what if he wins," Randi said in dismay, turning to look at the large, shaggy creature. "Would you follow him? Look at his eyes—he's crazy!"

"When we entered this place we gave up the right to reason. Such standards do not exist here," Allo said sadly. "At least not for us."

Septua joined the argument, his shrill, high-pitched voice adding to the confusion, but Braldt had ceased to listen to their words, realizing that the time for words had long since passed, if it had ever existed. He had met such men as Marin before. Confrontation, action, death—these were what mattered. Logic, reason, and words stood for nothing. The mistake was in thinking that such men were stupid. It was a mistake that could be fatal. While the heads of such men were empty of higher thoughts, they *were* filled with strategy and technique and their bodies were often trained to perfection. They made the best of allies and the very worst of enemies.

Braldt drew his sword and fell into the same shuffling sidestep employed by Marin. Matching each other stride for stride, they began to circle. Randi and Septua fell silent and pressed up against Allo's shaggy hide, watching the duel with fearful eyes.

The arena echoed with the sounds of combat, angry grunts, choked exhalations of effort, shrieks of agony, and the sobs of frightened men about to die. Braldt closed his mind to the noise and movement around him, focusing only on Marin's shiny body, studying the way he moved, taking note of the manner in which he held his trident, the rise and fall of the weighted net.

The weights increased the measure of their speed, whup, whup, whup, as they swiftly sped through the air, describing an even larger circle. Marin's eyes squinted more tightly and Braldt saw his fingers tighten on the haft of the trident. Stepping forward, Braldt broke through the circle and stepped directly inside Marin's guard, too close for him to use either trident or net and unable to reach for the short dagger in his belt without dropping one of his weapons. Without pausing, seeing Marin's eyes open wide with shock, seeing the small mind trying to decide what to do, Braldt reversed his sword and struck with all the power he possessed, striking Marin square between the eyes with the heavy, sheathed butt. Marin stopped cold as though he had run into a solid wall of stone. His tongue came out of his mouth and flicked back and forth as he tried to speak, but no words emerged. His eyes rolled back in their sockets, revealing hideous, gray-black corneas mottled with flecks of crimson, and he fell back without a sound, landing flat on the ground where he lay without moving.

"Is he dead?" cried Randi.

"No, just stunned, I think, although his brains, what few there are, will be addled for some time to come," Braldt said with satisfaction as he sheathed his sword and knelt at Marin's side, gathering up the big man's weapons just to be safe.

Before he could rise, two of the imperious blond men appeared beside him, although he had not sensed their advance. Four hard ones, armed with slender, metal staffs, stood behind them, flanking them on either side, their smooth faces impassive, devoid of any expression.

One of the men poked Marin with his toe. The big man did not move. The man raised his eyes to Braldt's— incredible eyes, eyes the color of the bluest of skies, eyes without guile or pretense or evil, the eyes of a child.

"Kill him," the man said gently, his eyes locked on Braldt's.

Braldt stared at him in shock, wondering if he had heard correctly. It seemed impossible that such words could have come from the man's lips. It was an abomination, an obscenity!

"Kill him," the man repeated, speaking slowly and clearly as though Braldt were incapable of understanding the words. Braldt shook his head dumbly.

The man sighed and shook his head sadly, then nodded to one of the hard ones. The metallic man raised his rod and positioned it delicately in the center of Marin's flanged ear. Braldt watched in disbelief, waiting for the man to counteract his command. But he did not speak; his eyes resting on Braldt, a small smile played at the corner of his mouth.

"No," cried Braldt as he flung himself at the hard one, striking it full in the chest as he tried to wrestle the rod from his grasp. The hard one swayed slightly as it balanced on its single wheel, but its grip on the metal rod never loosened, and even as Braldt seized it in his hands and pulled with all his strength, the metallic man drove the rod into the fallen team member's skull. The black man jerked spasmodically, his eyes came into focus, filled with agony and rage and fixed on the horrorstruck Braldt who clung helplessly to the cause of the man's death.

Black blood, thick and viscous, spewed from Marin's ear, drenching Braldt's feet and spattering his legs hotly as intelligence and life faded from the hate-filled eyes. Marin's arms and legs continued to thrash, long minutes after his brain had died, but the body remained firmly pinned to the ground by the thin, metal shaft.

Randi had uttered a shrill cry when the hard one drove the rod into Marin, a cry that had ended abruptly in a choked sob; Septua had doubled over and emptied his stomach of its content. Only Allo had remained silent, enfolding his two companions against his shaggy body, watching with saddened eyes, perhaps realizing more fully than any of the others the true nature of their captors and accepting with his stoical nature the futility of resistance.

But stoicism had no place in Braldt's vocabulary and he would have thrown himself at the blond man who had given the death order had Allo not realized his intent and wrapped his long arms around Braldt, firmly pinning his arms to his sides.

The hard one reacted swiftly, pulling the rod out of Marin's limp body and bracing the end, dripping with inky ichor, in the center of Braldt's chest. There was no doubt at all that it would have shoved the staff into Braldt with as little hesitation as it had used to dispatch Marin. All it lacked was the order to do so.

The blond man studied Braldt, the smile never leaving his lips. He turned to his companion who had until this moment remained silent.

"What think you, Jorund, will this one be more trouble than he's worth? Perhaps we would be wise to rid ourselves of him now."

The one called Jorund met Braldt's eyes. Braldt's eyes blazed with rage, his pulse beat furiously in his temples, and he struggled to free himself from Allo's embrace. Meeting the man's gaze was like being plunged into an icy stream, the shock was so great. Yet in that single, swift glance, he saw compassion and concern as well as a silent plea for caution. Braldt stiffened, wondering if he had imagined it. He studied the man's face, looking for confirmation, but the man known as Jorund had lowered his eyes and stared at the ground as though the matter was of little importance to him.

"No, Kiefer, I think it would be more amusing to let him live," he drawled. "Some of us are interested in this one."

Braldt's heart began to pound as he watched the man, wondering if he had been mistaken in believing that he had given a message as well as a warning.

The man known as Kiefer hesitated, and for the first time Braldt was able to read uncertainty in his stance. Abruptly, he dismissed the hard one who lowered his weapon and rolled off in reverse, balanced on his single wheel.

"I hope you are right, Jorund. I hope we are not

making a dreadful mistake. I—I had thought, had hoped that he would be the one to be winnowed. The black man was so much the stronger and it would have simplified matters.''

"Strength means nothing. Strength will fail every time when pitted against a determined, superior intelligence," said Jorund, and this time there was no denying it—as he spoke he looked directly at Braldt and the words were most certainly intended for him.

12

After Marin's death, events moved at a rapid rate.
The long hours of training grew longer still, often stretching
into the nights as the newly formed groups of four
learned to work together as a team, honing their skills
and their many different techniques. They learned much
they had not known about each other and grew to
appreciate each other's strengths.

Randi, they learned, had been a flight navigator on
an intergalactic, scientific expedition. Her vessel had
been struck by a cluster of meteorites which had penetrated the hull. The resulting loss of oxygen had killed
everyone aboard with the exception of Randi who had
had the good fortune to be wearing a space suit which
contained its own supply of oxygen. She had been
outside the hull of the ship, overseeing the repair of an
instrument, and had seen the shower of boulders hurtling
toward the ship but had been powerless to do anything
but shout a warning before they struck; her companions
were killed outright.

By using the air tanks of her dead shipmates, she
had piloted the dying craft to the nearest rescue station
which unfortunately was located on an uninhabited aster-
oid. She had activated the emergency distress call, hop-

ing against hope that someone would hear her signal in that desolate corner of the solar system and arrive before her supply of oxygen was depleted.

Her call was heard and a rescue ship did arrive, but to Randi's dismay it ignored the intergalactic code that governed the treatment of shipwrecked victims and immediately plundered her ship and took her prisoner.

Allo's story was not dissimilar. He had been the purser of a heavily loaded trading freighter that had been attacked by pirates. Their frantic calls for assistance had been heard and answered, but the armed robots who soon appeared on the scene had disarmed everyone and taken all of them, pirates and victims alike, prisoner.

Septua alone remained silent on the subject of his past, diverting them with bits of nonsense and clever chatter whenever they asked a question. For all his loquaciousness and glibness, he was strangely silent about his past and how he had come to be in his current predicament.

Their stories were told at night, bit by bit, as they came to know and trust one another, and it served to bind them more closely. Marin's death had changed that. After returning to their cell, Braldt had shared his thoughts with his companions and discussed with them what he thought he had heard, the veiled promise of help. Hearing the hope in Braldt's voice and the excitement of the others' responses finally broke Septua's silence.

"I know them," he said in a bitter voice. "They won't 'elp you."

"What are you talking about?" said Randi as they

turned to stare at the little man. "What do you mean, you know them?"

Septua seemed to shrink inside himself, drawing his large head down between his shoulders and twisting his hands in a manner quite unlike anything they had come to expect from the brash, little dwarf.

"I know 'em. Lived with 'em all my life on their 'ome planet. I know that you can't trust 'em, not none of 'em, no matter what they says."

They stared at him in silent disbelief, unwilling to think that he had valuable information that he had withheld from them, information that might have spared them pain and grief and perhaps even prevented their team member's death.

Septua felt the weight of their eyes upon him and averted his head. "You wouldn't 'ave understood. How could I 'ave told you, you're all so upright and fancy. Pilots and navigators and sons of chiefs and the like. 'Ow would you 'ave understood what it was like for me? You wouldn't 'ave, there's no way you could understand what it's like to be small and ugly. I never 'ad the chance to be nuthin' but what I become . . . a thief. Would you 'ave liked me if you 'ad known? Would you 'ave let me be one of you then? No, I'd be the one dead instead of Marin."

Septua's voice rose to an hysterical pitch and rang shrill in the cold darkness of the cell. The murmur of voices fell silent and watchful as the dwellers of the dungeon held their breath and waited to see or hear what would come next, thankful that it was not they themselves who were at the heart of the crisis.

Braldt held out his hands to the little man and tried to calm him, but Septua jerked away at his touch as though Braldt had struck him. He avoided Allo's reach and backed into a corner where he burrowed into the darkness as though trying to crawl into the stones themselves. Brushing Braldt and Allo aside, Randi knelt in front of Septua, making no attempt to touch him.

"I do not think it is fair to judge us by the treatment you have received in the past. Have we not been true friends and stood beside you from the start? Do you trust us so little that you would hold back information that might help us all to live? Come now, Septua, have we not shown ourselves to be honorable? What can it matter what one looks like in such a place as this? Survival is what matters and if not survival, then death with honor among friends. Do you not count me as a friend, Septua?"

"I wouldn't be your friend for long if you knew about me," sniveled the dwarf.

"I do not know or care what you have been before now," replied Randi, choosing her words carefully. "I know only that you have been a loyal companion to me here in this place. That you keep my spirits high when I am depressed and cheer me when I lose hope. What you did before we knew you matters not. Come, my friend, share your knowledge with us, help us to know what lies before us. Help us so that we may live."

Septua lowered his hands from his face, wiped his dripping nose with the back of his hand, and turned to look at Randi. His eyes were bright with tears and hope.

"I could do that, couldn't I, tell you about them, tell

you what I know, maybe some of it will help. Let us live a little longer.''

"Anything you tell us will help," Braldt said, crouching down, putting himself on a level with the dwarf. "The more we know about our captors, the better our chances of survival. Come, Septua, tell us what you know. And tell us why you suspect this offer of help."

"I don't suspect nuthin'," the dwarf said vehemently. "I know that you can't trust nuthin' they says. If they was offerin' to help, why there's got to be a trick in it somewhere's, some kind of joke, on us. They never does nuthin' to help no one but themselves. They're selfish an' cruel people with no thoughts for anyone else."

"You say you come from their home planet," urged Braldt, interrupting the dwarf's stream of invective. "Is this not their home?"

"Nah," spat the dwarf, beginning to regain some of his old confidence now that he had everyone's full attention and beginning to believe that he could avoid telling them of his own misdeeds. "Valhalla, that's where they come from, an' me too; it's a long, long ways from 'ere. This 'ere is where they do some of their business an' occupy themselves with stuff they couldn't get away with at 'ome, stuff like us."

"Valhalla," murmured Randi. "Isn't that one of earth's old colonies?"

"Yup," said the dwarf. "Started as an off-earth colony by a Scandinavian consortium way back in 2069. Businessmen an' engineers paid for it themselves; the government didn't 'ave nuthin' to do with it. Never 'ad no say in the matter. My grandfolks was part of it from the start. They was tall people. With 'air, too.''

"If they're businessmen and engineers, then what are they doing here?" Allo puzzled. "This is a very long way from earth."

"Mining," the dwarf said promptly. "Leases. The WWG opened this section for exploration and they claimed the whole sector. They don't 'ave to answer to no one about nuthin'. They can do whatever they wants and no one is goin' to say boo."

"That's not entirely true," said Allo. "There is the small matter of the WWG. They cannot possibly condone what is happening here. It is in direct contravention of every code in the galaxy."

"We're a long ways from the WWG," said Septua. "If they don't know nuthin', they can't say nuthin', an' who's gonna tell 'em?"

"Who or what is this WWG?" asked Braldt, filled with confusion by all of the strange terms and names he had heard, none of which meant anything to him.

"The Whole World Galaxy, it's a federation that governs all of the worlds and people of the various galaxies," explained Randi. "They make the rules that say what can and can't happen, otherwise it would be anarchy, the rule of the strongest."

"Something doesn't seem to be working right," Braldt said grimly. "These people certainly don't appear too concerned about this WWG of yours—unless this federation knows and approves of what is happening here."

"They don't have a clue to what's goin' on," said

Septua. "That's what got me put 'ere in this place and that's 'ow come I knows those folks won't 'elp us none, otherwise I wouldn't be 'ere, now would I? Tried to 'elp 'em, said I would if the price was right an' they agreed an' everything. But instead I get caught and wind up 'ere and don't even get paid!" the dwarf said indignantly, his eyes blazing at the injustice. "And where were they when I needed 'em? Nowheres, that's where! So don't you believe 'em when they say they're going to 'elp. We'll rot here 'til we die!"

"Well, my little friend, perhaps you had better tell us the whole story before the rot sets in," Braldt said dryly. "There is much that I do not understand. Share your story with us and then perhaps we can decide what is to be done."

The dwarf studied Braldt with a shrewd eye. "And why would I trust you?" he demanded coldly. "It's trustin' the likes of you that put me 'ere in the first place."

Braldt was taken aback, perplexed by the little man's words and his surprising display of hostility. "What do you mean, Septua?" he asked. "I have done you no wrong. Are we not friends?"

"You an' I can never be friends," Septua replied. "You 'aven't fooled me none. Everyone knows you're one of them."

13

Keri was stunned to see Braldt standing in the open doorway. Light streamed into the small, dark cell, blurring her eyes with tears, but still she was able to see that it was Braldt. She stumbled to her feet and flung herself at him, wrapping her arms around his waist, so glad to see him that she was willing to forego any pretense of independence.

"I knew you'd come I prayed to the Mother that you would find us and come to us and take us from this place. Where are we? What is this place and how did you find us?"

Only as she asked the question and received no reply did Keri began to realize that something was wrong. Braldt did not respond to her. His arm did not enfold her and draw her to him as it should have, and his body was stiff and unwelcoming. Nor did he speak the words of reassurance that she so desperately needed, words that would have told her that he had feared for her and felt her loss as strongly as she had grieved for him. The silence stretched on painfully, and at last, dreading what she would find, Keri raised her eyes. What she saw was more frightening than anything she might have imagined. It was Braldt, but it wasn't.

His eyes were the same shade of blue, his hair the same closely cropped mane of white gold, his body strong and well muscled. But the blue eyes were cold and dispassionate and studied her as one might study an interesting beetle rather than a cherished lover. She searched his eyes for some sign of caring and found none. The eyes remained as cold and distant as a mountain lake. The man who was Braldt but was not, turned his head and spoke in a language that Keri could not understand, a string of harsh, clipped sounds that had no meaning. It was then that she noticed for the first time that he was not alone. Her legs grew weak and nearly gave way beneath her when she saw that the two men who accompanied the first were so like him as to be indistinguishable!

The men spoke to one another, gesturing at her and smiling, even laughing at times. Only one of the men did not seem to share their amusement or enjoy her distress. This one looked the same as the others, but there was a small difference. Keri was not certain at first that it was real; she was afraid that it was only imagined, something that her mind devised to keep her from madness. But then as the agonizing heartbeats stretched longer and longer, she knew that it was true. This one did not really take pleasure in her discomfort, he was only pretending. Keri could not have said how she knew this to be true, but she did. Then their eyes connected and she felt the impact of his thoughts, wordless, yet somehow comforting, a message that said ''Be brave, you are not alone.''

She was still staring at the man, searching for some further confirmation of what she thought she had seen, when all four of the strangers stepped back hastily, something close to fear written on their faces. Keri looked up and saw that Batta Flor had wakened and now stood behind her, blinking against the bright light and frowning with concentration. Beast stood at his side.

"Who are they? What do they want? Why do they all look like Braldt?" asked Batta Flor, the words coming thickly.

"I do not know," Keri said as she stepped back, gladly placing the bulk of his body between herself and the strangers.

"Where are we? What is this place?" Batta Flor asked as he emerged from the small room that had entrapped them, walking forward and causing the men to step back still further. His action was apparently unexpected for the men seemed alarmed and almost fearful. One of them fumbled for a long, thin, silver wand hanging from a belt at his waist, but the man Keri had connected with held out a hand and stopped him, shaking his head firmly. Reluctantly, the man withdrew his hand although he continued to watch Batta Flor closely.

Keri's spirits rose. If they were afraid of Batta Flor, then perhaps things were not as hopeless as she had thought. But before she could share this thought with Batta Flor, two hard ones appeared, moving on silent wheels instead of legs, holding similar rods before them. Batta Flor jerked back, his face contorted in rage, the first real emotion Keri had seen since his ear had been so horribly mutilated. He roared in fury and the men scattered like leaves before a winter wind, leaving the hard ones to face him. This they did with precisely co-ordinated moves, coming at Keri and Batta Flor from both sides, rods extended. There was nowhere to go but back inside the dark cell where they would be trapped, but even as Keri glanced around behind her, the doors closed, removing even that unpleasant option.

Batta Flor struck out, one massive fist smashing down at a hard one. The hard one raised its metal rod, and as Batta Flor's arm touched its gleaming length, there was a sizzling arc of light. Batta Flor screamed as he was hurled through the air to smash against the doors of the cell and the stink of burned fur filled the air. Beast whimpered with uncertainty.

Keri dropped to her knees beside him and was glad to see that Batta Flor was only dazed. She lifted the arm that had been touched by the rod and saw that the fur had been burned away. Where the rod had touched his flesh, an angry weal was forming. "They burned you!" she cried in dismay. "Does it hurt?"

"It does not hurt at all," Batta Flor said, his small eyes bulging from his head. "I no longer feel pain. I was only surprised. They cannot hurt me with their toys."

One of the men nodded as though he had understood Batta Flor and uttered more of the guttural sounds. At his command, the hard ones swung away from Batta Flor and advanced upon Keri, rods held out before them like swords.

Having seen what the rods had done to Batta Flor and having no such protection from pain, Keri took several cautious steps backward. The men stood aside to let her pass. Unafraid, yet unwilling to be parted from Keri, Batta Flor and Beast followed, growling if the hard ones came too close. But the hard ones seemed content to trail behind them, brandishing their wands whenever they wanted Keri to move in one direction or the other.

They were traveling down a corridor carved out of red stone and lit by smoking torches stuck in stanchions in the wall. In spite of the light, the place was gloomy and dank. Occasionally, doors and other corridors opened off the passage, but the hard ones never deviated from the straight course they had set, herding Batta Flor, Beast, and Keri before them like grazing animals.

After a long time, the corridor began to slant upward and the rude, stone surfaces gave way to smooth-dressed brick, the smoking torches to globes of priest fire. In places, the walls were covered with brightly colored frescoes depicting scenes of battle, generally two groups of four warriors armed with a wide variety of weapons, pitted against one another. As concerned as Keri was with her own situation, she could not help but notice that the combatants were all different from one another. Some were people like herself, but those were in the minority. By far, most of those pictured were animals or animal-like, or unlike any life form Keri had ever known before. She tried to draw Batta Flor's attention to the pictures, but he was uninterested, preferring to keep his attention focused on the hard ones, enemies he knew and had good reason to hate.

After a time, they came to the end of the corridor and found only a set of double doors mounted flush against the wall. A feeling of dread filled Keri. She tried to resist, to stand firm, but at a command from one of the men, one of the hard ones jabbed Keri with the end of his rod. A bright, blue light sizzled against her skin and she screamed, nearly fainting from the intense pain that burned like fire and continued to sear its way into her flesh even after the rod had been removed. Batta Flor was there instantly, picking her up in his arms, cradling her against his shaggy chest and circling with a massive, balled fist extended, daring them to come closer.

The man barked out another command and the two hard ones, acting in unison, rolled silently forward. Batta Flor looked around, but there was no way to go except through the doors. He could not even attack the hated metallic men without letting go of Keri and this he refused to do. Teeth bared in a hideous grimace, rumbling growls emanating from his slavering lips, Batta Flor backed through the swinging doors.

As the doors swung shut behind them, they found themselves dazzled by a light far brighter than any they had ever known before, set in the ceiling like a captive sun. Even Batta Flor was stunned by the ceaseless glare. His arms dropped to his sides and Keri huddled against him, burying her face in his thick fur, closing her eyes against the painful light.

In that instant of helpless passivity, they were seized in a firm, unyielding grip, so strong that not even Batta Flor's incredible strength could break it. Tears streamed down their cheeks, blinding them, hiding the identity of their captors, which only served to increase Keri's terror. She flung herself hard against the implacable grip and screamed with fear and frustration. A tiny, sharp prick touched her arm, barely noticeable against the larger terrors, but immediately afterward, a strange lassitude filled her limbs, weighing her down, then carrying her away on a cloud of buoyant light.

When she awakened, it was to a headache even more blinding than the light had been. She put her hand to her head and touched the hated, metal plate fitted flush with her skin. It tingled with a life it had not had before. She rolled to one side and retched. When the bitter taste of bile filled her mouth, she spat and swung upright, gasping for air, wanting to know what had happened but too fearful to touch her head again.

"It appears to be some sort of receiving unit," said Batta Flor.

Keri raised her eyes and saw that Batta Flor was seated a short distance away atop a shiny, metal table. Implanted in his skull above his ear was the bright, silver disc which from the clipped fur around it had obviously been tended to. He seemed very calm and undisturbed by the fact that their flesh had been mutilated.

"But why?" cried Keri. "Why are they doing this to us? What do they want from us?" Before Batta Flor could reply, a voice spoke out inside her head.

"Welcome to our world. You are the newest combatants from those gathered from the farthest reaches of the star system. You will find honor and purpose in the arena and with each victory you will be rewarded."

Keri was too stunned to speak, all but overwhelmed by the voice that spoke from inside her skull. She clutched her head with both hands and screamed. Batta Flor slipped from the table and came to her instantly, supporting her and glaring around, searching for the source of the voice which had fallen silent.

"Why should we fight for you?" demanded Batta Flor, his voice harsh with anger.

"Because it is your destiny," the voice replied.

"My destiny?" queried Batta Flor. "According to who?"

"You are a creature of our making—we made you and your destiny is ours to command."

"And what about her?" asked Batta Flor. "Did you make her, too?"

"We have acquired her and she is ours. If you wish to be free, you have the right to fight for that privilege."

"You'll really free us if we win?"

"We honor our promises," the voice replied. "But know that no quarter is given. There can only be one victor."

"You mean if we lose we die?" Keri said in disbelief. "You'd actually kill us for losing?"

"The price is high," admitted the voice, "but so are the stakes—you are wagering your lives."

"What about Keri?" Batta Flor asked after a moment's pause. "I can take care of myself, but if I agree to fight, you have to leave her out of this."

"No, Batta Flor, if you fight, so will I," said Keri, placing her hand on his arm. "I learned a lot from Braldt, I know how to handle a sword and a knife and two of us stand a better chance than one alone. I am with you."

14

The dungeon was dark. The reptilian water carrier had long since trundled past, muttering to herself and doling out their meager allotment of water. Braldt had never been able to understand what she was saying, even with the aid of the translator. It seemed to be some grievous litany of woe, repeated over and over until it took on the cadence of a religious chant. The scaly creature was so wrapped up in the contemplation and recitation of her miseries that she barely seemed aware of them and at times would pass up one cell or another until their angry cries and the banging of metal cups against the bars broke into her musings and returned her to the present.

Braldt had come to feel a strange sense of sympathy for the odd creature and normally he tried to make out some of her words, but tonight all of his attention was focused on Septua and the tale he told.

"They came from old earth in the beginning," said the dwarf, looking round the circle at his rapt audience and taking the opportunity to slip his hand up the side of Randi's thigh. Randi's eyes flickered and a muscle tensed in her jaw but she allowed the dwarf's hand to remain.

"It was a long, long time ago, further back than any one alive can remember. They was a seafaring people, rode out on the waters in long, wooden boats and took what they wanted. No one could stand up against 'em. They were that fierce—big an' tall an' strong with eyes blue as the skies an' 'air as white as the sun. Some say they were the children of the sun god an' the sea.

"When earth began to die, they was among the very first to leave, sailing their ships to the stars. They called their new world Valhalla, the 'ome of the gods. Lots of people left earth then. The seas was dying an' so were the people, poisoned by their own greed and stupidity. Most of 'em went to the moon an' Mars an' other places that was close by an' spent most of their time figuring out how to 'elp those still left on earth.

"The Scandis though, they figured that earth was dead and they left it for good. They found Valhalla and settled it alone an' they wouldn't let no one who wasn't one of them set foot on the place.

"It be beautiful," said Septua, his voice heavy with emotion, "Valhalla is. It's easy to believe that the gods made it for their own selves. It 'as mountains so tall an' beautiful it breaks your heart to look at 'em. The sky is blue, too, not black or red like other places I've seen since. And it has water everywhere, lots an' lots of water, clear an' clean an' pure, too. But that was about all it 'ad. There was no life. No animals, no fish, no birds, no nothin'. An' then they found that the planet itself was made out of solid granite an' didn't have no minerals or nothin' that they needed to make things work. It was an empty world.

"They 'ad to figure out a way to make it work. They couldn't go back to earth—there was nothing there for them an' they 'ad already made folks mad 'cause they wouldn't 'elp out, send a tithe back to earth, like all the others. That's when they 'it on the plan. They would become as they 'ad been in the old days of glory. They would sail their ships among the stars an' take what they needed from those that 'ad. There was lots of folks travelin' the skies, even way back then.

"It worked good for a time, a long time, but then the different worlds came together an' formed the World Council. It was supposed to police the skies an' make sure no wrongs was done by nobody. The Scandis ignored 'em for as long as they could but eventually the Council caught up with 'em an' told 'em they 'ad to stop it or else they'd blast 'em outta the skies. They 'ad the force behind 'em, too, so us Scandis had to listen, even if we didn't like it.

"Times got grim then, an' we mighta' died out, but the Council, they relented and gived us a mining license, said we could learn to survive like everyone else, by workin' for our right to live. An' that's what they been doin' ever since, claimin' empty planets an' minin' 'em an' the meteors an' asteroids in the skies for the metals an' minerals."

"Seems to me like they decided to harvest a few more things, like other people's ships and people themselves," Randi said dryly.

"Salvage," Septua said defensively as he slid his hand a little higher. "We only take what's legally ours to claim. Laws of the Council, ain't none who could argue otherwise.''

"I could!'' Randi said bitterly.

"And I,'' added Allo. "We were attacked, plain and simple. We were no helpless, drifting hulk, no victim waiting to be salvaged.''

"And I,'' said Braldt, curious as to how he and his world figured into this scheme. "I was taken from my world by force. How do you explain that? And who are these hard ones? What is their role?''

Septua was obviously uneasy with the hostile confrontation of his companions. Defense of their captors was clearly an unwise course. Avoiding their pointed comments, he seized gratefully on the tail end of Braldt's question.

"The 'ard ones? You mean the 'bots? They just be mindless workers, no minds of their own. They takes their orders from us. Do what they're told to do. It be easier than tryin' to deal with real folks what can argue an' fight back. They does the mindless drudge work where a real person might get bored. An' you don't have to feed 'em or give 'em clothes or even a place to sleep. You just turns 'em off when you're done. They're real good 'cause they can work places that got poison air, or no air a'tall, places that would kill a real person. I had two of 'em once myself. Come in real 'andy.''

"So if you're one of them," Allo said slowly, "how come you're sitting here in this cell with us? And how come you don't look like them?''

Septua wriggled uncomfortably and stared down at the floor, the flaccid folds of his mobile face drooping sadly. He even removed his hand from Randi's thigh before replying in a low whisper that no one could hear.

"What?" asked Randi. "What did you say?"

"Caught me," he said in a slightly louder voice, but still he did not raise his eyes.

"Caught you? Caught you doing what?" asked Braldt, wondering what the little man could have done that would have been so bad as to be so cruelly punished by his own people.

"I ain't really a Scandi, guess you can tell. But me folks lived among 'em for generations until we almost become one of 'em. Called us lantsmen, let us come with 'em when they left earth. My dad and me mum, they were normal-sized and they 'ad 'air, too. But I always been small," Septua said in a soft voice. "I were even born small. All 'cept my head. My mum said it were big so it could hold all my brains. She always said I were smarter than anyone gived me credit for. It were 'er suggested to the Thanes that they could use me to salvage stuff in places that were too small for others to go. Places that even the 'bots couldn't go 'cause they don't bend too good an' of course, they can't think for themselves, don't always recognize somethin' of value when they see it.

"I worked for the Thanes 'til I was growed. Then my mum took sick, needed a new 'eart. But the Thanes, they decided she weren't important enough an' we didn't 'ave enough money to pay for it ourselves. She lasted for a time an' then she died. After she went, I quit salvagin' for the Thanes, just sat an' thought about things. An' then I got mad. It din't seem right, ya know? I'd worked for them since I were real little. Riskin' my life lots o' times, doin' dangerous stuff, goin' after somethin' they wanted. An' then when we needed somethin', well, we wasn't good enough for 'em and so they let her die. I decided it weren't goin' to be like that no more. If they would let my mum die, well, chances were they would chuck me out just as fast if I weren't no more use to 'em. I said to myself, Septua, it's just you now an' there's no one to look after you, so you gots to take care of yourself. Set somethin' aside for the 'ard times. An' so that's what I done.''

Fascinated by the dwarf's story, Randi urged him to continue. "How did you do that, my friend, and what did you do to get yourself thrown in here with us?''

Septua smiled, a gap-toothed grin full of satisfaction. "I went back to the Thanes. Told 'em I were ready to work again an' they was willin' to believe me. Had no reason not to, never crossed their minds that someone might dare to oppose them. After that, every time I did a job for them, I kept something back for myself, a bit of precious metal, some coins, a gem, something small that wouldn't be missed. It were easy an' they never suspected a thing. After a while, it came to be a goodly collection. I were rich, but I still lived like the poorest of the poor.

"One day I were out in the square an' I smiled at this woman, red hair, green eyes, an' legs that stretched until tomorrow. You know, the kind that would bring the gods back to life. Well, you'd thought that I had insulted her an' she starts screamin' at me, makin' fun of me an' callin' me all sorts of names. Said how dare I look at her, me being so puny an' all without the means to so much as dust the path before her.

"I don't know what happened to me," groaned the dwarf, burying his overlarge head in his broad palms. "Every bit of smarts I ever had went out of my head, I were that mad. I jerked my pouch off my belt, opened the drawstring, an' emptied it onto the ground at 'er feet. 'Er eyes got so big she actually choked an' couldn't say a word. It were worth it to see the look on 'er face. Me, I just turned an' walked away like it didn't mean nothin'. I never felt so good in my whole life. I felt . . . big.

"Well, she couldn't let me go, you know? She scooped up what was on the ground an' come after me. An' that were the start of it. The start of the end, even if I didn't know it then. Now don't get me wrong. I don't pretend to think that she liked me, I never fooled myself into believin' that. I always knowed it were the money an' the gems. But it were nice to 'ave a woman be good to me, even if it were just pretend.

"But she were expensive. First, mum's 'ouse weren't good for 'er, so she found a bigger place, one that suited 'er better. Then, she 'ad to 'ave new stuff to put in it. All the things that 'ad been good enough for me an' mum was garbage to 'er an' she tossed 'em out when I were gone salvaging an' bought new stuff that I 'ad to pay for. An' clothes! I never knew a woman could wear so many things or that they could cost so much! An' of course, there was jewelry an' presents, most of which she bought for herself any time somethin' took 'er fancy. But I ain't complainin', you understand," the little man said with an uptilted chin. "It were worth everythin' I gived. It were wonderful walkin' down the center of the chambers with a woman like that on my arm. Seein' all the others lookin' at me, wonderin' what I 'ad that could keep a woman like that 'appy. Seein' 'er smile at me like she really cared. It were worth it all. Even this.''

"So what went wrong?" Braldt asked softly, breaking into the dwarf's reverie of remembrance.

"Huh? Oh, well you know, she kept askin' for more of this an' more o' that an' I didn't 'ave no way of gettin' everything she wanted. I couldn't take too much at any one time or they was sure to catch on to me. I was down to the last of what I had put aside, an' Mirna, that were 'er name, Mirna, it were like she sensed it somehow an' she started to get restless, spent a lot of time talkin' to the captain of the guards, rollin' her eyes an' twitchin' 'er 'ips. I weren't dumb, I could see what was comin'. It's not like I couldn't 'ave let her go, you understand, go back to the way things 'ad been before, it's just, well, it's just I got used to having 'er around.

"So when this Thane came to me in the middle of the night with 'is big idea that were supposed to be so easy an' earn me lots of credits, why, you can see 'ow I had to say yes.''

"What was it that this Thane wanted you to do?" asked Allo.

"Nothin' so very 'ard, at least it didn't seem so in the tellin'. I were to sneak into the 'ome of the 'Igh Thane when 'e were gone an' find the program key for the 'bots.''

Randi and Allo murmured their understanding and exchanged meaningful glances. But Braldt was totally lost, failing to comprehend what Septua was talking about. It was like so much that had happened to him since his capture. He could hear the words, sometimes even put meaning to them, but they were seldom the right meaning and he was adrift on a sea of confusion, feeling no smarter than the dumbest of beasts who trained in the arena. How could this vast world filled with so many diverse life forms have existed without his knowledge? It made him feel small and insignificant.

"I do not understand what you are speaking of. Please explain the meaning of this program key," he said quietly.

"Oh, Braldt, I'm sorry, I should have explained," said Randi. "There's no way you could know. Programs are the brains of the 'bots, it's what tells them what to do and how to do it."

"I see," Braldt said, even though he was still very unclear about how such a thing might work. "What does this program look like? Is it difficult to build one?"

Randi could not stop herself from smiling, but there was no malice in her expression nor in Allo's chuckle. "Permit me," he said to Randi.

"I will try to explain, my young friend, even though it will be difficult to comprehend, coming as you do from a world that apparently has not advanced beyond the Bronze Age.

"I am what is known as a programmer, or I was before I was promoted to involuntary gladiator. It is my job to write the programs that the 'bots and other such wonders need to exist. I will not bore you with the details; perhaps at another time. Let it suffice to say that without these programs the robots and their fellow machines will not function.''

"You mean they will die?" Braldt asked incredulously. "All of these fancy machines and the hard ones will die, just like that!"

"It is a little more complex than that, but essentially that is correct," said Allo.

"Then why would this Scandi Master want Septua to steal the program?" Braldt asked.

"That's a very good question. Why would a Scandi want you to steal it?" Randi asked, turning her attention back to the dwarf.

"Don't know," replied Septua, raising his palms and shrugging broadly. 'E never said. Just told me where the programs was put an' gived me a time when the 'Igh Thane would be gone. 'Course 'e never mentioned no sensor beams nor no silent alarms. Caught me with a handful of programs an' a pocketful of saladium bars an' rough-cut zourmalines.

"As for the Thane what 'ired me, well, 'e were right there beside the 'Igh Thane when they sentenced me. Never said a word on my behalf. Not that I expected 'im to. An' Mirna, she were there, too, draped on the arm of the captain of the guards. Didn't waste no time a'tall. Got to hand it to 'er, she be enterprisin'!"

"Didn't you tell them about the Thane's role in the matter?" asked Allo. "Surely that would have helped you."

"Get serious—what kind of world do you come from anyway," hooted the dwarf, shaking with laughter. "Tell 'em a lord put me up to it. C'mon, who are they gonna believe, one of their own or a dwarf who spent 'is life thievin' for 'em? It weren't 'ard to guess 'ow it would go down. So I'm tellin' you, Big Guy, don't go trustin' 'im like I did 'cause 'e won't be there for you when things go wrong. An' I be livin' proof of that! An' for that matter, I ain't so sure I trust you! Ain't you the livin', breathin' copy of 'em? Tell me that's just a trick o' fate!''

"I can't tell you that, for I do not know myself," Braldt replied slowly. "I do not know how it is that we come to look so much alike. It troubles me more than you can know."

"Your parents?" asked Randi. "Do you not resemble them and are they from your home world?"

"Those that I call parents are not of my blood," said Braldt, his mind wandering back over the years to the little bit of information that had been told to him about his origins. "I was found in the desert as an infant, wrapped in a blue robe and shielded from the sun by my father's body. He was dead when they were found. My mother was still alive, although badly burned by the sun and the wind and she died without conveying any information.

"They carried nothing that would have given any hint of their origins for they were without any possessions other than the clothes that they wore. And a ring. A large, silver ring with a blue stone, worn in the manner of my people, at the shoulder, girding the ends of the robe together. There was nothing else."

"And your people...." queried Randi.

"Look nothing like me at all. They are short of

stature and dark of skin with curly, brown hair and eyes. There is no one on our world who looks like me. Although our priests, who have much to say about how the world is run, bear just such a device as this," he said, touching the silver implant in his skull.

"Is it possible that they are 'bots?" mused Allo.

"It is hard to believe, for I was taught to fear if not revere them," muttered Braldt, "and yet it would explain much that has puzzled me. They are always draped in heavy robes, their features never seen. If they are hard ones in disguise and not live, that would answer many questions. They are spared from death, that we know. Some of them are many lifetimes old. This is a thought that will take some getting used to."

"What do you think it means?" Randi asked, turning to Allo. "Why would they go to all the trouble of planting the 'bots on his world and giving them such an elaborate identity?"

"I don't know," he replied, shaking his furry head. "It could be that they colonized the planet with the 'bots, although it's strictly forbidden to colonize a planet that is inhabited by any sentient life form."

"That could not be!" Randi said in disbelief. "The Council would learn of it and censure them harshly."

The dwarf barked a mirthless chuckle. "Look around you, pretty lady. Does it look like they're worried about being censured? The Scandis, they do what they want, an' right now, lady, they wants us!"

"What you have told us will give us something to think on," said Braldt. "There is much here that must be puzzled out. But I still feel that one of those men was trying to send me a message, to hold out some form of hope. We must hold onto that belief and explore the possibility if it is so, for it is doubtful that we can escape this place without some form of outside help.''

Braldt's comments were interrupted by the dwarf's rude laughter. He laughed until he doubled over, sputtering with tears wetting his cheeks. ''That one,'' he said, ''the one you are looking to for 'elp . . . that one be the Thane who betrayed me!''

15

Batta Flor and Keri's existence took a strange, new turn. They were armed and outfitted with protective leather to which neither of them were accustomed, but recognizing their obvious value, they did their best to wear them without complaint. The weapons were exceptional in quality and staggering in the multitude of choice. In the end, both settled for weapons they were most familiar with—swords, knives, and shields. Batta Flor also chose a heavy club with a leather thong that wrapped securely around his thick wrist.

The two of them shared a cell with the lupebeast pup, a cell that had been carved out of the same red rock that everything else was built of. It was large and had a single, barred opening set high in the wall, and two broad, sleeping platforms laid with some sort of silvery fabric that was light and bouyant as well as warm. They were fed on a regular basis. It was strange food, unfamiliar to them in taste, texture, and origin, but it was hot and filling and the ewers of hot liquid imparted a tingling energy to their limbs. Other than their initial contact with the Masters, those who so looked like Braldt, they dealt entirely with the hard ones and a surly reptilian servant class that went about its business without speaking.

Keri was filled with a sense of shocked disbelief that stayed with her throughout her days and nights. She felt betrayed as well as bereft, but now there was the numbing ache of loss as well, for she truly felt as though Braldt had been taken from her forever. She could not explain how it was that the Masters looked so much like him, nor could Batta Flor offer any explanation, for he himself had never dealt with the Masters on their home world, only their minions, the hard ones. After his initial confrontation, he had sunk back into his silence and although he remained close to Keri, he had few if any words to offer.

On their fourth day of confinement, they were wakened by the roaring of beasts somewhere nearby and the woeful shrieks of a creature in mortal terror. Beast threw back his head and began a mournful accompaniment of his own. So unnerving were the eerie sounds, that Keri's stomach roiled and twisted and she was unable to eat her morning rations or even sip her cup of hot brew. Batta Flor lifted his shaggy head once, listened, and then returned to feeding, cramming the food in his mouth with both hands and downing Keri's portion as well when it became obvious that she had no interest in it.

When the guards came for them, even Batta Flor guessed that something was different. They donned their leather armor and received their weapons, but instead of being taken to the practice ring as they had been on previous days, they were led out into an immense arena, surrounded on all sides with tiers and tiers of redstone seats filled shoulder to shoulder with blond-haired, blue-eyed visages of Braldt. Beast pressed himself against

Keri's legs and slunk forward with his jaw nearly scraping the ground and his long, thin tail curled up beneath his belly.

She did not have long to contemplate her discomfort. There was a hideous scream behind her and turning, she saw a horrifying creature, neither animal nor human, but a strange combination of both, coming toward them at a swift lope.

It had six appendages on which it hurled itself over the loose sands of the arena, although all were not necessary for locomotion for one or more were frequently in the air waving long-hooked claws that flashed in the bloody sunlight. It was a grotesque thing with a semi-upright, man-like physique, but covered with coarse, mottled fur and possessing fangs and a horned protuberance on its forehead.

Batta Flor turned leisurely and studied the nasty thing as it drew ever closer. Beast growled nervously, showing all of his fangs, and crouched down ready to spring. Keri shivered with fear as the monster's ghastly cries preyed on her nerves, but she drew her sword and fell into a crouch as she had seen Braldt do countless times before.

It was very close now, close enough to see the maddened look in its eyes, small and bright without pupils or the light of intelligence. Blood-flecked slaver streamed from the edges of its mouth and the nerve-wracking ululation never ceased. It seemed to have no plan of attack other than to bowl them over with sheer momentum, then savage them with claw and fang.

It was close enough that Keri could smell the hot,

rank stink of its body before Batta Flor reacted, merely reaching out and seizing the thing in mid-air as it leapt for them. There was a single, high-pitched shriek as Batta Flor's fingers closed around its throat, then silence as the voice ended. The large, furred body flailed at Batta Flor's hand and hammered at his massive forearms. Blood poured from dozens of wounds as the beast's claws sliced through Batta Flor's flesh, but Batta Flor did not waver nor lower the thing to the ground until it hung limp and void of life, its claws dangling uselessly along the ground.

The lupebeast pup growled and tried to position itself to spring, but it could not seem to work up the courage. Its eyes rolled and flashed whitely and it whined with anxiety. The sight of Batta Flor's wounds was frightening and Keri attempted to aide him, maneuvering herself so that she could plunge her blade through the creature's body. But Batta Flor turned aside, removing the beast from her reach and shielding her from the danger of its wildly swinging claws. No matter what she did, he managed to keep his body between her and the dangerous creature. Only when it was dead did he allow her to approach him and even then he took the precaution of leading her away from the unmoving corpse. Only when it was dead could the pup work up the courage to approach the monster, nipping at its still body, then leaping away. When he realized that it really was dead, he fell on it and savaged it, dragging it around the dirt and growling ferociously.

The crowd had watched the action in near silence, but the intensity of its gaze carried an almost palpable weight. With the creature's death, there was a single, collective exhalation of breath emanating from the vast crowd and then as one, like some enormous, encompassing heartbeat, the spectators began to stomp in a rhythmic pulse on the stone tiers while humming deep in their throats. It was a disturbingly primitive sound and Keri was stunned by the waves of sound beating down on her. It was more terrifying than the beast had been, for that was a wild thing with little intelligence and violence and killing was its way of life, but these were supposedly intelligent beings exhibiting more of a blood thirst than the wildest of monsters. She dropped her sword and stared up at the chanting spectators, feeling the depth of their passions thrumming in her blood.

The noise frightened the pup away from the corpse of the monster and it quickly retreated to the safety of its friends. Batta Flor wrapped his arm around Keri's shoulders, scooped up her blade, and drew her away. Two hard ones sped toward them across the loose sands and a tall, majestic, blond male draped in a royal blue robe stood on a platform in the tiers holding two scarlet ribbons streaming in the hot wind. Batta Flor had other ideas though, and entertaining the Masters further held no interest.

Gently, Batta Flor guided Keri from the ring, ignoring the hard ones as they circled on their single wheels, metal wands pointed like swords, as they drew closer and closer, trying to force the combatants back to where their master waited. One came too close and Batta Flor acted swiftly, jamming his club into the center of the wheel and bracing himself with wideset feet. The hard one stopped abruptly, jerked forward, and fell face first onto the red Sand. Batta Flor was on it in an instant, planting his foot at the base of its neck, and yanking his club free, he brought it down in a crushing blow, shattering the hard covering like a brittle shell.

The crowd rose to its feet in a wave of motion, screaming and yelling with separate voices now, visible for the first time as individual beings.

The second hard one drove straight toward them, the metal rod pointed dead ahead. Batta Flor stood ready, his club in his hand. Suddenly a loud voice flooded their heads, commanding them to lay down their weapons and return to the dais. Batta Flor reached up and dug his fingers into the flesh of his skull. Blood spurted, staining his fingers and dripping down his face, but he gave no indication of any pain as he gripped the round, silver device and wrenched it free, trailing blood and bits of broken wires. Keri watched in horror as the voice inside her head grew shrill and incoherent, demanding that they come to the stands.

The hard one stopped, its rod lowered, staring impassively at them with its blank features. Batta Flor placed his arm around Keri and they made their way from the ring. The Madrelli stepped on the silver circle as they passed, grinding it into the sands with the heel of his foot. Keri was sick and dizzied by the frenetic screaming inside her head, but Batta Flor would not allow her to stop; when she stumbled, he picked her up and carried her from the ring.

The cool shadows under the arena were a soothing relief after the stunning glare of the double suns and the voice ceased once they left the ring, choked off as though the speaker had become too apoplectic to continue. Keri did not care what the reason was, it was enough that it had stopped.

Blood was dripping off Batta Flor's chin and trickling down her chest. She reached out to touch the gaping hole in his forehead, then drew back her hand when he looked down at her. She could see the broken ends of wire still protruding from the raw flesh like worms emerging from the soil after the grass had been stripped away.

Her face must have betrayed her dismay, for Batta Flor attempted to smile, his face responding somewhat woodenly as he placed her gently on the ground. "Do not worry, my friend, I feel no pain. Nor could I bear the sound of that one who looks like Braldt but is not, yammering inside my head. I will fight for them if I must, but I do not want to listen to them."

The speech, short as it was, was evidently difficult for Batta Flor, for the words came slower and slower and were slurred and thick toward the end, barely comprehensible, and the stiff smile had fallen from his face. He patted her awkwardly on the shoulder, then led the way to their cell, swinging the heavy, metal door shut himself before the startled reptilian attendants could do it for them. The pup had dashed for the safety of the sleeping platform, and huddled silently in the darkest corner.

In the days and nights that followed, Batta Flor sank further and further into an animalistic state, losing all of his more refined qualities. He ate with hands and fingers, shoveling food into his mouth by the handful, even eating bits off the floor when he dropped them, grunting and

snorting like some savage beast. He lost all sense of
dignity and propriety as well, defecating wherever and
whenever the need struck him, seemingly insensible to
the need for privacy. But far worst of all was the fact that
he ceased to speak and when he looked at Keri it was
with dull, animal-like eyes.

Such behavior unnerved Keri and depressed her
deeply, causing her to feel more alone than ever before.
The thing that shared the cell with her was not Batta Flor,
that good and noble being who had risked his life for her
more than once, but some primitive beast who inhabited
what was left of Batta Flor's body.

But despite his descent to base animality, the huge beast
was still gentle and considerate in his treatment of her. She
might have been afraid of him had it not been for that.
Occasionally he would stop and stare at her, his head to one
side, studying her as though he were trying to remember
something. At other times, he would pat her clumsily on top
of the head. But still, there was a sense of protection by
being near him. He still guarded her as zealously as ever,
perhaps even more so, growling viciously whenever anyone
approached the cell. The beast pup was her only companion.

Batta Flor's wounds had healed, scabbing roughly in
thick, brown welts which he ignored as he did most
everything. The blond men who were not Braldt appeared
outside the cell the evening of the fight and studied them
through slitted eyes, muttering among themselves. Keri
hoped that some hint of their conversation would come to
her through the hated, silver circlet, but it was not to be.
Batta Flor shoved her to the rear of the cell and showed

his fangs, daring them to come closer, but they made no attempt to do so, carefully remaining far out of his reach.

They did not replace the silver device that Batta Flor had removed so forcefully, perhaps realizing that it was futile. That one small fact remained as the single positive note in their existence, allowing her to feel that they had succeeded in thwarting the Masters' wishes at least in that small matter.

The games continued, and with them came continued success. Their opponents were as varied and numerous as the stars in the sky. Sometimes they looked almost human and fought in a familiar fashion with weapons that Keri could recognize. But often, they were life forms that were unlike anything she had ever seen before, even in her worst dreams. These were indeed the things of nightmares, fanged and clawed and open mawed, oft times possessing weapons that were not even recognizable or could be given a name. These were the most frightening opponents, for it was impossible to know how they would fight, what manner their attack would take. But it did not matter—regardless of their methods, Batta Flor killed them all.

As the games went on, they were at times confronted with more than one opponent, frequently they came at them in groups of four. When they fought one on one, Batta Flor refused to allow Keri to fight, but as the odds and the opponents increased, he was forced to do so.

Keri was frightened at first, but then strangely, she began to feel a sense of power, a fierce joy flowing with each confrontation, a joy that increased with each victory. She wondered why she did not feel more of a sense of kinship with her opponents, more of a sorrow at their deaths, for they were prisoners as well, and not really the enemy. But it was not so, she felt nothing but triumph when they died.

With the passage of time, even the lupebeast pup grew more and more daring until he was holding his own against all human types and many of the smaller animal beings.

The conclusion of every bout ended the same way, with Batta Flor and Keri making their way from the ring without pausing and without acknowledging the roars of the crowd or receiving their awards which awaited them at the dais.

The crowd by this time had come to expect an unusual show whenever they appeared, and the arena was always filled to capacity. The roars began before they even emerged from the darkness of the cells and continued undiminished until they left the ring.

Keri had fought awkwardly at first—"like a girl" as Braldt would have said—with her heart pounding in her chest and her knees feeling soft as jelly. But she swiftly realized that the majority of her opponents felt exactly the same and that knowledge gave her strength and courage. On days that games were not held, she began to practice in earnest and her time in the ring reflected that effort as she did her best to remember everything that she had ever heard Braldt and her brother discuss about fighting. Soon, she became a formidable opponent in her own right and was less and less willing to allow Batta Flor to bear the brunt of the battles.

Engrossed as she was in her own problems, Keri

never stopped thinking of Braldt, wondering if he still lived and if so, if he still thought of her.

Braldt's thoughts rested often on Keri and he carried the memory of her around like a weight in his chest. But other thoughts vied for his attention, thoughts of survival.

The games had begun in earnest, each of them a terror-filled, sickness-at-the-pit-of-the-stomach, gut-wrenching confrontation that ended in bloody death. So far they had survived the deadly games, pitted against less skilled adversaries, but with each round of combat, the chaff was being weeded out; soon only the toughest would remain and the victories would be harder won.

None of them had suffered anything more than surface wounds and a variety of painful bruises, but even these trifling injuries were enough to remind them of the fate that could so easily befall them.

Their last contest had very nearly been the end of them. At first, it had seemed that it would be their easiest one, for their opponents were four humans, albeit primitive in the extreme who wore no clothing other than leather loincloths and carried no weapons other than spears and knives; they had painted their lean, muscular bodies in bizarre colors and patterns. Their eyes and cheeks were a solid band of black and red stripes running horizontally through the eyes from brow to chin. Their long, black hair was caught up in twisted knots and fastened with vertebrae bones. Other bits of bone and claws were fastened at neck, wrist, and ankle with strips of leather. Since they were only human and not one of the more frightening alien creatures, Braldt and his companions made the mistake of thinking that the contest would be easy. It nearly cost them their lives.

From the beginning, the primitives had split up, circling round and round in a dizzying circuit, weaving, darting, never remaining in one place long enough for Randi to fix them in her laser beam. The ground was pocked with the impact of misfirings and the primitives were untouched. Emboldened by their luck, they grew ever more frenetic, darting in unexpectedly and striking out with the tips of their razor-sharp spears, drawing blood with every coup and screaming all the while, which served to further unnerve Braldt's group, especially Randi.

Finally, one of them made a mistake and a primitive came close enough to seize Braldt, pinning his arms against his sides so that he could not move and squeezing him against his barrel chest with arms that were bands of corded muscle.

As large as Braldt was, the primitive was both taller and heavier and, it seemed, stronger. Immediately after seizing Braldt, he skipped backward, covering his own body with that of his prisoner, presenting Braldt as the only possible target.

Braldt cursed himself for allowing the man to come so close, for thinking that he would stand a chance, and most of all, for underestimating the man's strength and speed. He could feel his breath straining in his chest, beginning to burn in his throat, and saw dots as his vision began to blur. He struggled to focus on the long, curved claws that were threaded around the primitive's neck. And then a desperate idea came to him. Drawing his head back as far as it would go, he slammed it forward with the last of his strength and drove the sharp, curving points of the claws into the base of the man's throat.

He was rewarded by a gout of dark, arterial blood which gushed into his face, drenching his throat and chest. The man screamed, a gargling, choking cry, and he dropped Braldt and fell to his knees as he attempted to pull the claws from his throat. As he did so, the blood began to shoot out in thick spurts and the man, realizing that he was about to die, lost all interest in Braldt and began to wail a death dirge. His companions were completely undone by his demise and hurried to his side, trying ineffectually to stop the flow of blood. Soon, he had collapsed on the ground, his blood a darker blot on the crimson earth. The three remaining men were overcome with grief and wailed and shrieked and tore at their hair and flesh.

Braldt and Randi stared at one another, uncertain of what to do. Septua, however, had no such reservations, not being adverse to stabbing an enemy in the back. He had advanced to within a pace of the grieving primitives with his dagger raised, when Allo leaned down and plucked him off the ground with two claws, depositing him between Randi and Braldt and removing his weapons as one might strip a child of harmful objects.

The dwarf screamed in rage, striking at Allo's knees and pummeling his massive, furred thighs, which the huge navigator ignored as one might ignore the rantings of an hysterical child. His cries blended in with those of the primitives and the angry spectators whose blood lust had not been satisfied. "Kill! Kill! Kill!" demanded the voices that spoke inside their heads.

"We do not kill those who do not defend themselves," Allo said firmly, tilting the dwarf's chin upward so that he could look into his eyes. The dwarf muttered one final curse and kicked sand over Allo's foot, but made no attempt to continue the hostilities once he was released.

Allo, Randi, and Braldt closed their minds to the insistent chorus that screamed from the silver circles, echoed by the thousands who crowded the stands and left the arena with Septua running so as not to be left behind. They had nearly reached the cool shadows of the arches when agonized screams ripped the air. Turning swiftly, they saw a group of hard ones surrounding the vanquished primitives and blue arcs of light coursing through the air. The screams ended abruptly and the hard ones wheeled about and left the arena, leaving the grotesquely sprawled bodies of the four dead men lying on the sand.

16

They had voted to wait, to do nothing until some definitive course of action had been decided upon, for there were still so many unknown factors and the danger was immense. If they were found out, it would mean their deaths and none of them were young enough to survive the arena.

But the woman named Lomi had been unable to rest with that decision, for long ago in her youth she had loved the man Bracca. And as she hurried along the dark corridor, her heart fluttering in her thin chest, she admitted to herself for the first time that she loved him still, had never ceased loving him even though he had been wed to another and banished offworld for daring to speak out against the Tribunal of Thanes.

She paused for a moment and leaned against the rough, stone wall, listening tensely for some hint that her flight had been noted, a sleeper wakened, a guard alerted to her presence, for it was not too late to stop, to return to her rooms and do nothing as she had done nothing so many years before. Once again, she pondered her actions, or her lack thereof, wondering whether or not some eloquent plea would have moved her father to rescind his judgment and the harsh sentence he had imposed on Bracca, her lover. But there were no answers now, no more than there had ever been. Her father had loved her as much as he had disliked and feared Bracca, and Lomi had always suspected that Bracca had been sent offworld more for the crime of having loved her than for having the courage to speak his mind.

No, she had failed him then by her cowardice and had suffered nights and years of torment; it would not happen again. Stiffening her resolve, she turned off the main corridor and slipped through the labyrinth of tunnels to the complex where the prisoners were housed.

She passed cage after cage of animals gathered by the roving starships from the furthest points of the galaxy, some of which hurled themselves against the bars, screaming with frustration at their inability to reach her. Others merely regarded her with quiet rage burning in their eyes, which was, in its way, even more terrifying.

Lomi clutched her cloak about her tightly and pulled the hood down to shutter the frightening sights as she hurried through the animal enclosure, but the resentment and hatred burned through her fragile defense and she carried its weight with her as she passed out of the area.

"I am not to blame," she whispered fiercely as hot tears stained her cheeks. "What could I do, one woman alone against so many. I did not cause them to be brought here." But her words did not expunge the burden of guilt that weighed on her like a stone cloak as she thought of the countless animals and life forms who had died in the ring for the pleasure of her jaded brethren. But that, too, was an ancient argument and one that had no more answer than her love for Bracca.

The door to the wing where the prisoners were kept stood before her. Such a small thing, that door. All that stood between her and the man she loved. To see him, to touch him, to be held in his arms after so long a time. . . . Her heart, grown uncertain in recent years, began to beat irregularly, fluttering against her ribs like a caged bird. She leaned against the wall and closed her eyes. Drawing deep within herself, she focused on an inner spot of warmth and slowed her breathing, her pulse, her erratic heart rate. It would not do to die now! At least, she was calm enough to continue. She opened the door and stepped through.

Braldt lay on the hard, stone floor feeling the deep stiffness that clenched his muscles and wishing that he could sleep, but knowing that he could not.

The enclosure was dark, lit only by the infrequent, smoky torches that by this late hour had burned so far down that they produced only a sullen glow. It was quiet, too, as quiet as it ever got in this place, the silence filled with the deep, slow breathing of exhausted beings, tiny moans, and the intermittent screams of the madman who never slept. The screams had bothered him at first, but now they barely penetrated his consciousness.

His mind tugged and pulled at the problem that kept him awake night after night despite his body's demands for sleep. Once more he went over Septua's strange story and tried to connect it to the feeling he had gotten from the man in the robe, the man who wore his face.

Braldt was certain that he had not imagined the unspoken message the man had imparted. Even though no words had been spoken, somehow he knew that the man was an ally, a friend. Coupled with the dwarf's tale, it could only mean that there were those among these people who were in opposition to someone or something in their government. Hopefully, they could be considered allies. But how could they be reached?

Braldt had seen the man several times. He was always present on the dais when they went forward to receive their token of victory, but other than maintaining a steady eye contact that seemed to hold an unspoken promise, yet urged caution, there had been no solid contact and Braldt was growing ever more frustrated.

True to their original promise, they had been granted a wish with every victory. Putting his own fears and worries aside, Braldt had allowed Randi to make the first request. Even though Septua squawked his disagreement, it seemed the honorable thing to do.

Randi had asked after the fate of her family, and for the first time, Braldt caught a glimpse of the real woman hidden beneath the tough, competent exterior. She had been granted her wish, although what she had learned was not revealed to the rest of them for the information had been some sort of personal revelation received by Randi alone. Nor would she speak of what she had learned. Her eyes were bright with unshed tears. "All is well," was all that she would say. Braldt found himself wondering belatedly whether she had a mate, children, a lover on her home planet, but he did not force himself on her, seeing that she desired her privacy.

They had assumed that each of them would be given this privilege upon winning a contest, but it was not to be so. To their angered dismay, they learned that only one of them would be granted the knowledge they desired and that further enlightenment would depend upon further victories.

Septua railed and screeched at the unfairness of the decision and would have hurled himself at the three men above him on the dais, had Braldt and Allo not restrained him. The dwarf seemed to have lost his fear of his countrymen and he lost no opportunity to heap abuse on them whenever he saw them. If his words troubled them, there was no sign of it on their impassive features. He stopped short of mentioning the foiled plot he had supposedly shared with the man who always stood to the right of the dais. Although whether out of fear of going too far or whether as Braldt half suspected, the whole story was a hoax, he could not have said.

It was decided among them that Allo would be granted the next favor if they won, which they did, for he had two mates and three children and was much concerned about how they were dealing with his absence. But at the last moment, Septua stepped in front of Allo and took his place.

What he learned brought him no pleasure. His stolen knowledge informed him that his home, his possessions, and the lovely Mirna were all being enjoyed by none other than the captain of the guards who had arrested him. Further, it appeared that Mirna had helped bring about Septua's downfall by sharing his most secret plans with that same muscular captain who had also been rewarded with an advancement of rank due to the seriousness of Septua's crime.

Not even Allo could bring himself to chastise the dwarf who was completely devastated by the information, which he told them in a bleak monotone once they had been returned to their cell. Immediately after, he had rolled himself in his blanket and lay facing the wall, refusing to speak or even grope Randi when she knelt to offer him solace.

He was still sunk within himself when they won their next victory. He fought well enough, for even depressed he could grasp the fact that if they did not fight and win, they died.

When Allo finally received his turn, he, too, came away despondent for it seemed that his mates and children believed him dead. One of his mates, the one he loved most dearly, had ceased to eat and had apparently lost the desire to live, and furthermore, his youngest son was deeply distraught and angered by his loss and was creating a good deal of trouble by demanding that the company that had commissioned Allo, as well as the WWF starfleet command, do something to find the missing ship and bring home their dead. It was not making him popular with the authorities.

All of this was confided in bits and pieces as Allo paced back and forth in their cell. "I've got to get out of here. Got to find some way of sending a transmission. I have to let them know that I'm alive! Matek is not strong. She will perish! Allovie is so impetuous. I know that one—he will not stop until he has provoked someone into taking action which will most likely be to throw him into a cell somewhere! I must get out of here! I must help them!''

Allo's long, orange fur stood on end, spiked and peaked in shaggy tufts all over his body, and his eyes were wild. There was no evidence of the gentle creature who always urged them to practice caution and self-control. But none of them could offer Allo any hope for they had none themselves.

Upon their fourth victory, the death of the team of painted primitives, it was Braldt's turn at last.

There was a swirling inside his head, similar to the passage of clouds swirling at a rapid rate of speed, then they cleared away and it was as though he were hovering in mid-air above the city that had been his home.

His thoughts immediately conjured up the image of Auslic, the chief of their city state, and Auslic appeared before him. It was as though he were standing in Auslic's bed chamber and could actually have reached out and touched the man who was like a father to him. But Auslic gave no sign of seeing him, despite Braldt's clarity of vision. Auslic appeared to be in better health than the last time Braldt had seen him. Then he had been close to death. Now he paced his chambers with his hands tucked behind his back, sighing deeply and often as if a great weight rested on his shoulders. His face was creased and careworn and his mouth sagged in sorrow.

Braldt spoke to him, but it was obvious that Auslic did not know he was there. Braldt was desperate to know what terrible events had brought such grief on Auslic and he turned his thoughts to Carn, his adopted brother. Surely Carn would know.

The mists swirled and parted a second time and the sight that was revealed to him was so terrible that at first he could scarcely comprehend what he was seeing. It was Carn, as he was when last he saw him, horribly scarred and disfigured. Their torturous path, the one that had ultimately brought him here to this place, had taken them inside a mountain which housed an active volcano trapped in its depths. The unstable ground had fractured, grievously wounding Batta Flor and scalding and burning Carn.

The exposure to the volcano and his close brush with death had evidently shaken Carn deeply, altering his life in some radical way, for he had become crazed and had attempted to kill Braldt, but had only succeeded in plunging him into the void that had delivered him to this place.

But now, here was Carn again, inside the mountain at the heart of the volcano once more, spewing religious madness. Only this time he was not alone, he was wearing the robes of a priest, and behind him, their faces shining with fear or religious fervor, were a multitude of Braldt's clan.

He was so stunned at the sight of this revelation that his mind refused to function and he stared at the awful scene until it was shrouded by mists and disappeared. Only then did he come back to himself with a jerk and think to ask about Keri and Batta Flor, the two who occupied his thoughts the most. But it was too late. The world swam into focus around him, his companions staring at him with concern, Randi leaning forward and saying something he could not hear, and Allo shaking his shoulder gently. The men on the dais were watching him intently.

He closed his eyes, desperate to bring back the

swirling clouds, to learn about Keri and Batta Flor. But it was no good, the present came flooding in on all fronts, the heat of the suns beating down on his head, the stink of fresh blood smeared on his chest, Randi's voice in his ears. He sagged, overcome with sorrow. At once he understood how his companions had felt. The gift of knowledge was a bitter gift, one that brought no comfort, only pain. Perhaps that was why it was granted.

17

Keri ran her fingers through her hair, tugging on the tight, dark curls, trying to work the knots out but scarcely aware of her own actions as she contemplated her companion. Beast whined as though sensing the darkness of her mood and lay his head across her lap, an unusual bit of familiarity from the wild creature who normally kept his distance. Keri reached down and stroked his coarse fur, feeling him tremble beneath her touch, realizing that this strange captivity was hard on him as well.

But Batta Flor occupied most of her thoughts, for without the red berries that supplied the complex chemicals that were necessary to maintain his genetically altered brain, her companion, that noble and gentle being, was visibly sinking further and further into a primitive animalistic state. Without the berry in his diet, all signs of a civilized nature had vanished. He walked on all fours far more often than upright. He no longer spoke at all, only grunted, growled, and made other animal sounds. The damage to his ear, the center of pain for those of his species, had eliminated pain as a deterrent; now there was little or nothing that could sway him from a decided course of action. Further, the glint of intelligence that used to come into his eyes whenever he saw her was gone as well. Now he would look at her in puzzlement as though unable to figure out who or what she was.

But even more upsetting than the fact that he no longer recognized her was the attraction he now seemed to feel for her—that of an active, adult male for an available female. So far, he had done nothing more than sniff her from head to toe, but once he had seized her and held her tight, refusing to release her even when she struggled. He had carried her around beneath his arm like a package, finally losing interest and abandoning her. This had frightened her badly and she did her best to keep as much distance between them as possible, although it was difficult to do in such small quarters.

Beast sensed that something was wrong and once when Batta Flor approached Keri, the lupebeast pup bared his considerable double rows of fangs and growled at his former friend. Batta Flor stopped short and stared at the pup, then ambled off and began to feed. Keri hugged the pup to her chest, afraid for him as well as for herself, for it would take no more than a casual backhand from Batta Flor's immense fist to break the pup's spine or neck.

Batta Flor's lapse into animality had one good side effect—he had become an even more powerful fighter. Now he seemed to sense a coming battle as soon as he wakened, and paced the cell, eager for the coming fight. He entered the arena, shoulders hunched, his long eyeteeth bared in a fierce grimace, pounding on his broad, powerful chest with his fists, producing a hollow booming sound that could be heard across the ring. His roars of rage and defiance spoke of death and dying and struck terror into the hearts of their opponents. Even Keri was terrified and at such times she was glad that Batta Flor was not her enemy.

He had ceased to use any of his weapons other than the cudgel which he used as an extension of his arm, cracking heads, crushing flesh, and pulverizing bones. His reputation preceded him and often their opponents fled in fear only to be hunted down and ruthlessly slaughtered one by one around the perimeters of the ring. Often times it was not even necessary for Keri and Beast to fight.

The trio of men with Braldt's face still waited for them on the dais after each contest, but as always, Batta Flor had no interest in them and exited from the arena as soon as the last opponent was slain.

Their entrance into the ring was always met with a mighty roar, chanting their names over and over and over. They had clearly captured the hearts of the audience and become ring favorites. Keri wondered if they would cheer their deaths as well.

With every victory, their physical circumstances improved for it seemed that victors were rewarded for their performance. The quality of their food improved as did their physical comforts. Softer blankets were provided as well as thick cushions to sleep upon. Batta Flor took no notice of the amenities, and seemed more concerned with the quantity of the food rather than the quality.

Keri could not stop worrying and wondering about Braldt, but in this, too, as with everything else, there was no answer.

* * *

Her heart thudding within her chest, Lomi approached the bars of the cell, wondering if it would contain Bracca. She had greeted the reptilian crone who crouched before the fire burning in the low hearth, seeing the recognition come to the single, rheumy eye. The old one had patted her hand with a scaly paw and murmured a low question. Lomi had long known that this one was the custodian of the cells and had gone out of her way to show the crone kindness simply because she was the last to have come into contact with Bracca before he was sent offworld. The old one now regarded her with an affection that went far beyond gratitude for the simple kindnesses Lomi had extended to her over the years.

The woman's tongue was difficult to master, for her mouth had been disfigured by an injury at some point in her long distant youth. But with the passage of time, Lomi had learned her story and their mutual sorrow had drawn them closer than would normally have been possible.

The crone was a native of the planet. Her brethren had resisted the invasion of men who descended out of the skies, but they had fallen before the superior weapons and technology. Theirs had been a fledgling civilization and they had been easily subjugated. Those who dared to oppose them were killed outright or sent to labor in the mines which the invaders quickly established.

The Rototarans, as they called themselves, were the cause of the origin of the games. A rudimentary ring existed at the time of the conquest, used for a stylized, ritualistic form of courtship. But the invaders were quick to turn it into something completely different for their own amusement. At first they used it as a means of getting rid of Rototarans who proved difficult.

The crone, known as Saviq, who was young and courting at the time, saw her betrothed dispatched in this manner. She had gone berserk with grief and rage and had attacked the Thanes. Her life was spared, for her actions had amused the Scandis, but she had been grievously wounded and ever after had spoken in a garbled manner. The two women had been drawn together by the magnitude of their losses which was a far greater bond than the sum of their differences.

Now it took but a murmured request which Saviq honored without hesitation, pointing out a large cell at the far end of the corridor.

Lomi could not understand how such a thing could have happened. What could Bracca have done to have brought himself back to face the ring? And what of his mate and his child? All of these questions and more hammered in her head as she gripped the bars and peered into the dark enclosure. "Bracca," she whispered tremulously. "Bracca, it is I, Lomi."

At first there was no response, but she called out a second time, and before the words were out of her mouth, a horrid little man who stood barely waist high, pressed up against the bars leering at her, his hand sliding up the inside of her thigh. She jerked away out of his reach and crossed her arms across her chest, waves of revulsion coursing through her body. She could feel her cheeks burning red under the dwarf's salacious gaze.

And then he was there, Bracca Jocobe Brandtson, tall and handsome and miraculously untouched by the passage of time. He gripped the dwarf by the shoulders and lifted him away, ignoring the sputtering of colorful curses that spewed from the little man's mouth. Then there was nothing between them but the bars and the deep welling emotion of her memories. Lomi's eyes filled with tears as her hand reached for his. He spoke.

"Is there something wrong, Lady? Are you in some distress?" His voice was kind, but something was wrong. Even the long years of separation could not rob her of the memory of Bracca's voice, strong and deep and resonant. This voice was all of those things, but different. It was not the voice she had held in her heart.

She grasped the hand that reached for hers and knew without a doubt that the fates had not seen fit to smile upon her but were merely playing out some cosmic joke for their own amusement. Lomi was an intelligent, intuitive, and discerning woman, and the hand that held hers did so out of good manners and gentle concern. There was no hint of love or the memory of such. This was not Bracca. At that moment, she sagged and would have collapsed had Braldt not wrapped his arms around her slender body and called out in alarm. To his amazement, the old woman who tended the water cart was there in an instant, reaching for the woman and cradling her in her scaly arms, crooning to her and uttering words of comfort. Braldt and his companions gathered at the bars and watched the strange scene in total confusion, unsure of what was happening.

The old crone attempted to revive the woman, but her skin was a curious ashen-blue shade and her breathing was ragged and steterous. It was obvious that she was in great distress. The old one's cries grew frantic and she looked about in terror, clearly divided about going for help or remaining with the woman.

Braldt felt responsible in some way, even though he could not have said how. The woman had reached for him and he had failed her in some way as was apparent from her reaction. "Let me out!" he cried to the crone. "Let me help."

The old reptile looked up and tried to focus on Braldt with her single eye which dripped with tears. She wrung her scaled hands and rocked back and forth, moaning. She was clearly terrified, although whether for herself or for the fallen woman was impossible to say. Randi added her voice to Braldt's and Allo spoke up as well. The crone stumbled to her feet and unlocked the door to the cell, urging them toward the woman whose eyes had rolled back into her skull.

Braldt laid his hands upon the woman's chest and felt the thready tremble of the uncertain heart within. He spoke to Randi who immediately pushed him aside and began a complex routine of breathing and manual expression of the woman's chest. After a long, uncomfortable period, Lomi gave a long sigh, choked, and began to breath more evenly.

It was a long time before she was strong enough to sit up, leaning against and supported by Allo's shaggy body. The water carrier had hobbled off and returned as fast as her legs could carry her, bringing a gourd of hot, herbal brew which the woman sipped in shallow draughts.

"Did he send you?" Septua asked, without waiting for the woman to speak.

"Who?" she replied, obviously confused by the dwarf's question.

" 'Im. Jorund, that's who. 'Im what got me in 'ere. 'Im what Braldt thinks is gonna save us. That's who."

"Braldt? Is that your name? Yes, now that I see you close . . . I can see the difference. But you are so much like him. I thought . . . I wanted to think . . ." Her voice trailed off.

"Hey, lady! Don't die, huh! We got enough trouble now without you croakin'!" cried the dwarf.

"I would not think to cause you further difficulty," the woman said with a wry smile as she struggled upright. "Nor would I wish to misrepresent my intentions. As to Jorund's intentions I cannot say, I can but speak for my own. I did not come here to save you for I did not even know you existed. I came here to see this man whom I mistook for one I once knew and cared for long ago. I thought it was he, and while they are much alike, they are not the same. I thought . . . we all thought . . . but it seems we were wrong."

" 'Ow can you tell?" argued Septua, unwilling to relinquish even this one small thread of hope. " 'Ow can you tell? It might be 'im, whoever 'e was. You all look the same!"

"No." The woman smiled gently at the dwarf. "There are differences among us, slight though they might be. This is not the one called Bracca Jocobe. I fear that he is long dead on another world."

"What world?" Braldt asked sharply, and Lomi looked at him in surprise, considering once again the shape of his head and the sound of his voice. "A world

without a name, K7 as the star charts call it. A distant
world rich in precious minerals.''

"Rhodium," said Braldt.

"Yes, rhodium! How did you know?" asked Lomi,
her voice filled with amazement.

"Because this uninhabited world, this K7 as you
call it, is my home. I think that we have much to talk
about."

Before the leading edge of the primary sun advanced
over the edge of the horizon, Lomi and Braldt had talked
and explored the mystery of the past. Much had been
revealed and sorrow had accompanied enlightenment.

They had pieced together their bits of information
and come to the unavoidable conclusion that Braldt was
the son of Bracca Jocobe and the woman Mirim. Braldt
had learned that his father had been the high-born son of
a powerful Thane. Always an outspoken youth, Bracca
had involved himself in dissident issues as he grew older
and eventually incurred the wrath of the rest of the high
council by arguing against the colonization of K7, a
populated world, which was in direct contravention of the
Whole World Federation's directives.

Bracca's charismatic personality had earned him the
respect and loyalty of many of the younger Thanesons as
well as Lomi's quiet, unspoken love. The High Thanes
had seen the light of a dangerous rebellion in the young
Bracca, a threat to all their carefully laid plans. In vain
did they try to convince the young Thaneson that the
colonization of K7 was necessary for their own planet's
existence.

What possible harm, they argued, could come from

the taking of a mineral from a world whose inhabitants were thousands of years away from its possible use. Inhabitants who had barely progressed beyond the age of bronze, who placed their belief in animistic spirits and dieties of the earth.

But the young idealist would not be convinced and threatened to report the Thanes to the World Federation. If Bracca had not been the son of a reigning Thane, he might have been dispatched without conscience, but his father had been a member of the ruling council for a score of years and still had many powerful friends. These friends dissuaded other, angrier voices from killing Bracca outright, but everyone knew that something had to be done.

Bracca and his young wife and newborn son had been imprisoned in these same cells for safekeeping, to prevent either side from taking hasty, improper action before a rational compromise had been agreed upon.

Unfortunately, irrational behavior existed on both sides, and one dark night, Bracca's friends set a number of explosives at the mine's processing plants, hoping to frighten the Thanes into releasing their leader. Their plan backfired.

Worried that the young Thanesons were indeed a serious threat, another group of the Thanes spirited Bracca and his wife and child out of the prison and into the transmission chamber. In one swift, irreversible move, they sent the defenseless trio hurtling through time and space to the planet K7 to live or die as fate and their wits would have it, depriving the young rebellion of its heart and soul and themselves of their worst enemy.

This action caused serious uprisings on the small waystation called Rototara as well as their home planet, Valhalla. The young militants, as well as the thinkers and dreamers, united over the cause which had brought about the banishment of their young leader.

Lomi's quiet voice held them all in thrall as she explained how the Thane tried desperately to calm the unexpected rebellion. Although it was not their habit to explain their actions, those who were defying them were their own sons and others of their blood.

They explained to all who would listen that they had believed K7 to be uninhabited, only discovering the primitive population after they had already established a mine for the extraction of rhodium. Rhodium was a rare mineral essential for space travel and its discovery was the answer to their own barren planet's problems, for while Valhalla was indeed a magnificent planet, it possessed absolutely no resources which would make it economically viable or able to support its burgeoning population.

Literally everything needed for life had to be brought in from other worlds, and to do so cost a great deal of money. The Thanes were desperate to find a means to support their world. It was impossible to return to the old, dying earth and before the discovery of rhodium, they had been forced to return to their ancient heritage and become pirates.

But the Thanes were worried. Piracy was profitable and had worked for a time, but eventually, other offworlders came together to create the Whole World Federation which regulated the rules of the galaxy, the rules by which all offworlders were governed. It was impossible to defy the WWF for it possessed a superior war fleet capable of blasting transgressors into stardust.

The Thanes still looted and raided when it was deemed safe, but they could no longer depend on such actions to support their world which had grown larger and larger and far more complex, requiring vast amounts of money to survive, much less compete in the galactic market.

Rhodium and K7 were the answers to their problems for rhodium was needed by every race capable of space travel. In all the known universe, only rhodium was capable of protecting hulls from the intense heat encountered when departing or re-entering atmospheres. It was a dream come true, financial solvency that would make Valhalla the richest planet in the galaxy.

It was the revelation of the financial benefits that finally put out the fires of the rebellion, for even the young idealists were able to recognize the fact that their own lives were at risk. When faced with the concern for an unknown race of primitive people on a far distant planet or the continuance of their own pleasant lifestyle, there was really no choice.

A small, hard-core band of resisters including Lomi and Jorund remained, but for their own safety, they were forced to remain silent. They had watched and waited over the years, inheriting positions of power as they came available and carefully and quietly inducting new members to their cause.

Unaware of their existence, the Thanes had continued on with their work on K7, excavating the mine, installing the expensive equipment necessary for the extraction of the rhodium and staffing it with robots. They also sent along the Madrelli, an apelike race which they had genetically and chemically manipulated to make them the perfect slave worker.

The Thanes had been telling the truth. It was only after the mine was fully operational and an enthusiastic and captive market established for their high-grade rhodium, that they had discovered that the planet was inhabited by not one or two but a score of primitive yet intelligent races.

It was a disaster of staggering proportions. The Thanes conferred and after long discussion decided that they had only three options. They could abide by the WWF's rules and abandon K7 which would mean planetary ruin. They could kill off the native population which no one besides themselves even knew existed. Or, they could devise some elaborate plan which would keep the two civilizations apart.

In the end, there was really no argument, for deception was far more preferable to wholesale murder. An elaborate fiction was composed, rather simplistic actually, but in the case of a civilization that had barely advanced beyond the Bronze Age, more than adequate. They had composed a pastiche of old earth religions based on weather and natural events and animistic deities that would appeal to the primitive mind and put it all in place with the introduction of black-robed "priests" who were, in fact, nothing more than robots draped in voluminous robes that concealed their non-human features.

The Thanes were able to monitor all happenings via

small "seeing eyes" and silver discs implanted in the palms of the robots' hands and chests that were listening devices. When it was necessary to sway the natives in one direction or another, "visions" were miraculously created by a robot priest placing his hand directly against the forehead of one selected to receive the "vision." Group visions were projections of holograms which had never failed to convince the impressionable natives who held the mysterious priests in reverential awe.

To complete the religion and further protect themselves, the Thanes erected immense, stone monoliths, much in the image of themselves, and placed them at the edges of the natives' land, creating a buffer zone and separating them from the previous mines as well as from the Madrelli who knew all too well of their existence.

The scheme had worked brilliantly. The care and handling of native affairs was overseen by a small group of Thanes who maintained a close watch on the lives of their charges and saw to it that they remained wrapped in the heavy cloak of the religion that had been created for them. They also saw to it that the natives did not advance too swiftly, purposely holding them at a semi-primitive state, for advanced thinkers and skeptics could mean nothing but trouble.

But of course such thinkers and skeptics did arise from time to time and these were dealt with swiftly and harshly. They seldom lived long enough to cause anyone any trouble.

The last thing the Thanes had expected was trouble on their own world. So alert were they to trouble on K7 that they were taken entirely by surprise by Bracca's incipient rebellion and they acted foolishly. An intelligent solution would have been to have offered the young idealist a position on the Council for Native Affairs—a position with high rank and title and very little actual power, but enough to convince the young firebrand that there was the possibility of progress in his cause.

Instead, they had reacted swiftly and without thought, setting in motion events that would have far-reaching implications.

This much was known to Lomi and she shared her knowledge with Braldt, but that was far from all of the story. There was no way she could have known that Bracca and his young wife had perished almost immediately on the hostile and unfamiliar planet, having the misfortune to arrive in the desert in the middle of the hot season. Unfortunately and inexplicably, the infant sheltered by his father's body survived long enough to be found by the natives.

By this time, the Thanes' misguided actions had come to light and Bracca's enraged and grief-stricken father, although unable to retrieve the child, refused to permit its death. The child's existence was a closely guarded secret, one that Brandtson had no reason to share with Lomi, but of great importance to the old man.

Brandtson had manipulated events and caused the child to be given into the care of the chief's family. His grief over the loss of his son and daughter-in-law was somewhat comforted by his ability to oversee the child's progress as Braldt and the chief, Auslic, a fine and noble leader, developed a close and loving bond.

But his fellow Thanes did not share his happiness. Far from it. They were nervous and concerned over the existence of the child, viewing him as a terrible threat. How could one of their race fail to be superior in every way, even when surrounded by an inferior, primitive species? And indeed that proved to be the case. They made certain that the child was closely watched from his very youngest days on, so that they would be forewarned of any danger.

And so began a ballet of sorts with Brandtson overseeing his grandson from afar and his fellow Thanes, not powerful enough to kill him or depose him, attempting to control the child as well. They tried to steer him into the priesthood, for there, surrounded by their robots, they would have been able to exert the most control over his actions. But Braldt was not cut from a priestly cloth. From the very first, it was clear that true to his ancient lineage, he was a warrior.

In spite of the Thanes' efforts to hold him back, Braldt excelled in everything. His skills in weaponry were unmatched by anyone, even his teachers. He had made remarkable strides in education, absorbing everything he was taught and yearning for more. He carried abstract deduction to levels that astounded his mentors, advancing the study of mathematics into areas that had never even been thought of, and he developed a new process of smelting that produced harder metal capable of holding a keener edge than had ever been possible.

But the thing that had worried the Thanes most was Braldt's continuing close relationship to the aging chief, Auslic. Although childless (a situation created by the

Thanes), Auslic had stepped beyond the established chain of command and publicly chosen Braldt as his successor. This could not be allowed, for whom among them could say how far Braldt would be able to take the primitive society. Far enough to begin to question the old rules and the religion that dictated so much of their lives. Far enough to disregard the borders and venture into the Forbidden Lands, far enough to discover the mines and the Madrelli, which would be the beginning of the end.

The Thanes took steps to see that such a thing did not happen. With the priests' help, they augmented Auslic's diet with life-extending potions that had long been known to them, enabling him to outlive his contemporaries and put off Braldt's ascendance to power.

They used the time they had gained as best they were able, seeing to it that Braldt was given the most dangerous of assignments, hoping that he would be killed by one of the dangerous creatures or other species that inhabited the planet. But such did not happen; Braldt survived all obstacles thrown his way, and in doing so, grew even more adept.

And so they were stalemated, Braldt and Auslic alive and well and the Thanes watching nervously for a day they knew must come. That day arrived in a way none had imagined. An old man, warming his bones in the rising sun, had been slain by a wild beast. Unfortunate as the death was, it was made worse by the fact that he had been a close friend of Auslic's. Also slain by the beast was a young comrade of Braldt's.

At first, the deaths, totally natural in their occurrence, had been hailed as positive, for Braldt had set out after the beast, determined to slay it. The Thanes hoped with all their hearts that the beast would kill Braldt, solving all of their problems. But in this, too, they were to be foiled. Although Braldt was badly injured, he succeeded in killing the beast and acquired one of her young who attached itself to him with a fierce loyalty.

To make matters worse, Auslic, already old and frail, kept alive long beyond his natural lifespan by unnatural means, had suffered a failure of his heart brought on by the shock of the death of his oldest friend. The Thanes were in turmoil, for if Auslic died, Braldt would accede to the throne, an impossible situation!

But their problems did not stop there. The Thanes found themselves beset by problems on all sides. After thousands of years of domination, the Madrelli were rebelling. Their level of intelligence was closely controlled by the administration of a pill that contained all they needed to maintain their genetic advances. In the past, all that had been necessary to control the Madrelli was to withhold the vital pill. But in this, too, they were frustrated, for as impossible as it seemed, the Madrelli had found a berry on K7 that replicated the pill that was so essential to their existence.

It was at this point that a faction of the Thanes, sensing that they were losing control of the situation, had begun to advocate that all of their problems would be solved if neither the Madrelli, the natives, or the troublesome Braldt existed. From there it was but a single leap to the thought of total annihilation. After all, they still possessed many more captive Madrelli on Valhalla and Rototara and other worlds that they firmly controlled.

What was the loss of a few thousand when others could easily be cloned? Also, if the planet were destroyed, it would be far easier to collect, extract, and process the valuable rhodium.

This plan was certain to be opposed by any number of their fellow Scandis; the Council for Native Affairs had, over time, come to take itself rather seriously and was sure to resent such a plan to eradicate their charges. And most importantly, there was the venerable Brandtson who still wielded considerable power. There was also the small matter of the WWF which would mete out harsh judgment if it ever discovered that the Scandis had purposely destroyed a world that contained intelligent life.

If the planet was to be destroyed, it would have to look like a natural occurrence. The planet, like so many others, contained an active belt of volcanos, dangerous in the extreme unless one knew how to manage them by bleeding off the excess amounts of pressure. It was also possible to increase the pressure, which one never did since it could cause a planetary cataclysm of disastrous proportions; this was exactly what the Scandis had in mind.

Steps were taken to shut down the mine and all but a caretaking staff of robots were withdrawn, for unlike the Madrelli who could be endlessly and inexpensively cloned, the robots were intensely complicated and incredibly expensive bits of technology and not easily or quickly replaced.

The Madrelli, however, learned of the Thanes' plans and reasonably enough, objected and took steps to foil the plot. At a great loss of Madrelli life and robots, the Madrelli flooded the control chamber of the mine and shut down the equipment which allowed the Scandis to come and go undetected. This was a serious problem for the planet could not be destroyed from space in a manner that would not be suspect. Somehow, it was imperative to drain the chamber and reverse the piece of equipment that concealed the arrivals and departures of their ships.

To the ironic amusement of those still possessing a sense of humor, it was decided that Braldt was the only one capable of carrying out the difficult and dangerous mission of crossing over into the hostile Madrelli lands and finding his way to the heart of the volcanic mountain that contained the cloaking device.

Braldt had been sent on this "holy" mission by the priests who told him that Auslic's only chance for survival lay in the retrieval of a medical kit that could be found in the mountain's interior. He was also instructed to reverse the crucial lever. The medical kit was but a cover story to conceal the true mission, throwing the lever, for if Braldt did as they directed, it would not matter if he succeeded in bringing the kit back to his tribe. There was nothing in its contents which could save Auslic and by that time, the planet would have ceased to exist.

Once again, the fates, which not even the Scandis had managed to control, intervened and all of their plans went awry. Braldt and his adopted siblings, Keri and Carn, had crossed over into the Forbidden Lands as directed and then were lost to the Thanes for they had no way of observing them. When next they appeared inside the mountain and were subject to remote scanning, the

Thanes received an unpleasant shock. Somehow, Braldt and the Madrelli had discovered each other and appeared to be working in concert. Even worse, it appeared that the Madrelli had shared their knowledge of the Scandis with Braldt which could not fail to lead to horrific problems.

Then, those same fickle fates had swung in their direction. Volcanic activity had increased, and without their assistance in relieving the build-up of pressure, the mountain suffered ground shifts which all but killed Carn and severely injured the Madrelli known as Batta Flor. Carn, exposed to the great heat at the heart of the volcano, experienced what his fevered mind interpreted as a religious revelation that directed him on a specific course of action.

After great difficulty, Braldt, Keri, and Batta Flor succeeded in reaching the flooded chamber and retrieved the sought-after medical box. Then Carn arrived, and following the whisperings of his heat-demented mind, threw the lever that allowed the Scandis to come and go and also transported Braldt off K7 and directly onto Rototara in an ironic blink of fate's eye.

The watching Thanes were thunderstruck! Not only had they succeeded in reversing the lever, but here was Braldt delivered into their hands as well! Now they could not take the chance of allowing the Madrelli to return to his village, for there was still the possibility that his tribe would sabotage the machinery a second time. As it was, they would not know that it had been reversed until the ships arrived and then it would be too late. But if the Madrelli did not return, it could only be assumed that he had perished in his brave attempt. And so it was that the machinery had been activated a second time, seizing Batta Flor, Keri, and even the lupebeast pup in its inexorable grasp and delivering them to the Thanes.

Now, fate would be allowed to play its part again, for no matter how good Braldt was, no matter how strong and resistent to pain was the Madrelli, neither of them could survive the ring forever. And if they did, they could always be pitted against each other. There was, of course, the small risk that someone would recognize Braldt, but it was unlikely. Brandtson had been sent back to Valhalla on a quickly contrived affair of business and no one else on Rototara had the necessary strength to oppose them. *At last,* thought the Thanes, *things were going our way.*

If the Thanes had known what was happening beneath the arena, their carefully coiffed, silvery, blond hair would have turned gray overnight.

18

Concluding their long conversation, Lomi returned to her quarters just before dawn, barely escaping detection by the roving guards who took careful note of those who were not where they were supposed to be. Her tired heart beat erratically and she willed it to be calm, chiding herself for being a foolish old woman with a case of the flutters. Braldt and his friends depended on her. His life was in her hands. She had been unable to help Bracca, but she would not fail his son.

There was much to be done. First, she had to tell Jorund and the others what she had learned, and somehow they must get a message to Brandtson, for his help would be badly needed. No one, not even the Thanes of Rototara would be able to stand against Brandtson. When he learned that he had nearly lost his grandson...the mere thought of his rage was staggering. No, Lomi smiled to herself. Telling Brandtson was the answer. He would fix everything.

She had to find Jorund. Lomi turned to the door, then sunk to the foot of her bed, pressing the tips of her fingers hard against her breastbone, willing her ragged heartbeat to return to normal, to cease its uncertain patter. This was no time for such nonsense, she was needed! But she could not rise. Darkness crowded in at the edges of her eyes, dimming her vision, and the air seemed thick and heavy . . . it was difficult to breathe. Maybe if she rested for just a moment, gathered her strength. . . . She collapsed slowly against the cushions of her bed, her slight figure seeming no more than a bed ornament, and the rise and fall of her chest came slower and slower and slower.

Braldt, Randi, Allo, and Septua were all but overwhelmed by what they had learned; alternately overjoyed, angered, and dismayed. Braldt was deeply moved, hearing about his father and mother, and he grieved anew for their deaths. His anger burned ever more deeply over that long distant decision that had sent them plummeting out of their world to die in a strange and hostile land.

He wanted to know the man who was the father of his father, felt his heart race at the thought. Were there others of his blood as well? Questions whirled inside his head, so many questions that he had failed to ask.

But he could not discount the matter of his enemies who now appeared to be more numerous than he had imagined and the reason for his imprisonment all the more dangerous. They would not feel safe until he was dead, nor would they have risked submitting him to the arena unless they felt safe from discovery. Which meant what he already knew: that he had few allies and slim hope of survival.

Just how much of a chance depended heavily on the woman Lomi and her compatriots, although it seemed clear that they, too, were operating against the odds.

Well, so be it, Braldt thought with a grim smile. The odds had improved greatly in just the span of a single night and if he had not had reason to hate the Thanes before, he certainly had cause now.

Septua was practically hopping up and down, dancing from foot to foot, unable to contain his excitement. "See, I told ya it were true! 'E set me up to 'elp 'em! I knew it were a real plot! Mebbe we can do it again! An' it'll work this time! All we gotta do is get the chance! When we get outta 'ere, we'll show 'em they can't push us around!"

Braldt stopped listening after a time and gave up trying to convince the dwarf to be still, for it was an impossible situation. Whatever the plan might have been on Valhalla, it was unlikely that such a plot would work here and now.

The woman had said that she would speak to those who were allied to their cause immediately upon her return and set in motion whatever events were necessary to free them. She had promised that Jorund would speak to them himself before the day began and all of them anxiously awaited his arrival. Even Braldt felt a thrill of anticipation with every new footstep in the corridor.

But the sun rose over the edge of the distant horizon and the guards arrived to herd them from their cells, beginning the long day's routine. Septua lagged behind and looked about desperately as though somehow imagining that Jorund might be hiding in the shadows. Braldt felt a chill of premonition. Something had gone wrong. The woman had seemed so certain, so determined to help. Despite his strength, Braldt felt a moment of deep despair for he had allowed himself to hope, to believe. It was a bitter pill to swallow. Randi turned and looked at him and he could see his own bleak thoughts reflected in her eyes. He could not even offer her a smile of hope.

The day was like all others, but because of its very ordinariness when they had hoped for so much more, it seemed to have no end. There was only one unexpected occurrence during the day—an alien being, stranger than any they had encountered as yet attacked the guards. The thing stood more than seven feet tall and was deep blue in color. It was squarish in shape and no thicker than Braldt's hand. It propelled itself through the air by a curious rippling which appeared along its lower edge and took it in whatever direction it aimed. It was capable of reversing itself instantly, with its edges fluttering in both directions, then flowing all together at once. Hands or some form of appendages appeared wherever they were needed along any of the edges or even growing out of the main body if it were necessary; they were as short or as long as required. The thing did not appear to have a head and even though it was impossibly thin, it was incredibly strong.

The guards had never been able to make the thing do anything they wanted it to do. Nor were they able to communicate with it despite the silver disc which had been attached to the upper left quadrant of its body. Perhaps it had no language. It took no nourishment that anyone could discover and had no apparent needs. Its cell was next to Braldt's and at night it merely rolled itself up into a tight cylinder and lay still and unmoving until morning. Nor would it fight.

The guards grew increasingly frustrated with their lack of ability to control it, and on this particular morning had begun to beat the creature and prod it with the points of their spears, all to no effect. One of the guards, more aggravated than the others, lost control and plunged his spear completely through the thin, blue body. All around the arena, guards and prisoners alike stopped to watch the strange conflict.

For a long moment nothing seemed to happen. The arena fell silent. The guard looked around, uncertain what to do, for while the guards were there to guard the prisoners, and violence was always implicit, the blue being had done nothing to warrant the severity of his action. Yet all wondered just what if anything it would do.

The blue alien stood unmoving, the spear sticking out of its body. The guard, feeling the weight of eyes upon him, felt it imperative to pretend that he had intended his action. He swaggered forward, and bracing his foot on the body of the creature, made as if to pull his spear free. Instead, his foot slowly sank, drawn inexorably inward as the guard stared at his entrapped limb in horrified disbelief. And then he began to scream.

At the sound of his voice, everyone rushed toward him. Some of his friends grabbed him around the upper body and began to pull backward, trying to free him, but it was hopeless. Inch by screaming, struggling inch, he was pulled forward, sucked in, absorbed by the impossibly thin, blue body. No sign of him appeared on the other side, nor did the blue square grow any larger. Several of the guards began hacking at the blue being with swords, knives, clubs, and even the metal lightning arcs; nothing seemed to affect it. The blades merely penetrated its thin body, emerging on the other side. Clubs and blunt weapons bounced off and the blue arc of light sizzled along the edges without seeming to bother the being in the slightest. But in the end, despite all his friends' efforts, the guard was taken, every single bit of him, leather, metal, flesh, and bone, until he was completely gone.

Septua watched the entire happening with wide eyes. When it was over, he gave a long, low whistle of appreciation. "Whew, wotta we 'ave to do to get that guy on our side, I wonder! Wotta technique! I never seen nothin' like it! Did you see the way it just sort' slurped 'im in, I mean it was nothin' short of amazin'! Oh, sorry, Randi, 'ere, lemme 'elp you sit down!"

Randi gave Septua a black look, and deftly avoided his hand which had already inched upward from her waist to the side of her breast. "You're disgusting! A man was just killed and all you can think about is the technique!"

"Well, 'ey, better 'im than us!" Septua exclaimed in his own defense, placing his hand on his breast and trying to look offended.

"Enough," said Braldt as he stepped between the two. "Much as I hate to admit it, Septua is right. It was an amazing technique. Think about it," he said to Randi. "When else has anyone ever been able to stand up to the guards? Never. Many have tried and some of them have been very good warriors indeed, but no one has ever succeeded. How does one speak to this being? Has anyone ever tried?"

His question went unanswered because the day was brought to an abrupt halt as they were herded back to their cells and locked down without food or water. There was none of the banter and casual talk that normally accompanied this procedure. It was clear that the guards were badly shaken. No further action was taken against the blue alien who returned to his cell, coiled itself tightly, and promptly went to sleep, or whatever it was that it did at such times.

Braldt sat down as near as he could get to the creature and studied it, pondering how they could persuade such a thing to help them in their fight for freedom.

Lomi struggled back to consciousness and fought off the waves of darkness that threatened to envelope her by sheer strength of will. Her flagging body infuriated her. She could not, would not die now, now that she was needed! She rose from her bed, and using the walls for assistance, made her way out into the hall. The corridors were thronged as always; so many people hurrying about their business, everything so very important. So many people, but who among them could be trusted? Despite her resolve, she felt her knees weaken, and still clinging to the doorframe, slid gently to the floor.

Before she could struggle upright, a crowd had gathered around her, murmuring sounds of concern. A grim-looking, take-charge sort of fellow leaned over and peered into her eyes, then listened to her hesitant heart. Guards shouted orders. She tried to speak, to tell them it wasn't necessary, but somehow, her voice never quite left her lips, or if it did, it went unheard. She felt herself lifted by efficient hands and carried down the corridor. She had led such a quiet life, it seemed odd to have such a fuss made over her. It was quite nice, actually. A pity one had to nearly die to have it happen.

Lights streamed past and fragments of conversation came to her. It seemed that they did not think she would live to reach the infirmary. She closed her eyes and smiled. She would live long enough to do what was needed, but she wished she could stay around to see what would follow. Quite irreverently she wondered if there weren't someone you could complain to. It was like having a mystery novel taken away at the last chapter. As the darkness closed in again, she wondered why life had to be so unfair.

19

There was trouble. Something was wrong. Even Keri could feel it. It was in the air. Batta Flor had been pacing back and forth all morning from one end of the cell to the other, pounding on the bars of the door and shaking them violently. No guards came to yell threats or strike his fingers with their clubs and that in itself was odd. They had seen no guards other than a small guard that had raced through the cellblock early that morning. They had been fully armed.

They were supposed to have fought this morning, but as yet there were no sounds to indicate that a game day had begun. No blaring of horns, no pounding of drums, no sound of the crowds. Batta Flor's constant motion was making her nervous; she wanted to scream at him to stop, but she was afraid to. More and more she felt fear. The way he looked at her now frightened her. She was certain that he had lost all memory of their past existence, their friendship. The look in his eyes was quite different now. A cunning look and something else as well, a look of ownership.

He had begun to lash out at the lupebeast pup whenever it came too close. But Beast was now the only thing that kept her sane, a link with Braldt and what had been, and she was not about to relinquish him to Batta Flor's moodiness. She did her best to keep him by her at all times, even sleeping beside him at night. She hugged him to her now and felt the tension in his body. She drew her legs up under her and huddled against the coarse-furred pup. Hot tears pricked behind her eyelids and she closed her eyes, unable to bear the sight of Batta Flor pacing off the steps of their captivity.

Young Leif Arndtson, a Thaneson of the first circle, had hoped to make a name for himself on this mission. He had hoped to acquit himself well enough so that he could erase the memory of the shameful manner in which he had disgraced himself during the skirmish on the captive freighter. It had been his first real fight. No one was more surprised than he to find that he could not stomach the sights and sounds of battle. Before he could strike a single blow, he became hopelessly nauseous and spent the rest of the brief affair emptying his stomach of its contents. Although there had been a few awkward attempts at joking about the situation, even his men had been embarrassed over his behavior and not anxious to remain under his command. Most had transferred out within the month that followed.

He had hoped to remedy that blot on his career by following his instructions to the letter, winning the commendation of his superiors and making his father proud. It hadn't seemed so much to wish for, but now he would settle for escaping with his life, or at the very least, the chance to kill himself and avoid dishonor and betrayal. A bitter taste filled his mouth as he began to realize how slender were his chances of doing even that.

He had stepped through the transmission chamber with a contingent of twelve men, fully armed and ready and willing to do his bidding. He had also been entrusted with the safety of two tectonic specialists, the men who would set the charges that would cause the planet known as K7 to self-destruct in a manner that would seem entirely natural. He had been assured that there would be more than ample time for him and his men to return in safety.

At no time had there been any mention of crazed natives and swarms of hostile, armed Madrelli, which was what they had found waiting for them. . . . Now there would be no honor, nothing but ignominious death at the hands of primitives.

Leif Arndtson closed his eyes and sighed, closing his mind against the pain of his tightly bound wrists and ankles, trying to think of what they might have done to have prevented this debacle from happening.

He had known about the Madrelli of course, for he had often organized new shipments of the shaggy, cloned workers to replace those killed in the mines. But the Madrelli had always been a placid, abiding race and it had never occurred to him to fear them. One merely ordered them to do something and they did it. Only these Madrelli didn't.

They had emerged from the transmission chamber in the ruined control room on K7, astonished at the degree of destruction they found. Pipes and ceiling panels, ductwork and bits of machinery were strewn all over.

There were watermarks all along the edges of the walls indicating the depth of the water as the river poured through the chamber.

The Madrelli had done this; this Leif and his men had been told. But they had thought it had been the work of a few rogues who were themselves killed in the fierce deluge they had caused. Or so they had been told. There were several robots lying about as well, violently disassembled. This should have given them a clue what to expect, but instead, they had merely been horrified at the waste and cost of replacement.

Leif and his men made their way through the maze of broken and semi-collapsed tunnels following the carefully drawn schematics which would bring them to the heart of the mountain where they would set their charges.

They had met no one on the way in and that was unfortunate, for in the tangled mass of fallen debris that clogged the corridors, some of them might have escaped. The mountain had rumbled continuously and bits of rock and broken panels rained down on them incessantly which made them increasingly nervous. Occasionally, the mountain would shake so hard that they would be unable to keep their footing. Several of the men had been injured and their lights lost or broken.

The thunderous rumble that accompanied these shakings was even more terrifying, for all of them were aware of the vast mountain of rock above them. It was all too easy to picture a sideways slip of rock or the collapse of an already weakened corridor, crushing the life out of them as easily as one might swat an annoying insect. Many had wanted to turn back, and even though Leif

Arndtson had held them in place, in his heart he had wanted to flee as well.

Would that they had. He could have reported to his superiors that interior damage had prevented him from reaching his goal. They might even have believed him.

Instead, fearing that he would forever be branded a coward, he had pressed on and had led his men unerringly to the throat of the volcano. The fiery maw had yawned beneath them, churning, boiling, spitting out chunks of flaming rock that leaped high into the air above them only to return and be swallowed by the crimson flood once again. Here, the shaking and rumbling roar had been constant, the noise too loud for them to be heard even if they shouted. They crept from place to place, clinging to every knob and projection, holding their bodies flat against the heated ground to avoid being thrown into the flaming cauldron. They made their needs known by signs though they feared letting go long enough to do so. At last, the technicians set their charges and they were free to go, which they did with all possible speed.

It was then that the disaster happened. The mountain growled and shook itself—a mere twitch really compared to some of the tremors that had gone before—but it was enough to bring down the roof of the tunnel. Four of the men were killed outright, several others badly injured. There was no hope of digging through the fall, for it appeared to be solid rock and they had no equipment. They discussed setting a charge but the thought of all that unstable rock just waiting to be dislodged dissuaded them, for they could not be certain that they could control a fall once it had started.

Even more frightening was the thought of the charge behind them, already activated and ticking down toward total annihilation. They had backtracked and found another tunnel, one that seemed to lead in the direction they needed to go, but they had been wrong. They took several turns, none of which appeared on the schematic and then the ground opened beneath their feet with no warning and they fell into the stifling darkness, crashing into hidden rocks, breaking bones, splitting skulls, and losing lights and crucial life-saving equipment.

Then there were but five of the original party left alive and all of the survivors were injured in one way or another. They had but a single light left among them and even though they could see another light burning on the slope above them, no one had the courage to retrieve it.

Their map was gone as well. They staggered along, helping one another until they came to the bottom of the rock fall and found the outer wall of another corridor. They had used rocks to batter their way through it, terrified all the while that their light would fail and they would be left in the dark until the final blossom of light that would accompany the moment of their deaths.

The joy they felt at breeching the wall was only surpassed by that with which they greeted the sight of the dim, flickering light and the flow of fresh air. They had forced their way through the hole in the wall and literally stampeded forward without any thought for formation or their years of training, so great was their desire to be out of the treacherous tunnels. Turning a sharp corner, they had run headlong into a large party of natives, all of them armed to the teeth.

So totally were they taken unaware that they were surrounded before they could even think of defense, had they still possessed the weaponry and the wits to do so, which was doubtful.

The natives, a dark-skinned, handsome people, were led by a hideously deformed man whose skin was ruched and eroded as though it had melted and hardened not once but several times. He had no hair on his head or face and the shiny skin on his eyelids was stretched taut, giving him an ominous, sleepy look.

There had been no hope of communication; the natives were in a surly, militant mood. They carried swords and spears made of some inferior metal and they certainly looked like they knew how to use them and would do so if given the least provocation. They jabbered among themselves in some unintelligible language and hurried Leif Arndtson and his men along the tunnel in the opposite direction from which they had come, deeper into the mountain, and if the advancing degree of heat was any indication, closer to the volcano. Not at all the way they wanted to go.

Leif attempted to communicate with their captors, to tell them what was going to happen. He would have been willing to take them through the transmitter with him in order to save himself and his men, but at the first sound of his voice, he was viciously clubbed in the mouth. He could feel the sharp, broken ends of his teeth rubbing against his swollen lips and his mouth was filled with the coppery taste of his own blood. He had not tried to speak again.

They had been hurried along the corridor at a fast pace. It was then that he had become aware that the natives were looking about them in a furtive manner that did not seem to have anything to do with the shaking of the earth. Far from it, in fact, for when the mountain shook, the scarred man stopped, opened his arms wide, and spoke with respect and awe, not fear.

He wanted desperately to ask the tectonic men how long the charge had been set for, but when he was able to turn and look back he found that neither of the experts was with them. He did not know when the men had been lost.

Black despair filled his heart and he trudged through the tunnels almost without caring. Now even if they found themselves back at the mouth of the volcano, they would be unable to defuse the charge for none of them had the skills. It seemed certain they would die.

Then the inconceivable had happened, as though any of this had made any sense. Turning yet another corner, they had literally bumped into an even larger party of armed Madrelli!

Both groups had stood electrified for a brief, thunderstruck moment as though neither could believe their eyes. Then the true insanity began, with natives and Madrelli raging against each other in the narrow corridor with Leif and his men standing helpless in between.

It was an odd sort of battle, almost a shadow play, and might have been very entertaining had he not been a participant. The mountain had begun to rumble and shake once again. The noise was so loud that nothing else could be heard. Eyes flashed, mouths gaped, lips formed silent, comic words, and arms and legs seemed to move in slow motion as the lights flickered on and off, on and off.

At first Leif had thought that he and his men might possibly sneak away during the heat of battle, but that thought was soon squelched for things went badly for the natives from the very first. They were heavily outnumbered and could not stand up to the superior strength and longer reach of the Madrelli.

These were Madrelli unlike any others he had ever known before. They were not the placid, docile creatures he had directed on many a menial course. Rather, they were taller and stronger than usual and had adorned themselves with elaborate headbands set with handsome stones and bits of feather. They looked regal and fierce and warlike. Leif Arndtson felt his broken teeth and tasted the blood of his wounds and could not bring himself to speak.

He had lost track of the time since then. All he knew was that they had reversed themselves once again. They had passed the hole in the wall a long time ago. The lights had failed and they had traveled through darkened corridors which did not seem to slow the Madrelli at all.

Leif Arndtson did not know where they were or how much longer they had to live. He thought that they might be somewhere near the control room for they had climbed several levels and the heat had diminished greatly even though the seismic activity had not.

Leif Arndtson lay in the darkness, the weight of his

cowardice troubling him far more than the pain of his wounds or even fear of death. Then he heard a sound that struck to the very heart of him. It was the sound of crying; soft sobs that Leif knew came from young Thorson who was to have been married in a fortnight. Somehow, the sound of someone else's grief strengthened him, and when the Madrelli came for him, jerking him to his feet after their brief rest, he was determined to speak.

20

Brandtson stared down at the scrap of material he held in his hand and frowned, wondering what to make of it. For a brief moment he wondered if it were some odd prank although he was many, many years past the age when he and his friends had indulged in such activities. And, if it were a joke, well, it was a cruel one.

Even after all these years, the mere thought of his son was enough to clench his heart into a fist of pain. He had had such hopes for Bracca. Seldom was there one as brilliant and gifted as his son had been; even allowing for an old man's pride, it was true.

He had tried to tell the council that the young man would calm down in time, that the agitation for social reform was harmless and could be controlled. In vain did he suggest it was a positive note that the young man concerned himself with affairs of state rather than showing no interest at all as was the case with so many of their children. But his fellow Thanes had barely acknowledged his arguments and their stiff faces and worried eyes revealed their true feelings.

The Thanes of Valhalla had good reason to be concerned over the actions of their young. For many long centuries, they and those who had gone before them had been involved in a struggle for life. First, on old earth with the planet dying around them, there had been serious competition for the materials and food that made life possible. Only the strongest and most ruthless had survived those difficult days as the planet grew increasingly warmer, the seas became lifeless bodies of pollution, and the acid rains killed off most forms of plants and wildlife.

In the generations that followed, the much diminished Scandinavian nations had come together to protect what little they had left against the more aggressive and desperate hordes to the north. They had united as never before and forged a tight-knit community based on a single tenet, survival.

When it became obvious that it would take earth many thousands of years to heal, if such a thing could even be done, the Scandis had decided to leave earth, to search the stars for a new world.

The problems had been overwhelming: technology, financing, and the ability to adapt to strange, new conditions. All of it had been hard, almost beyond bearing; many had not been able to make the transition. But in the end, the Scandis did it.

The new planet had been claimed from the heavens and they had started building a new world, a way of life, an entire civilization from scratch. And succeeded.

They had done what was necessary, taken what they needed for survival by force, by the sweat of their brow, and finally by sheer guts, building a mining conglomerate that could make them rich enough to never worry again.

Who among them could have imagined that all of it, all the centuries of backbreaking, hard work, of fighting tooth and nail for the right to survive, could be turned around and brought to ruin within a single generation, not by their enemies but by their own children. But that was exactly what had nearly happened. It was the most bitter of pills.

In the span of one lifetime, their children had turned their backs on all the generations of deprivation and struggle that had gone before them. They had availed themselves of the comforts that their parents provided without asking or caring where they had come from or what they had cost. They took everything, all the hard-won gains for granted and took them as their due.

Insult followed injury as the youngest generation not only rejected its parents' and leaders' values, but actively set about undermining them and bringing them down.

The Thanes had reacted harshly, rightly or wrongly seeing the youngsters' words and actions as a condemnation of their very existence. They had forbidden the young people the right to form any group that did not have Council approval and of course none of their groups received such approval.

Brandtson thought about those years of travail and the unhappy years that had followed with a heavy heart. Where had they gone wrong? Perhaps if they had not reacted so harshly, but had allowed the young men and women the opportunity to talk freely, perhaps things would have been different.

Their stern actions had gained them nothing and had lost them everything. The best and brightest of the

younger generation had turned militant, vanished underground to oppose them at every turn. The others, those
who were left, were merely walking bodies with none of
the fire and courage of their ancestors. These were the
vapid, young faces that filled the tiers of the arena on
game days. These were the empty young minds that had
never experienced the thrill of danger themselves but
were willing and anxious to experience it vicariously, by
having others spill their blood and endanger their lives
for their amusement.

It made Brandtson sick to see what they had become. More and more he found it difficult if not impossible to remain on Rototara. More and more often he found
himself in agreement with the angry young rebels for
there was much about their world that could do with
change. But he was too old to bring about such changes
and if he were to suggest it, he would lose what power he
had left in the Council. Nor would the young ones accept
him as their advocate for he was both old and a Thane as
well.

Increasingly he thought about taking himself off to
some desolate spit of land along the edge of the inland
ocean, building a high-prowed boat such as the old books
pictured and leaving his life behind. He was an old man
and few would miss him, except one whom he had never
known.

This was what had held him to life for so long. He
summoned up the image of young Braldt, the son of his
son—he who looked so much like Bracca that it was like
reliving those distant days again. It had been hard watching
the young life emerge on that distant planet, hard to

relinquish the vital care and loving to another when he so yearned to provide it himself. But knowing that the young Braldt was safe and well-loved was almost enough to still the pain.

He had observed the young man's progress over the years, taken pride in his considerable accomplishments, and wracked his brain for a way to bring the boy back to a world he had never known. It had never seemed possible, for even if he could be returned, Brandtson knew that the Thanes would see Braldt as a threat, a symbol of all they feared the most—revolt from within.

And now this. Brandtson opened his fist and stared at the crumpled bit of fabric that lay there. Not a holotransfer, not a vocal transcript, not an encoding, but a primitive note—large, childish, block printing on a torn fragment of fabric—furtively pressed into his hand as he made his way through the crowded marketplace.

Was it a trick of some sort? Did the Council suspect his true sympathies? What could they do to him at his age, put him in the ring? He almost smiled at the thought. But if it was not a trick, then what did it mean? Was it possible . . . could it possibly be true? Brandtson's heart began to pound and the blood roared in his temples. He grew dizzy and was forced to sit down, then stared at the note again, although he had already committed the single word to memory. It was a scrap of primitively woven cloth, woven from organic fibers, like nothing worn on Valhalla, but identical to the robes worn by the natives on K7. Drawn onto the fabric with some inky dye was the single word, "BRALDT."

*   *   *

Keri was frightened. Nothing had gone right for the last two days. Twice they had been readied for the arena and then hastily returned to their cell without any explanation. There seemed to be a great deal of coming and going and furtive whispers between guards, shifty looks that observed them when they were not looking, then turned away swiftly. Several of the white-robed men who wore Braldt's face came and studied them, standing back from the bars, well out of Batta Flor's long reach. They were the subject of intense scrutiny and it seemed that some momentous decision was being made that concerned them. Keri wished that she knew what was happening. Even more, she wished that she could talk about it, but there was no one to talk to except Batta Flor and the lupebeast pup, which meant that she might as well talk to herself for all the good they would do her.

And then the visits stopped. There were no more game days, for which Keri was thankful, but neither was there any explanation of what was happening. Their guards, never talkative to begin with, were even less eager to speak. They merely arrived bearing larger quantities of food than normal and of a far better quality. Their diet included meat for the first time and Batta Flor, who had always been a devout vegetarian, devoured the bloody cuts with gusto.

His behavior became even more bestial with every passing day and Keri found it increasingly difficult to fend off his advances. Often, he would become surly and snarl at her, baring his long eyeteeth when she refused to let him stroke or pat her.

Once, Beast had snapped at the Madrelli when he

came too close to Keri and Batta Flor swatted him with the back of his hand, sending the pup crashing into a wall where he lay whimpering. Keri had rushed to his side, fearing the worst, but the pup was merely bruised and dazed. She had turned on Batta Flor and screamed at him, terrified that he might actually kill the pup at some point and then she would be all alone. Batta Flor had roared back at her and pounded his chest in fury. Both of them had retreated to opposite corners and ignored each other for the rest of the day.

Keri knew that something unusual was going on, something that concerned them; she just didn't know what and there was nothing she could do but wait to find out.

Septua was furious. He strode back and forth inside the cell, pacing twenty steps in one direction then twenty steps in the other, cursing all the while.

"I told you we couldn't trust 'er!" he ranted. "That old bitch! Lyin' to us, sayin' she was gonna 'elp. Then, nothin', nothin' a'tall, just leaving us 'ere to rot! I told you they was all alike, but no, you believed 'er, was taken in by 'er faintin', by 'er sad, sad story. It was all a joke, I tell you! She never 'ad no intention of 'elpin' us!"

Randi sighed and shot a quick look at Braldt who was staring at the ground, his hands hanging limp. He had not reacted to the dwarf's words, yet Randi knew that he had heard them and had probably thought them all himself as had they all. Several days had passed since Lomi's clandestine visit and all of them had been buoyed by an almost euphoric sense of hope. Their hopes had been so high that the descent into reality was all the more painful.

"Maybe something happened to the woman," Allo suggested. "She was not well; perhaps she was taken ill. She did not seem the type to break a promise."

"Yeah, sure, take 'er side," spat the dwarf as he whirled around to face Allo. "It's no fur off your ugly 'ide; you probably like it 'ere. But I 'ave a life I'd like to get back to!"

Randi's head snapped up and her green eyes grew bright with anger. She was at Septua's side in two long strides, and picking him up by the back of his neck, shook him back and forth so hard his vertebrae cracked.

"How dare you, you—you little piece of slime, you! How dare you speak to us that way. We all have lives we'd like to get back to. Lives that are far more significant than yours will ever be and people who love us and care what happens to us! What do you have waiting for you? Does anyone even give a damn whether you live or die?" The astonished dwarf hung limp from the end of her fingers and stared up at her, too stunned to speak.

"And another thing, you little piece of space garbage, you ever touch me again, it had better be to shake my hand. Got that?"

Septua did his best to nod and Randi dropped him abruptly. She turned on her heel and walked away without a backward glance as the dwarf crashed to the floor, still too wrapped in her own anger to notice the admiring glances that followed the amazing byplay.

"I hope you did not feel the need to defend me," Braldt said as Randi thumped down onto the floor beside him. "His words no longer trouble me."

"His words trouble me, damm it," Randi snapped angrily. "That little slime! I have a husband and a child I would like to see again. And parents. And who's he got, a paid floxie who betrayed him the first chance she got!

"And I'm worried about Lomi," she said in a quieter tone, her green eyes luminous with unshed tears. "I cannot believe that it was all a hoax. I'm afraid that something has happened to her."

"I, too, fear that some misfortune has befallen her," Braldt said heavily. "It took great courage for her to come here alone. But what can we do? We can do nothing trapped in this place. We cannot even help ourselves, much less another."

He thought a moment, then rose to his feet and crossed to the front of the cell. "Water!" he cried loudly, rapping his cup on the bars. He continued to call until the water carrier trundled into view pushing her cart before her, grumbling loudly at every step.

It was most unusual for the crone to answer anyone's request, for more than half the time she ignored her charges during even her normal rounds. But as soon as Braldt saw the sharp gleam in Saviq's single eye, he knew that she was aware of the situation and was as concerned as they were.

"Have you any news of the woman, Lomi?" Braldt asked softly as he held his cup out to be filled.

Saviq focused on his face, listening intently to the

words as she poured water that missed his cup entirely and splattered onto the ground.

"Nuzzing," she replied in a thick accent, made all the more difficult to understand because of her deformed muzzle.

"We are worried about her," Braldt said, speaking slowly and carefully. "She promised to return. To help us. Can you find out if she is all right?"

Saviq started to tremble and water splashed everywhere but into the cup. "Go to Scandi quarters?" Those were the last words that Braldt was able to understand, for the old crone's words became jumbled and a bewildering juxtaposition of noises and words. She started to leave, but Braldt dropped his cup, and reaching through the bars seized her rough, scaly wrist and held on tightly, forcing her to turn around and look at him.

"You said you were her friend. We are her friends, too. She risked a great deal by coming here and she trusted you to help her. If she is hurt or in danger, we must find out. We must help. That is what friends are for."

Saviq tried to pull away, but Braldt would not release her wrist. Finally, she stammered out a reply which Braldt interpreted as saying that she would try to find out what had happened. He let her go, fixing her with a steely glare and hoping that she would do as she said. If she did not, there was really nothing he could do to convince her otherwise.

But Saviq had indeed given her word, even though Braldt had guessed more than understood her meaning. She fretted over the indignity of being seized by the young man, yet, still, it was very bold and daring of him and she could not help but admire him for his courage. None of the other prisoners would dared to have touched her for fear of reprisals. Little did they know that she hated and feared the guards as much as they did. She pushed her heavy cart back to her cubbyhole, ignoring the cries of thirsty inmates which she seldom allowed to penetrate her consciousness, far preferring to ruminate on her own dark thoughts.

She sighed deeply as she sank down next to the fire and felt the deep ache in her ancient bones. She was tired. She was old and alone and had no one to love her. Did it matter if she was killed? There were none who would mourn her, except perhaps the woman Lomi, she who should have been her enemy but was her only friend. She wrapped her scaly limbs in yet another blanket and shivered. She was cold all the time now and it was a cold that no amount of blankets or fire could warm.

The old gods spoke of a place where all those who died were reunited. In her youth, when old age and death were but a foreign concept, she had scoffed at such beliefs. It seemed so obvious—when one died, one died, there was nothing more. But now, after a lifetime of sorrow, with pain her constant companion and all she had loved gone, Saviq wanted nothing more than to believe that the old gods knew what they were talking about. Briefly, she wondered if she would still be old and ugly and her lover young and handsome as the day he died when they met again. She banished the thought from her mind.

She resolved that she would venture into the vast complex that housed the Scandis as soon as night fell and attempt to find the woman who had been her friend. That much she would do, and if she was killed, well, life had been anything but good; one could only pray that death would be more kind.

It was many hours before darkness fell and traffic lessened in the corridors. It was not an ordinary day. It seemed that things had been strange ever since the night that Lomi came. There had been no games since that day and it was obvious even to her that the Scandis were worried about something. Briefly, she wondered what it could be.

She tried to tell herself that the sight of one old water carrier would not alarm anyone and that she would be allowed to pass simply because she was no one of importance. But it did not work that way. She passed through the last of the prisoner and animal quarters and immediately found herself challenged by a pair of nervous young guards. They were not Scandis but aliens from another world, and although fearful of making a mistake, they were not as alert as a Scandi would have been.

Saviq knew they would not be able to understand her. It was a knack she had cultivated when she discovered how much it annoyed the Scandis. They were so superior, it was almost beyond their comprehension that one of their brilliant devices would fail to do as they wished. It pleased her immensely to foil them with even such a little matter, speaking so that nothing she said could be understood. Now, she looked the two guards in the eyes and babbled at them, saying nothing that made sense, but

dropping an occasional word that could be understood—
the name of the Lady Lomi, order, urgent, angry, council.
The guards looked at each other in confusion. Saviq
repeated her message a second time, in a slightly louder
voice, and stepped toward the guards, bumping them
slightly. She hid her amusement as the guards parted,
allowing her to pass, asking each other what she had
said.

This ploy worked well and allowed her to penetrate
into the heart of the Scandi complex, passing two more
sets of guards and leaving them in confusion. *Authority
worked the same everywhere*, she mused, *on all races no
matter what their planet of origin*. Everyone was afraid
of making a mistake and equally afraid of making a
decision. So long as one acted confident and slightly
demanding, the odds were in your favor that you could
force your will on others.

Now that she had succeeded in finding her way into
the heart of enemy territory, there was another problem.
She had no idea of how to go about finding the Lady
Lomi. A figure scurried toward her, a shriveled-up, little,
old woman, even tinier and older than she was, clinging
to the wall and seemingly fearful of her own shadow. A
thought took shape in Saviq's mind, one that brought a
sly grin to her misshapen muzzle. She hobbled over to
the woman, smiling to herself as the woman cringed back
in fear, her serving tray and the silver objects that it held
rattling loudly.

"Where is the Lady Lomi?" Saviq demanded, taking care to speak clearly.

The woman began to speak, her words tumbling

over themselves in a breathless rush, the fear apparent in her eyes. For the first time ever, Saviq was glad for her frightening appearance. At first she could make no sense of the woman's words, for she seemed to be saying that Lomi's rooms were in one direction, but Lomi herself in another. Saviq frowned with impatience, then reached out and grabbed the woman who dropped the tray and shrieked loudly.

"Stop that, old fool," Saviq snarled. "Stop that or I will eat you," she said, although she would never have done such a thing. The woman ceased her screeching instantly. "Better. Now take me to the Lady Lomi, and no tricks or I will nibble your fingers one by one. Understand?"

The woman nodded, her head bobbing up and down rapidly, her eyes as big as the saucers she had dropped. Together, the old serving woman and the ancient reptile made their way down the darkened hall.

21

"We must get rid of him; there is too much danger in allowing him to live." There was a murmur of agreement.

"How would it be done?" asked one of the men gathered around the circular table, quirking one perfectly shaped blond eyebrow.

"I say make no fuss about it, quick and simple, do away with him. It does not matter how—poison, a knife in the back, or for that matter, transport him out to space," said another, smoothing his already immaculately groomed pale, blond hair back from his high forehead.

"I don't think you understand the delicacy of the problem," said the first speaker, who appeared on the top step of the dais every game day, the man known as Kiefer.

"Why don't you explain it to us, Kiefer," said Jorund as he smiled at his superior, the man who was in charge of the entire installation on Rototara.

Kiefer frowned at Jorund, unable as always to decide whether his second-in-command was being purposely disrespectful. But Jorund met his gaze openly and smiled encouragingly, leaning forward as though anxious to hear what words of wisdom Kiefer might convey. Kiefer frowned again, wondering for perhaps the millionth time how he had been so unlucky as to be saddled with one whose loyalties he did not command.

In Jorund's youth, there had been that business with the rebels. The association alone would have condemned a lesser man to dismal duty on some farflung outpost, but Jorund had been powerfully connected, his father being old Brandtson's best friend and a highborn Thane himself. The two old men had protected Jorund from the reprisals that had shaken the Council following the uprisings and they had guided and safeguarded his career ever since.

Jorund had never given Kiefer any reason to distrust him, following his every order with alacrity, but still, there was no sense of camaraderie with the man, no real friendship, and always, there was the suspicion of mockery. It made a man uncomfortable. Now, here was a challenge of sorts, having to explain himself when just the order itself should have been sufficient. Still, the older men would probably need to have it spelled out for them.

"I do not believe that it is wise to make a martyr out of this man, this Braldt," Kiefer said smoothly. "If he were to die under suspicious circumstances, who knows what mischief might arise because of it."

"What are you saying, Kiefer?" demanded one of the oldest members of their circle, his bushy eyebrows lowered in a dark scowl.

"I'm saying that even after all these years there are those who still remember and would rally around the cause if they were given the opportunity. I'm sure that I do not need to remind you that we are not without our enemies, those who would welcome the chance to bring us down."

Another of the older members cleared his throat

nervously and stroked his white beard. "You think they still live, those who believed in this business?"

"I am certain they still live," replied Kiefer. "Many of them were highborn and protected by their birth. Their identities were unknown to us in most instances. Many years have passed since those days, but I do not doubt that they still harbor their beliefs. Many of them have doubtless inherited or attained positions of power in the intervening years. They will be more powerful and more difficult to vanquish this time. That is why I believe that we must arrange it so that this Braldt dies in the ring, having been given a fair chance to survive."

"How will you arrange that?" asked Jorund. "After all, he and his team have been quite successful at staying alive, and far longer than the norm, I might add."

"Thank you for that observation," Kiefer said dryly. "Yes, it's true that he and his team have defeated others whom we thought would put an end to them early on. It has surprised many of us who wagered against them. They've managed to develop an effective technique that has served them well against all manner of opponents. Furthermore, none of them are stupid and this has been an advantage over those who depend on sheer strength to win. But I have a plan that I do not think can fail. I think it's rather clever, if I do say so myself, and if we are lucky, the problem will resolve itself."

"What is this final solution?" asked Jorund, tenting his fingers and resting his chin upon them.

"The Madrelli," Kiefer answered. "As you know, we brought the apeman through the transmitter shortly after Braldt arrived. A woman was with him, a woman whom we believe this Braldt cares about. Putting the two teams in the ring together should give us a fairly good chance of them killing each other off.''

"Am I missing something here?" rumbled the older man with the beard. "If they are friends and lovers, why would they fight, much less kill each other?"

"Forgive me," said Kiefer. "I have been following this matter so closely, I forget that the details are not more widely known. But again, that is to our advantage.

"As you know, the pain center in the Madrelli is located in a narrow channel in their ears. Our ancestors designed them this way when they first manipulated their genetics to give them a way of controlling the beasts; pain is a most effective control. But the Madrelli was injured shortly before he left K7; one of his ears was torn off, making him impervious to pain.

"Also, he has gone without formicase, the additive which make the Madrelli sapient and tractable. He has been without it now for more than a month. Our doctors have been most interested at the speed with which he has regressed. He is now barely above his natural animalistic state, which as you know is very quick to anger and easily driven into manic rages."

"Interesting," murmured the older man. "But what does the woman have to do with this and why should young Braldt fight the Madrelli? There is nothing wrong with him and he has no reason to fight one who has been his friend."

"Another interesting turn of events," said Kiefer. "As the Madrelli lapsed into his primitive state, he seemed to forget who the woman is or what she had meant to him. He forgot that they were platonic friends.''

"Surely you don't mean that—that! . . ." exclaimed the older man, half rising to his feet.

"No, no," said Kiefer. "Not yet, at any rate, although I would not doubt that such a thing might eventually happen . . . but you see, that's just the point. The Madrelli no longer recognizes the woman, so there is no reason to think that he will recognize young Braldt, he will merely see an enemy who must be killed if he himself is to live.''

"But the woman will recognize Braldt," said Jorund.

"Precisely," said Kiefer. "Now do you understand? The woman will see Braldt and attempt to go to him. The Madrelli will do everything to stop his woman from leaving him. And if she succeeds and makes her way to Braldt, well then, the Madrelli will be more determined than ever to kill Braldt and get her back.''

"But there are four on Braldt's team and only two on the other.''

"It will not matter," Kiefer said with a humorless smile. "The Madrelli is unbelievably strong, stronger than all four of his opponents added together.''

"But they are armed with blades and the Madrelli has never used more than a single club!'' protested the older man.

"With the Madrelli's longer reach," Kiefer explained patiently, "he can keep the others at bay so that they cannot use their weapons, and bash their heads in before they can think of another plan.''

"If he succeeds in killing them, this Madrelli," the

older man said thoughtfully, "what will we do about him and the woman? Will we have to kill them, too?"

Kiefer shrugged. "We will not have to kill him. All we have to do is continue to withhold the formicase. Soon he will regress to a total animal state. He has already lost all but the most primitive bits of language; in a short time, he will have lost even that. How can he do us any damage if he cannot speak?"

"But the woman has not lost intelligence or the ability to speak," Jorund pointed out helpfully. Kiefer shot him a black look.

"I think our young beauty will have her hands full," said Kiefer. "Having won her away from Braldt, the Madrelli will surely claim her as his own. No, I do not think she will have time for talking."

The news of their next bout was delivered to them by the captain of the guards, that same overly muscled hulk who had seldom missed the opportunity to make their lives miserable. It sometimes seemed that he resented their success and the fact that they were still alive. He stood in front of their cell smiling at them in a manner that boded no good.

"You fight in the morning," he said in the odd, sibilant garble that was the language of his home world. The translating device issued the pronouncement inside their heads in clipped, accentless tones. "You will not be so lucky this time, I think. I think I will see none of your faces here tomorrow night. At least they will no longer look like the same faces!" He laughed uproariously at his own humor.

Randi blanched, but took care not to let her fear show. "What is so special about this fight?" she asked casually. "We have fought many opponents—most of whom you bet upon—and we defeated them. Why should tomorrow be any different? We will win again, as always."

"Ho, ho, I think not," laughed the guard. "This one is undefeated as well, and from what I hear, you don't stand a chance. He's fighting for his mate, too, so that should make him twice as mean. Good luck, or I think I will say, good-bye!" His laughter bounced off the walls and echoed back as he walked away.

"Do you think it's true?" Septua asked anxiously, his face puckering up in a grimace of worry.

"He has no reason to lie," Braldt said with a shrug. "He hates us because he has bet against us and we have always won. He would tell us the truth if it made us unhappy."

"Well, who is it, do you suppose?" Septua persisted. "I thought we were the only ones undefeated. How come we have not met this one as yet? I thought we knew everyone there was. Why are they adding someone new to the games now?"

"I have heard that there was another," Allo said thoughtfully. "I heard the healers speaking of him when they were working on me. They either did not know or did not care that I was listening."

"What did they say?" Septua asked impatiently.

"I did not understand a lot of what they said," Allo said slowly, casting his mind back to that time of pain. "They spoke about an injury to the creature's ear. Some grievous accident had occurred to the ear and they seemed to regard it more seriously than I would have expected. After all, an ear is only an ear and not as important as an arm or a leg. They talked about it a good deal."

Braldt began to smile. "If it is the creature I am thinking of, an injury to its ear would matter greatly and also explain why it is undefeated. The Madrelli's ability to feel pain is governed by delicate crystals in their ears. If the ears are damaged, or in this case all but removed, the Madrelli are incapable of feeling pain. Their strength is legendary. I fear that our good friends the Masters are in for a surprise, and once again, the captain has bet on the wrong side, or the contestants will be the only winners in this bout."

"What are you saying?" Randi asked.

"This one with the injured ear can be none other than my good friend, the Madrelli, Batta Flor. I myself would be willing to bet on it. Somehow, he came through the transmitter after me; perhaps it sucked him through. By the gods! That means . . . I wonder if Keri and Beast! . . . Allo, did the healers mention any others who might be with the injured one?"

Allo shook his head in the negative and Braldt looked downcast. "Still," he said, "having Batta Flor on our side can only be a positive step. We must try to think how we can turn this to our advantage. With Batta Flor fighting alongside us, we cannot help but win. If Keri and my lupebeast are with him, we will be invincible!"

"Who is this Keri?" Randi asked, and Braldt realized that while he had told the others the story of how he had come to be on Rototara, for some reason he had made no specific mention of Keri, at least not by name. He could not explain the strange omission, not even to himself. With Randi's large, green eyes studying him intently, he stammered through an awkward explanation, stressing the fact that Keri was his adopted sister. The more he tried to explain, the more awkward and uncomfortable he became. Randi said nothing, but her eyes seemed to spark with anger. Braldt's voice trailed off and he wondered why he felt as though he had done something wrong.

Septua guffawed loudly, but when Randi turned and shot him a dark, angry look, he swallowed his laughter in a series of feigned coughs. Allo wisely held his tongue.

The night passed in an uneasy sense of anticipation. There was none of the camaraderie that had bound them together through so many ordeals. Everyone in the cell was aware of Randi's anger which seemed to radiate through the air. Septua was careful to avoid her glance and kept well out of her reach. Braldt sat down next to Allo and spoke in a low tone. "I do not understand why she is so angry. We are not mated, and even if I did forget to tell her about Keri, she herself has a mate and children of her own. It is not logical that she should feel anger against me."

Allo looked amused and rubbed his hands over his face. "Ah, my good friend, you may be well versed in the art of battle, but you have much to learn about women. I do not care what their race or the origin of their home planet, I believe they are all the same, and emotion, not logic, rules their heads as well as their hearts. My own mate is as wonderful a woman as ever existed, but even she . . ."

Allo began the telling of a long, involved story.

Braldt listened for a while, then his thoughts began to drift. He listened with one ear, nodding whenever Allo paused, but let his mind roam free, thinking of Batta Flor, Keri, and Beast, wishing that the dawn would come.

Saviq was enjoying herself immensely. No one had even given her a second glance as she made her way through the dim corridors following the terrified serving maid. The longer she escaped detection, the more courageous she became. Twice, she had actually walked quite close to a guard when she might have hugged the far wall. She even coughed to waken the second guard who was slumbering at his post. He blinked and frowned at her in a dazed manner, then cleared his throat, pretending to be awake.

Saviq wondered how it was that she had never realized how easy such a venture would be. She had always thought that she would be challenged and intimidated. This was simple as well as exhilarating! She stopped the drudge with a gesture and filled her pockets from a tray of rich pastries sitting in an alcove. The thick, sweet cream slid down her throat, imparting waves of luxurious pleasure.

The drudge was all but gibbering with fear. She cringed and ducked down, wringing her hands as Saviq caught up with her. She whined and pointed at a doorway at the junction of another corridor just ahead of them. Saviq nodded her understanding and turned to speak to the slave, but the woman was already scuttling away, anxious to be gone.

Saviq shrugged and hurried to the doorway, her task

once more foremost in her mind, wondering why Lomi had moved her quarters, wondering if everything was all right.

The doorway was dark, the room within even darker, and the air was heavy with the sharp, bitter scent of medicines. As her eyes grew accustomed to the darkness, Saviq saw that a faint night-light glowed on the far side of the room. It did little to alleviate the darkness; merely accentuated the lack of light. She felt her way into the room cautiously, her clawed hand extended out before her, reaching for unseen obstacles. "Lomi?" she whispered softly, hoping for a reply, suddenly fearful.

She advanced further into the room, once bumping into a small table that capsized before she could catch it, dumping a metal object onto the floor where it clattered and banged, sounding twice as loud in the darkness as it would have in the light. But still, no one reacted or challenged her right to be there. A terrible feeling came over Saviq and a lump formed in her throat. Suddenly she did not want to find Lomi and was afraid to find out why Lomi had moved.

She started to move toward the door before the words of her promise brought her up short. She had given her word, and even if it were to one of them who did not know the meaning of honor, such things were still important to her. Stiffening her resolve, she turned and walked straight to the night-light and plucked it from the wall, holding it before her. Driving back the darkness, she began to make a systematic sweep of the room.

The room was larger than she had first thought and was filled with beds, most of which were empty. Those that were not had sleepers in them who would not be wakened by any sounds Saviq might make. Her heart grew heavy and her legs felt weak and tremulous. The next bed she came to nearly frightened her out of her scales. An old man lay in the bed, his head cradled on a fat pillow, and as she held the light over him, he turned his head and looked directly at her. She all but dropped the light. Then the old man raised his hand and asked for a drink of water in a quavery voice and she knew that he was not yet dead. She helped him drink, then lay him back down on his pillow. He closed his eyes with a sigh and once again looked as though his spirit had left his body.

Saviq moved on, her heart in her throat, afraid of what she would find. Two more of the beds contained ancient Scandis, either deep in sleep or coma, who did not waken when she held the light over their somnolent faces.

Lomi was in the last bed, a slender figure, barely raising the blankets that covered her. Her eyes were still the brightest of blues, the eyes of a young, vibrant girl rather than the eyes of a woman on the verge of death. She smiled at Saviq and held out her hand to grasp the scaled paw. "I knew you would come," she whispered in a breathy voice.

"What is the matter with you?" Saviq asked in a blustery, accusatory tone. "It is not yet your time. We have many years left to live, and we have yet to bask in the sun as we have so often said we would do. Why are you in this place, old friend? Let me take you from here. It is a place for dying, not for living."

Lomi smiled, a gentle, sweet smile that struck sorrow into Saviq's breast. She squeezed Saviq's hand, a slight pressure that could barely be felt. "You will have to bask alone, old friend, but think of me and of the time when we were young and strong and still believed in life and love."

"Do we not still believe in life and love?" Saviq asked, the tears crowding to her eyes.

"Neither life nor love have been very kind to us. Why is it that women are always left to mourn? I have always felt it was a mistake to leave the world in the keeping of men; they are too—too irresponsible for such an important task. Women should run the worlds. Women do not declare wars or spend their days and nights planning death and ruin. Life is too precious to us."

"Do not fret about such things," replied Saviq, patting Lomi's hand. "Perhaps things will be more just in our next life. And if they are not, well, we will not wait around for the men to come to their senses. You and I will have to tell them how things should be."

Lomi's eyes twinkled, and she smiled at the scaly old reptile crone who was her most loyal friend. "Before we can address the problems of the next world, dear Saviq, we must deal with the troubles of this one. I have been thinking as I lay here, just how we can put an end to all these senseless deaths, all this killing, once and for all. This is how I think it should be done."

The two heads, one scaled and scarred, the other pale and drawn, drew close together over the dim, glowing light and together, they laid their plans.

22

Dawn came more slowly than ever before. Braldt had tried to sleep, wrapping himself in the thin blanket he had earned through his trials in the ring, but sleep would not come.

He stared into the darkness, thinking about all that had happened to him since he had come to this world, and began to wonder if something were not coming unraveled, for it did not seem as though things were going according to a plan.

There were many signs of wrongness, if one knew how to read them. They had first been told they would have a question answered for every contest they won, but after their first few victories, those rewards had ceased with no explanations given. Instead, they were offered extra rations and meager tokens of luxury such as the threadbare blanket which now covered a portion of his body. They had also managed to gain the cell exclusively for their own use. Several of their cellmates had been lost to the ring, others had died, and the guards had removed the few who remained. That was an improvement in itself, for it was difficult to sleep if one was constantly worried about waking up with a knife between one's ribs. Or perhaps not waking up at all.

Then, too, there was the nervousness of the guards who seemed ill at ease and troubled, often gathering in small groups to murmur among themselves with many a furtive, sidelong glance, making certain they were not being overheard. Braldt recognized the signs of unrest all too well and had often wondered what was at the bottom of it. The guards were a collection of many races and worlds and seemed to have no inherent loyalties to the Scandis. Braldt wondered how they were paid and what incentives could be used to turn them against their masters.

He also wondered how it might be possible to unite the many hundreds of prisoners into a force that would rise up against the guards and the Scandis. There had to be a way, surely, for even the most dense among them would realize there was no percentage in fighting. There could only be one set of victors, and eventually all of them, even the best, would die.

Sleep was impossible. Braldt tossed off the annoying, too-short blanket, and noticed the odd, blue alien in the next cell standing next to the bars looking directly at him. At least he thought it was looking at him, even though he could see nothing that resembled eyes. The silver translation disc caught a stray bit of torchlight and flashed in the darkness, drawing his gaze.

"Now, you," said Braldt as he pondered the impossibly thin, blue rectangle. "If I could figure out how to communicate with you, then I could probably talk to anyone. If only there were a way. I know we could fight back. I do not want to be here. I want to go home!"

No sooner had the words been said, then Braldt

raised his hand to his head; something strange was happening. He grew dizzy, and for a moment thought he would fall. Things swirled inside his head and there was the sense of movement, of swirls of color. There was a voice—no, not a voice, but somehow there were words or rather the sensation of words.

"It is not hard to speak to me," said the voice that was not a voice. "Speak, say your words. I will answer."

Braldt took a step back and looked around him, wondering if someone else had spoken or at least heard what he had heard. But everyone else was asleep with the single exception of the blue rectangle which rippled along its lower edge and moved closer to the bars as though to remove any lingering doubts as to who had spoken.

"You!" said Braldt. "Well, well, so you can speak. But if you can talk, why did you not reply to the guards?"

"One does not dignify their presence with conversation. The only thing one can do is deny their very existence. What good can come of speaking with such intemperate barbarians? I regret my hasty actions and have prayed for the wisdom and the strength to resist any future provocations."

The words echoed and bounced inside Braldt's head and he closed his eyes to steady himself, it was such a strange sensation. "What are you saying?" he asked, moving to the bars. "Don't you realize that you are the only one who has ever been able to defeat a guard? They were actually afraid of you! Do you think you could do that with the hard ones. I—I mean, the robots?"

"The metal men? Yes, of course it could be done. But why should I do such a thing? Taking the one life will cost me many yantreks of repentence; I do not wish to add on others."

"I do not understand yantreks of repentence," Braldt said apologetically. "But tell me this, the metal rods that the 'bots carry, they shoot lightning. Swords and spears did not hurt you; will the lightning rods injure you?"

"Nothing they do can hurt me," said the voice.

"Will you help us?"

The blue being was silent.

Braldt stared at it in frustration, trying to think of what he could do or say that would prompt the being to help them. "Do you like being here?" he asked. "Do you not miss your home?"

"The great Yantra did not place us here so that we might enjoy ourselves, but to learn wisdom and attain enlightenment," replied the blue rectangle, its edges rippling gently. "Everything happens for a reason. If we are here, Yantra must expect that we will learn some valuable lesson that will advance us toward the ultimate wisdom."

"Us?" queried Braldt. "Do you mean that this Yantra expects all of us to learn the ultimate wisdom from our imprisonment?"

"I do not doubt that Yantra knows of your existence, but I cannot say what his expectations are of you and your companions. I was speaking only for myself and my brothers."

"There are more of you?" Braldt asked sharply. "Where?"

"I do not know where they are, I merely know that they exist. We were separated soon after our arrival."

"Probably wanted to see what they could do with one of you," mused Braldt. "No good for morale to have a bunch of blue things around who make fools out of the guards; might give the rest of us ideas. How do you know that the others are still alive?"

"Why, we speak!" replied the alien, with something close to surprise in its voice. "Much as you and I are speaking now. Distance does not affect our ability to communicate. Do you not share this ability with your own people?"

"Sadly, no," said Braldt. "Now tell me, is it not possible that this is not part of the great Yantra's plan for your enlightenment? Is it not possible that he would like for you to take some action yourself to get out of this place? After all, what good will it do if you sit here 'til you rot? What will that teach you?"

"Patience," replied the blue creature.

"I'd say you've already mastered that one," said Braldt, thinking of the way the being sat day after day in its cell, refusing to react to anything the guards did to force it to fight. "Listen, aren't you getting even a little bit homesick? Wouldn't you like to see your world again? You can die here, locked away in this cell, but wouldn't it be nice to go home and pursue the great Yantra's teachings?"

"It would be nice to sit in the talek again and discuss the finite ramifications of Yantra's 1,227 musings," admitted the blue alien. "And it would also be pleasant to see Mutar once again, to—to compare musings, of course," he added, his skin turning an even darker shade of blue, perhaps the alien equivalent of a blush.

"Of course," agreed Braldt. "Even an unenlightened one such as I, recognizes the value of comparing musings." He started to speak again, but held off as it seemed that the alien was deep in thought.

At last it spoke. "I would have to confer with my brothers. I cannot say what they would do and I am certain there are many among them who would not wish to regress with such impetuous behavior. But if there are those who agree to join you, what would you have us do?"

"I'm afraid that all of this is merely wishful thinking," Braldt said with a sigh. "We would need to find your companions and think of some way to free them before we could even begin to plan."

The blue being sighed as well. "I may never reach a state of enlightenment, I fear. Already, I am filled with excitement at the thought of action, at the thought of being reunited with Mutar once again. Perhaps I should remain here to teach myself patience."

"No!" cried Braldt, seizing the bars and pressing up against them. "Freedom first, then patience! Yantra helps those who help themselves!"

"That is true!" exclaimed the blue rectangle, his perimeter fairly quivering with excitement. "And you know what he says about self-determination!"

"I will be glad to discuss it later; have you teach me all 1,522 of his musings, but after we are free!"

"One thousand two hundred twenty-seven," murmured the creature.

"Right," said Braldt. "Now, how many of you are there and how many can we count on for help, if we can figure out a way to find them and get them out?"

"There are many of us," said the blue being. "Not so many as Yantra's musings, but nearly. Perhaps three-fourths of those would be willing to assist us, for they are young like myself and not older and wise enough to resist such temptations."

"Three-fourths of Yantra's musings!" exclaimed Braldt. "Are you certain? That's more than all the guards and Scandis put together!"

"Oh, yes, I am quite certain. The barbarians came upon us when we were on a Yantran retreat. They took us quite by surprise, and while we were trying to decide what Yantra wished for us to learn from the experience, they removed us from the Yanek and brought us here. And as to freeing ourselves, why that is no problem at all."

And as Braldt stared in astonishment, the blue alien simply walked through the bars—which passed through its body—and emerged unharmed on the other side.

"How did you do that!" cried Braldt, touching the bars and finding that they were still as solid as ever.

"It is nothing, merely a matter of concentration and rearranging one's molecules," the blue being said modestly.

"Can all of you do this?" asked Braldt.

"Oh, yes. It is quite basic," replied the being.

"Listen, do what you have to do. Talk to the others and convince them to help us in order to help themselves.

It is nearly dawn and we must go to the ring and fight. But we fight friends and allies who can be counted on to help. If you can persuade your friends to aid us as well, we can begin to put together a plan. We will talk again tonight.''

The blue rectangle nodded, bending its entire body in a bow, then reversed itself and flowed backward through the bars. Once in its own cell, it curled into its customary cylinder and was silent, although Braldt thought he heard it murmur "Mutar" once, in a dreamy tone.

He had intended to tell Allo and the others about the odd conversation, but while he was turning it over in his mind, he fell into a sound sleep and did not waken until the guards pounded on the bars with the butts of their spears. There was no time for talk from that point on, for they were shepherded to and from the dining hall and the weapons room by a full contingent of guards, all of whom seemed to watch them more closely than usual. There was an odd aura of tension in the air and the guards seemed to look about them as often as they watched their prisoners. It was almost as though they were expecting to be attacked. Braldt could not help but notice that there were more than the usual number of armed 'bots roaming the corridors as well, some rolling silently on their heavy, single wheel, other striding about on two legs.

Even though there was much to be optimistic about, Braldt had been unable to eat or drink anything, and his belly churned with excitement. Randi would not meet his eyes and she seemed more downcast than angry. He tried to speak to her, but the guards took care to keep them apart. He wished he had the blue alien's ability to speak inside his head.

Allo and Septua seemed untroubled; the large furred creature was as mild-mannered and calm as always. Septua appeared slightly more nervous and flexed his stubby fingers and immense arm muscles to discharge the gathered tension.

And then, as the twin red suns rose above the edge of the amphitheater and the crowds began to stamp in cadence, the horns blared, and once again, it was game time.

Saviq was exhausted. Her stubby legs trembled with fatigue and she longed for the comfort of her woolly blankets and her fire. But there was much to be done before she could sleep. She wondered if she would be able to accomplish all that she had been charged with. Tears filled her eye even as she snuffled and berated herself for being a silly old woman. She would not fail Lomi, no matter what it took. Then her single eye filled with tears at the thought of her friend, channeled down her scarred, lumpy muzzle, and dripped onto the floor. No, she would not fail.

She had refused to leave Lomi's side, watching the frail chest rise and fall, patting the thin, pale hand with her own scaled paw until the last breath had passed from the tired body. Saviq had tucked the blankets around her old friend, crooning gently and cradling the pale, silvery, blond head against her chest, rocking back and forth with the pain and grief that threatened to overwhelm her. She had stayed there holding the empty body far longer than had been wise, remembering how very beautiful Lomi had been in her youth, beautiful by Scandi standards. And how very beautiful her spirit had been by any measure.

She thought it unfair that Lomi's love had gone unfulfilled, that she had been forced to love from afar one who had barely been aware of her existence. Yet she had loved long and hard, and even with her death, thought only of Braldt, the child of her love.

A small smile lifted the lips of her muzzle as she thought about Lomi's plan. There was irony in it as well as satisfaction. How odd that those who had destroyed her people and her world would themselves be brought down by one of their own, one who had been of little importance during her life, but would gain renown with her death. The thought lent speed to Saviq's tired feet, and steeling herself for the difficulties that still lay ahead, she hurried forward.

23

Keri had never seen Batta Flor in such a state. Even before the suns rose, the Madrelli had risen and begun pacing back and forth within the confines of the cell. And then it had happened, the thing she had dreaded most. Batta Flor had approached her as she lay huddled beneath her blanket and gently stroked her hair with one giant paw. She had cringed away from his touch and this had seemed to enrage him. He had swept her off the pallet and gathered her to his chest. She had cried out with fear and pushed against his mammoth muscles, struggling to free herself.

Beast had wakened instantly at the first sound of trouble and flung himself at the Madrelli, sinking his wickedly sharp, double rows of teeth into Batta Flor's calf muscle.

The Madrelli could not have been hurt by the pup's attack, for his damaged ear rendered him impervious to pain, but he was enraged at the defiance shown by the pup, infuriated at any effort to foil him in his intent. He had slapped at the pup with one fist while holding Keri close to his side. The pup had managed to evade his blow and dark blood poured down the Madrelli's leg and pooled on the floor.

Keri continued to beat her fists against Batta Flor's shaggy hide, knowing she could not hurt him, but hoping to distract him so that he would not kill the pup. She screamed at him as well, and tears of fear and frustration flooded her face as hysteria threatened to overcome her.

Batta Flor stopped trying to strike the pup and lifted Keri, bringing her face level with his own. She stared tearfully into his face, reading fury and confusion as well as hopeless despair in his dark eyes. He roared full into her face, all but deafening her with the depth of his rage and sorrow, and then he flung her from him, threw her like a useless bit of fluff that he no longer had need of or interest in. She struck the edge of the sleeping platform and felt the pain of impact across her shoulders and spine. She scrambled onto the platform and gathered the blankets in her arms, shielding herself as best she was able.

Beast growled a warning, then released the bloody leg, scurrying away from the Madrelli and leaping onto the platform to huddle next to Keri. His ruff was fully extended, and the line of fur that marked his spine stood straight up, making him look larger than he really was. His eyes glowed yellow, his teeth were coated with the Madrelli's blood, and crimson-tinged slaver drooled from his mouth as he snarled his hatred.

Batta Flor took no notice of either of them, but strode about in the center of the cell, pounding on his massive chest and screaming in rage and defiance. Then he stopped still, and throwing back his head, bellowed with such sorrow and pain that Keri nearly forgot her own fear and rushed to his side.

The terrible sound filled the cell and echoed through-out the prison, silencing the usual early morning sounds of activity. Those who shared their captivity were accus-tomed to sounds of rage and sorrow, but this cry touched emotions that most of them struggled to deny. All those within hearing of the terrible cry shivered and fell silent, for the sound mirrored all too accurately, for prisoners and guards alike, the depth of their own despair.

Horns blared and the crowded tiers echoed with the sound of feet pounding in cadence on the red stone. Tension was palpable in the chill morning air. The dual suns ascended the crimson sky, bathing the arena and its occupants with a bloody hue, an omen of what was to come.

The first bout included four reptilian monsters, thickly armored with overlapping, ridged scales who bore no other weapons than their own four-inch claws and scissoring fangs. Their long, powerful tails ended in a large, solid ball of muscle which they wielded like a club.

Their opponents were oddly jointed creatures with eight legs who were able to move in any direction with equal dexterity. Their centrally spaced bodies were small in comparison to their legs and covered completely with a gleaming, metallic carapace. These creatures bore no weapons at all, but jutting out just above the first seg-ment of each leg was a wicked, curving sickle-like projection.

The two groups of combatants swept toward each other as soon as the arches were opened, and met with a clash of bodies in the center of the ring. For a moment it was difficult to tell what was happening, for the opponents were so closely meshed. Then they swirled apart and it could be seen that the reptiles were bleeding from a number of wounds while the insectlike creatures appeared to be unharmed.

They came together a second time, and this time the reptiles had learned from their first encounter and struck upward at the insects' bellies with their scythe-like claws, drenching themselves in their opponents' blood which was a pale, watery fluid. This seemed to give the reptiles an impetus, for they pushed forward, beating the insects back, lashing out at them with claws and clubbed tails.

The insects fell back and clustered together, their forelegs waving in the air before them, holding the reptiles at bay. Then, surprisingly, they shot a stream of fine spray at the armored reptiles who screamed and fell to the red sand, writhing in agony. While their opponents were indisposed, the insects rushed forward and straddled them, spraying more and more of the caustic substance on their fallen foes. The louder the reptiles screamed, the louder the crowd stamped until the arena reverberated with the sound.

The segmented creatures slowly lowered their bodies until they were positioned just above the agonized reptiles, and a cloudy, insubstantial substance began to drift downward. It coated the reptiles with a fine mist which whitened upon contact. Layer after layer of mist fell upon the fallen reptiles whose movements slowed and grew stiffer with every passing moment.

The crowd quieted inexplicably, for they had never before seen such a technique. The reptiles were all but buried in the strange, cottony, white swaddling and their limbs twitched and jerked spastically. The insects crouched down over their hapless prey, and with neat, surgical strokes began to slice off bits and pieces of the armored flesh and consume it, despite the fact that their victims were still alive.

The guards and robots entered the ring, weapons drawn and ready to herd the jointed creatures from the arena. The insects did not seem afraid of the guards in the least, but folded themselves down, gathered up the remains of the reptiles, and allowed themselves to be escorted from the ring.

Next came four amorphous shapes which flowed and stretched like gummy pools of water. They seemed to have no specific boundaries and defied gravity by flowing horizontally and hanging in mid-air with nothing to support them. They were nearly transparent, and when the sun shone full upon them, they cast dazzling rainbows of light.

Their opponents were four small, human-like creatures with long, matted, fuzzy hair, their bodies covered with filth. Their heads were exceptionally large with small foreheads and large jaws; their features were small and nearly flat with little definition. They wore no clothing at all and it could be clearly seen that their spines continued beyond their bodies, ending in a primitive, fleshy tail. They bore a variety of clubs and spiked cudgels, and they crept into the ring, their eyes wide and fearful.

The translucent shapes drifted toward the frightened manthings, grouping together, then drifting apart in no apparent pattern. As they came close to the men, they rose upward, joining together like a shimmering cloud. The suns rode high above them and shone down through the crystalline clouds, and as they did so the beams of light that emerged fell upon the men who instantly began to scream in agony. They swatted at the clouds of light with their clubs, accomplishing little as the clouds merely drifted aside or temporarily broke apart, only to reform.

The beams of light were constant and it could be seen that the skin on the screaming manthings was blistering and rising up in bubbles of flesh.

And then the unlikely happened. The sky, which was always clear on Rototara, began to fill with clouds. At first it was the merest shred of gauze, then, with impossible speed, more and more clouds began to appear until the blood-red sky was all but filled with them, great, towering, billowing thunderheads which cut off the light of the suns and chilled the ground below. Vagrant flicks of wind licked downward, as though sampling the earth, spraying the combatants with stinging shards of sand and stone.

The drifting forms seemed to falter, then sagged lower and lower as the light disappeared from the sky. The suns were obliterated, covered by dark, threatening clouds. The light faded from the odd, floating shapes, leaving them no more than tiny, pale clouds. The manthings reacted with surprising alacrity, striking at the clouds with their clubs.

Without the light, the shapes seemed heavier and they moved with difficulty. They were unable to evade the clubs and one of them was batted out of the air. One

burned manthing screamed and beat the transparent cloud
with its club until it was driven into the red earth. The
others, seeing that it could be done, rallied and struck out
at the enemy that had inflicted such cruel pain upon
them.

A second of the cloud figures was dashed to the
ground and disintegrated under the blows of the spiked
cudgel. The two remaining forms did not wait to meet
their fate but broke up into countless tiny shreds, too
small to be struck by a club, and allowed themselves to
be whisked away by the wind. They reformed at the edge
of the arena, and without waiting for the guards to arrive,
drifted through an open arch and were gone.

The tailed manthings leaped up and down like animals, banging their clubs on the ground and screaming
taunts at the vanished enemy. Blood and fluid streamed
down their bodies, streaking the filth that covered them
and painting them in bizarre patterns. When the robots
and guards arrived to shepherd them away, they brandished
their weapons and screamed in defiance. They swatted at
the guards' spears and hurled insults, and were finally
brought to bay by the lightning rods of the robots.

Braldt and his group had watched the two contests
that had gone before them with fingers of nervousness
plucking at their stomachs. Even though Braldt had
assured them that they would be facing friends and not
enemies, they could not entirely abandon their fear.
What would happen when the two groups met and would
not fight? What would the guards and robots do?

Braldt had tried to explain about his encounter and
conversation with the blue being in the adjoining cell, but

the others had stared at him as though he had lost his mind. Septua had gone so far as to suggest that Braldt had dreamed the entire episode. Braldt could think of nothing that would convince them. He had told them of the 1,227 musings of Yantra, thinking that such a strange detail would lend credence to his story, but they stared at him even more dubiously. In the end, Braldt gave up, for it was quite possible that the strange, blue aliens would all opt for learning the value of patience rather than risk earning themselves yantreks of repentance. Briefly, Braldt found himself wondering just how many yantreks one would be penalized for killing a robot. But if robots were not living beings, did killing them count as taking a life?

Braldt's musings were brought to an abrupt halt by the arrival of the guards who shoved them toward the archway, poking and prodding them with the points of their spears. The door to the arch rumbled upward into the thick, stone walls and the wind gusted into the chamber, filling it with a stinging haze of red sand. Even the guards were driven back by the sudden, unexpected assault of the wind.

Then they were being urged into the ring, the guards anxious to be rid of them and out of the force of the stinging onslaught which scoured their flesh with sharp-edged, minuscule grains of sand.

The door rumbled shut behind them, thudding into the earth with a jarring impact that could be felt through the soles of their feet. For some reason, it conveyed a feeling of great finality. They looked at one another and drew closer together. It was impossible to look up into the force of the wind. None of them had ever experienced weather such as this on Rototara. The days were endlessly alike, one after the other, clear, crimson skies, tremendous heat bearing down on them from the dual suns, and then cool, crisp, clear nights with the stars of their distant worlds shining in the dark.

All around them was a world gone mad. The suns were gone, covered by clouds the likes of which none of them had ever seen before. These were not mere thunderheads which foretold of rain or even heavy storms, these were the harbingers of some colossal catastrophe. The clouds were backlit by the unseen suns and glowed an ominous red in their centers, like hot blood waiting to drip from the sky. The edges were darker, tinged with black and streaks of yellow like old bruises and painful to view. They roiled and seethed, constantly growing, becoming ever more threatening.

The guards, what few remained around the edges of the arena, were clearly terrified, looking upward, mouths agape, their weapons held slack at their sides. Septua whimpered in fear and would have run back to the archway, but it had closed behind them.

They could barely make out the tiers of seats for the blowing sheets of sand. The Scandis were cowering beneath their cloaks. Many were fleeing the stands, others were standing still, staring up in awe and disbelief, as stunned as the guards.

Randi crouched down and curled into a ball, putting her arms over her face and head, trying to protect her eyes from the driving sand. Allo seemed the least affected, for he was well protected by his thick covering of fur.

Septua scurried over to Randi and squatted down beside her, clearly too terrified to practice any rude behavior.

Braldt wondered why they had been brought into the ring at all during such a threatening bit of weather, but then as the wind increased, throwing up sheets of red sand and blowing it in horizontal waves across the arena, he began to see it as the opportunity they had been searching for. They could barely see. The guards and the Scandis were looking out for their own welfare; no one would abandon their search for shelter to stop and look for them.

Braldt reached down for Randi, grasped her arm, and began to pull her toward him. She looked at him through slitted fingers, then rose when he gestured urgently. Septua grabbed her leg and she turned to smack him, but the dwarf's eyes rolled in terror and it was obvious that he clung to her out of fear rather than lecherous thoughts. Allo quickly realized what Braldt was trying to do and seized the dwarf by the scruff of his neck, dragging him away from Randi. They bent low to get beneath the force of the wind and hurried forward, running with weapons before them in case they encountered a foolhardy guard.

And then the skies opened, parting with a thunderous crack that all but knocked them from their feet with the force of its impact. With that, bolts of malevolent, red lightning zigzagged from the pregnant underbellies of the clouds and struck the ground of the arena, as well as the tiers and whatever high points rose into the dark sky. There were screams of fear and cries that ended abruptly as the bodies containing them were struck down and scorched to shriveled husks.

Bolts slammed down on either side of the fleeing group and behind them as well, one coming so close that they could smell the acrid, bitter stink of it and feel its heat upon their flesh. It lent speed to their feet.

Then, before they could take another step, the clouds delivered their load, and rain, rain such as they had never seen before, began to pelt down, striking them with tremendous force, each drop painfully felt, like sleet. They stopped and stared at the moisture coating their bare arms. It was a clear fluid, but as red as blood and unpleasantly warm as well. The chill wind blew against them, causing the drops of red rain to course in rivulets, looking too much like blood for comfort. It coated their heads, soaked their hair, and dripped down into their eyes, nostrils, and mouths. It had a salty, coppery taste, much like blood itself. It was unsettling. Braldt could feel the fear rising in all of them, feel his own anxiety, and knew that he had to get them out of there quickly before their fear immobilized them.

Braldt literally jerked Randi off her feet. She was standing still, looking down in horror at her silver uniform which ran red, seemingly dripping with blood. She looked up at him with wide eyes that did not seem to see him. He shook her hard, and slowly, reason came back into her eyes. She blinked and nodded, giving him a weak grin to show that she was all right. Allo was shaken, but his phlegmatic nature prevented him from lapsing into hysteria. He stroked his moustache and tried to keep it from sticking together. It was a comic sight under the circumstances.

It was the dwarf that worried Braldt the most.

Septua was obviously stricken by the sight of blood coating his flesh. He kept turning his hand over in front of his face, riven by the horrific sight. Braldt wasted no time in subtleties, but slapped the dwarf hard across the face, then seized him by the nape of the neck and propelled him across the arena, leaving the others to follow.

They had nearly reached the other side when a figure loomed up out of the rain and wind-driven sand in front of Braldt, a huge, dark figure. Braldt grasped his sword and tried to get a firm grip on Septua while changing his course. He would much rather avoid an encounter—which seemed possible given the circumstances—than fight. The dark figure altered its course and moved directly into his path. Braldt cursed, wondering if it had been intentional, then shifted again. But the earth was growing slippery, the red sands soaking up the warm, red rain, becoming glutinous, and his feet slipped, causing him to lose his grip on the dwarf's neck. Septua wrenched free and slipped away from him, vanishing behind the curtains of rain without a backward glance, running like a rabbit runs from the lupebeast. Randi and Allo crashed into Braldt's back and the three of them struggled to keep their footing.

The dark figure moved toward them as they did what they could to regain their balance, draw their weapons, and choose a battle stance, for they had lost the opportunity to drift away under the cover of the rain.

The wind, which had died down once the rain began to fall, rose in a capricious swirl and blew aside the heavy folds of moisture, revealing the figure behind it. Batta Flor.

Braldt had never been so glad to see anyone in his life. The huge, shaggy Madrelli was the most welcome of sights. His heart leapt within his breast and he strode forward with a smile on his lips.

His steps faltered and he stopped and took a second look at the Madrelli, taking in many details that had escaped him at first glance. The Madrelli wore no sign of welcome on his face which was fixed in a dark scowl. One lip was raised, exposing a long, sharp incisor. But it was his eyes that caused Braldt to grip his sword more tightly and bring it up across his chest. The Madrelli's eyes gave no hint of warmth, of the deep friendship that had existed between them, no sign of intelligence. They were the eyes of an animal, the eyes of a dangerous animal, one who would attack and most certainly kill.

Braldt stared at him, wondering if there was some mistake, wondering if this could be some other Madrelli. This Madrelli seemed larger, more hulking and muscular than Batta Flor who far preferred peace to bloodshed and violence. It seemed almost impossible that this could be his gentle friend, but there was the matter of the ear which was torn from the head in a ragged line. Surely no two Madrelli bore the same terrible wound.

Then the wind whipped the rain aside and Braldt saw Keri, her wrist gripped tightly in the Madrelli's enormous paw, pulling against him, struggling futilely against his vast strength. Her eyes were wide and full of fear and her face was drawn and lined. There were dark circles under her eyes and black, blue, and yellowing bruises on her arms. She was thin, almost emaciated, and her torn and dirty garment hung on her like she was made out of sticks.

There was movement at her feet and Braldt saw a bloody figure inch along the muddy ground. It was Beast, one ear crushed against his head, an eye swollen shut, and his fur crusted with dark blood that in actual comparison looked nothing like the crimson rain. Beast raised his battered head and scented the air, his muzzle casting back and forth, searching. Braldt called his name and the lupebeast leaped forward, staggering on wobbly legs, and collapsed at Braldt's feet.

"Run, Braldt, run before he kills you!" Keri screamed, and as Braldt raised the whimpering pup in his arms, an immense club came sweeping down upon him.

Braldt ducked and lurched to one side as the red mud squelched beneath his feet. He lost his balance, though, and slipped, and it was this that saved him, for as he fell, still cradling the lupebeast pup in his arms, the huge club slammed down alongside his head and thudded into the earth.

Keri screamed, a high, thin sound filled with despair. Braldt rolled to the side, unwilling to relinquish the pup, for in its weakened condition, it would be an easy target. He scrambled to his feet and reached for his sword, realizing he had dropped it when he grabbed up the pup. Then Allo and Randi were at his side with weapons drawn, holding the enraged Madrelli at bay as he brandished his club before him and bellowed wordlessly.

Keri struggled against his grip, but it was like a gnat attacking an armored reptile and the Madrelli took no notice of her at all. But seeing Keri in such a state threw Braldt into a frenzy, and it was all he could do to prevent himself from running to her defense. He tried to remain calm, telling himself that Batta Flor was using her as bait, hoping to cause him to lose his rationality and draw him in close so that he could kill him. He reminded himself of the Madrelli's deep affection for Keri and tried to believe that it was all a sham and that Batta Flor would not really hurt her. But looking at the expressions of fear and rage he had trouble believing it.

Randi sidled close. "Friend, huh!" she hissed. "Heavens save us from your enemies!"

"I don't know what's wrong," said Braldt, trying to understand what could have caused the drastic change in the once gentle, pacifistic Madrelli.

"Well, it looks as though we'd better rescue your friend from King Kong, then figure out what went wrong later," Randi said dryly.

"King Kong?" asked Braldt.

"Never mind, old earth joke," muttered Randi. "Before your time, or mine, for that matter."

The three of them spread out, offering less of a target to the swinging club, which if it connected, could easily separate their heads from their shoulders.

Allo was very nearly identical in size to Batta Flor, but lacked his powerful musculature and the rage that seemed to drive him. Braldt wondered if Allo would be able to hold the Madrelli if they succeeded in separating him from the vicious club. Beast whimpered and struggled in Braldt's arms; Braldt put him down and the pup immediately began to bark and growl at the Madrelli.

The rain came down harder and harder and the lightning increased, striking on all sides, accompanied by tremendous claps of thunder louder than anything Braldt had ever heard. It was louder than mere sound; his ears ached and he was stunned by its depth and power. He could feel the vibration of each stroke in his bones and teeth. The intensity of the wind increased as well, whining and shrieking around the arena, tearing at their hair and clothes, plucking at their eyelids, pelting them with hard pellets of rain and sand.

Randi said something, but the words were torn from her mouth and scattered by the winds. It was impossible to hear anything except the sound of the storm. Braldt wanted nothing more than to run for cover or shield his head with his arms, for he felt as much danger from the storm as he did for Batta Flor. A bolt of lightning crackled out of the sky and plunged into the red earth no more than two feet in front of him.

The accompanying thunderclap was immediate and they reeled under its force; they staggered off balance and would have made easy victims except for the fact that Batta Flor and Keri were affected as well. Batta Flor was thrown to the ground, striking his elbow and losing his grip on Keri. Keri, who had been just as badly stunned by the thunderous detonation, nonetheless dropped to all fours and scrambled across the short distance that separated them, crawling behind Braldt, placing him between her and Batta Flor, clinging to him in desperation.

Batta Flor leaped to his feet, his mouth open in a scream of frenzied fury. He raised his club again and swung it high above his head. Braldt tried to shove Keri back out of reach, but she was frozen, her arms and legs rigid; her fingers digging into his arms so hard that it was impossible to dislodge her.

Randi raised her gun and pointed it at the Madrelli, a grim, determined look on her face. *"No!"* screamed Braldt, for despite all that had happened, he could not allow Batta Flor to be killed. But Randi ignored him completely and from the set of her jaw, Braldt knew that if Batta Flor followed through with his swing, she would surely fire. He had seen her dispatch a number of combatants with the gun and knew how accurate her aim was.

Batta Flor raised up on the balls of his feet, his eyes glittering with a manic rage, the club standing straight up. He was not deterred by the sight of the gun; he may not have even been aware of it for his eyes had never left Braldt and Keri.

Then it happened. An enormous, jagged bolt of lightning slammed down out of the seething clouds and struck the tip of the club. It shimmered and danced along the length of the weapon with a vivid, flaming light, then flowed around the massive paws that gripped the base of the club so tightly. The glowing incandescence traveled swiftly, progressing down the length of the Madrelli's enormous arms and jolting into the body itself.

Keri cried out and buried her face in Braldt's back, sobbing hysterically. Randi lowered her gun and looked at her intended target in horror, her face pale. She staggered back from the Madrelli, for the lightning was crackling around his body in all directions, causing his limbs to twitch and fly about wildly. He was out of control, flailing and thrashing, his teeth clenched and bared in agony, his eyes rolled back into his skull. The bolt released the Madrelli and disappeared as swiftly as it had appeared, leaving Batta Flor to collapse upon the wet earth, his body still with rictus.

He was arched backward, resting on head and heels, his body bowed above the muddy ground. Not even the pouring rain could cover the stench of burned flesh and singed fur. Tiny wisps of heat rose from the agonized corpse before being dissipated by the rain. The four witnesses hung back, held in place by the horror of what they had viewed, then Braldt flung himself forward, breaking the spell, and ran to the side of the one who had been his friend.

It was even worse up close. Braldt hurled himself on the Madrelli's chest, feeling the incredible heat that had charred the life from the immense body. He placed his head flat upon the arched chest, but could hear no heartbeat, no sound of life. He swung himself astride the contorted figure and began to pound Batta Flor's chest, screaming at him to breathe, to live. So frantic were his actions, so deep was his grief, that he did not even notice that every time he pushed down on Batta Flor's ribcage, chunks of burned fur and flesh sloughed off.

It was Keri's hysterical crying that brought him back to his senses. She had sunk to the sodden ground and was clutching her head with both hands, rocking back and forth and alternately screaming and crying. Randi knelt at her side and tried to calm her, tried to gather her in her arms, all animosity vanished, but Keri could not be comforted. Allo and the lupebeast pup stood to one side, the pup growling and whining with uncertainty, his lips drawn away from his teeth in an odd grin. Allo stroked the pup and watched with sad eyes, recognizing death and knowing it could not be reversed.

Braldt stumbled back from the thing that had once been his friend and took Keri in his arms. The rain bathed them in red streaks, the color of death and sorrow.

Suddenly Septua was there, running at full speed into the center of them, nearly tripping over Batta Flor's body. "Whoa!" he gasped, circling the charred corpse with wide eyes and cautious steps as he hurried to Braldt's side. "Gotta 'urry! C'mon, gotta get outta 'ere! The 'bots an' the guards, they're coming!"

"I'm surprised you bothered to think of us," Randi said dryly. "What's the matter, don't you think you can make it by yourself?"

" 'Ey, it's not that!" Septua squeaked with indignation. "It's just I di'n't want to leave you guys 'ere after all we been through together. We're friends, ain't we? Friends stick together!"

"So, you didn't think you could do it alone, right?" Randi repeated.

"Yeah, all right. So you know everything. Make you feel better? C'mon! We gotta get outta 'ere now, or you can tell the 'bots 'ow smart you are. See 'ow much it impresses 'em. An' somethin' weird is goin' on—there's a bunch a' blue guys everywhere!"

Braldt raised his head from Keri's shoulder. "Blue guys?" he said dully, then nodded to himself. "Yantra helps those who help themselves." He gripped Keri by her shoulders and shook her gently. "Come," he said. "There is nothing more we can do for Batta Flor; he is gone from this body. We can only help ourselves now. You know that he would not want us to stand and grieve for him if it costs us our lives."

"But—but, he . . ." Keri said tearfully.

"That was not Batta Flor," Braldt said firmly. "We

must remember him as he was and forgive him for what happened here. He was not himself.''

"Can you jabber later?'' Septua asked, jiggling nervously from foot to foot and looking around in all directions. "We ain't got all day!''

Allo placed a large hand in the center of Braldt's and Keri's backs and propelled them forward, away from the Madrelli's ruined body. The rain soon hid it from sight and as it disappeared behind them, they were somehow freed.

Now they could hear the sounds of combat, screams and yells and the clash of steel on steel. It grew steadily louder as they drew closer to the far side of the arena, although they were unable as yet to see anything other than the sheets of crimson rain.

It was not the sound of typical combat. There was confusion and hysteria in the cacophony of voices that could now be heard from all sides. The rain and lightning continued with undiminished ferocity, but now through the rain, they were able to make out a frieze of odd figures locked in combat around the edges of the tiers and spilling down over the walls into the arena itself. As they advanced, they could see that Septua had told the truth for once—there were indeed blue aliens everywhere.

They were not fighting so much as they were being fought—the blue rectangles did nothing but advance, or in some instances, stand still and allow the guards to come to them. In any event, the outcome was the same. Spears, swords, clubs, and fists had no effect on the strange creatures. No matter what touched them, it either passed through their slender bodies unharmed or was completely absorbed. The guards seemed to learn the lesson quickly as several of their number were sucked into the blue beings to vanish without a trace, and one after the other they turned and ran, their fear spreading like contagion.

The Scandis turned them back, forcing them to fight the blue aliens who rippled forward, implacable, undisturbed by anything, human or nonhuman. The Scandis stood tall and firm, ringing the guards, armed with weapons of their own, giving an indication of the strength they had once possessed, the strength they had used to carve an empire out of the heavens. They stood between the guards and escape, but they were not alone—standing before the Scandis was a line of hard ones wielding their rods of lightning. The guards were caught on the horns of a dilemma—no matter what they did, they could not win.

Then one guard, smarter than his companions, lay down his weapons and stood with arms outstretched, showing his empty hands as the alien drew close. The oncoming blue being did not even pause, but flowed over him, and the fearstricken guard passed through its body and emerged safe and unharmed on the other side. Seeing this, those guards around him immediately dropped their weapons and were spared the fate of those who continued to fight.

The blue aliens then advanced on the hard ones and the Scandis beyond, rippling their way over rows of stone seats and the bodies of the dead. Occasionally, one of them was struck by lightning. Their bodies, if that was what they could be called, seemed to absorb the charge, glowing briefly, bathed in a warm light that seemed to caress them; certainly they were not harmed. The guards, the robots, and the Scandis were not so lucky. The lightning was as fatal to them as it had been to Batta Flor, but it was little comfort watching them contort in the agonies of death.

The small group stood huddled at the base of the arena and conferred hurriedly, trying to decide what to do. Septua was in favor of heading off through the arches and finding a transmission station while the "blue guys" and their various enemies occupied each others' attention. Allo wanted to free the prisoners and Randi agreed. Keri was downcast and did not speak; Braldt did not want to leave her. He urged Allo and Randi toward the cells and took a threatening step toward the dwarf who squealed in fear and turned and ran after Allo, calling for him to wait.

Braldt settled Keri on a stone in the shelter of an arch, out of the driving rain, and chafed her hands between his own. Beast crawled between her feet and whined, pawing at her knees for attention. Braldt examined the pup quickly and saw that none of his injuries were critical; he would heal with time, although certainly his ear would never stand erect again.

At length, Keri seemed to bring herself under control and her tears diminished; she gave Braldt a tremulous smile and hiccuped. Braldt helped her to her feet, knowing a decision must be made. Even if they could defeat the Scandis, their task would not be done. Somehow, they had to return everyone to their home planet and this could not be done without the Scandis' cooperation. Furthermore, once all their mischief was undone, some way had to be found to ensure that it would not happen again.

Braldt was staring up at the tiers, watching the blue aliens advance on the hard ones, thinking that victory was within their grasp when something inexplicable happened. One blue alien after another stopped its rippling and stood slightly bowed as though listening. Then, in chain-like command, they lay down where they stood and rolled themselves into tight, motionless cylinders. The guards stared in astonishment, and after gaping at each other to see that they were not mistaken quickly retrieved their weapons.

The Scandis lost no time in directing the robots and the guards to gather up the now quiescent aliens like so many rolled rugs and take them away, back to whatever form of confinement they had shared before the outbreak. Only this time, Braldt had no doubt that the Scandis would find a way to keep them under control.

"Come on, we've got to get out of here," Braldt said to Keri, grabbing her by the hands and dragging her deeper into the arch, knowing that they had to vanish before the guards and Scandis found them, wondering what had gone wrong, why the aliens had ceased their attack. Perhaps they would never know; Yantra seemed to be a difficult god to understand.

The corridors echoed with voices as they plunged deeper into the immense labyrinth that lay under the arena. Almost immediately they began meeting prisoners freed by Randi, Allo, and Septua, rampaging toward the arena in search of weapons and retribution.

Keri and Braldt joined a group already armed; several members wore silver uniforms similar to Randi's. They were heavily bearded and their uniforms frayed and torn; it was obvious that they had been on Rototara longer than the others. One who appeared to be the leader sized Braldt up with a swift glance. "You Braldt?" he asked tersely. Braldt nodded. "Randi told me about you. Sent me to find you. Transmission station this way. Follow me."

Braldt looked around, seeing the hordes of prisoners pouring past him into the arena; hatred and the need to inflict pain burning in their eyes and scored on their tortured flesh. Braldt realized he would never be able to stop them, to convince them that they could not win and for all he knew, perhaps they could. Randi's friend had not stopped to see if Braldt was following him and was already a good distance away. Braldt made his decision, and pulling Keri by the wrist, hurried to catch up.

The flow of released prisoners increased as did clots of guards, bunched together, fighting desperately to stay alive and for the most part not succeeding. Braldt almost felt a moment's pity for them, for most of the guards had had no choice in the role they played, their only decision being guard duty or death in the arena.

They pushed their way through the struggling masses and soon found themselves traveling empty corridors with doors gaping open on either side, mute testimony to the panic which had seized the inhabitants. There were numerous bodies strewn on the floors in grotesque postures of death, the blood still flowing across the stone floor and swirling in thick pools. A few Scandis had met their deaths as well, and these corpses all seemed to wear stunned looks of surprise in their staring, blue eyes as though they could not believe their fate.

There was yet another corpse sitting with its back against the wall, swaddled in ragged layers of coarse robes. Braldt leaped over the outstretched legs and when he heard the whisper of his name thought at first that he had been mistaken. He stopped with difficulty and turned to see who had called him. At first he saw no one, then his attention was drawn to the bundle of rags on the floor, for it seemed to move slightly. One hand raised and signaled weakly, then fell back to the ground.

Braldt's heart sank and there was a leaden feeling in the pit of his stomach. There had been so much death already and there was no reason for this one to die. He was ashamed that he had forgotten about her. And Lomi—what of Lomi? "Saviq?" he said softly, dropping to one knee and gently pushing back the heavy folds of fabric that swathed her head.

He had half expected to see some horrendous wound, but there was nothing to be seen except the rheumy, filmed eye and the torment of ancient scarring that warped the old reptile's muzzle.

"I—I am glad you came," Saviq said quietly. "I do not know what is the matter with these old legs, they just refuse to go anymore. I sat down here to rest, but now I think it will be a longer rest than I had planned. But we did it, Lomi and I, we brought about the downfall. We have saved you, the two of us. Will you remember us, two old ones, after we have gone? No, that is too much to ask, you owe us nothing. Forget us, but do good things with your life and do not take the lives of others for granted."

"What are you saying?" asked Braldt. "I will not forget either one of you, and I will not leave here without you, do not fear. But tell me what it is that you and Lomi have done."

"It is too late for Lomi," Saviq said with a sad smile. "She is freed from her pain and sorrow. I was with her until the end. She is happy now."

"Lomi is dead?" Braldt asked numbly. "Why? How?"

Saviq shrugged. "She was old. We are both old. Our time has come. But we have done it, we have fixed the Scandis, she and I; their time here is over."

"What have you done?" Braldt asked again, seeing that Saviq was fading quickly, needing to know what was going to happen.

"Sent a message to Brandtson, your grandfather. Asked for help. He will come. Took a message to Jorund, he will stop the robots if he has the courage. One thing remains. Must open outer doors for the true ones. No time left for me. You must do it for me."

Then, even as Braldt bent over the ancient crone, trying to ease her labored breathing, her mouth twisted to one side and her single eye lit up as though it were receiving some private vision of joy. She was gone from them now; no one would ever be able to hurt her again.

Keri looked up at Braldt with a question in her eyes, wanting to know, but not daring to ask.

"A friend," Braldt said quietly, looking down on Saviq who had perhaps given her life to help people she did not even know. There was nothing more he could do to help her. He would follow her instructions even though he did not understand them. His grandfather! His heart leapt at the thought and he pulled Keri to her feet after saying a silent prayer over Saviq's still form.

Saviq was not aware of their departure, nor was she aware of the aches and pains of her weary body. Her flesh was still of the earth but her spirit was free. She was young and beautiful and her body lithe and graceful. She was not alone. She was lying atop a flat rock, reveling in the heat of the two suns beside her beloved. Soon the rains would come, the rains that would liberate her brethren from their dens, the dens where they had gone with the first of the great heat. The rains would free them and they would roam the land filled with a rage and madness, a blood lust that would only be satisfied when they had fought for the mate of their choice. She had already been won. She was beloved. She turned toward her lover, opened her arms wide, and gave herself up to his embrace.

25

Braldt pondered the meaning of Saviq's directive as he and Keri continued on down the corridor. Open the outer doors for the true ones? What did that mean? Who were the true ones and what outer doors did she mean? Would Jorund be able to disarm the robots? Only time would tell.

"We saw outer doors, I'm sure, when we first came," Keri said softly, scarcely daring to interrupt his thoughts. Braldt stopped abruptly. "Where?"

"I—I don't know," she said uncertainly, touching her throat with her hand. "Somewhere over there," she replied, gesturing to the warren of outer corridors.

Braldt was undecided. What to do? Randi and the others were waiting for him at the transmission station. He could go back to his own world and tell them what he had learned, try to convince them of all that he had seen and of the danger they were in. He wondered if they would believe him.

Or, he could do as Saviq said and open the outer doors for "the true ones." He yearned to return home. He wanted nothing more than to see the blue sky and the single sun of his own world as well as the faces of those he loved. But did he dare turn his back on so many of those who had given their lives to help them? His heart grew heavy and he knew what his choice must be.

"I must do as I was bid," he told Keri. "You and Beast are free to go if you wish. Find Randi and the others. They will send you home."

"I will not leave you," Keri said stubbornly, her eyes growing bright and the old determined sound coming back into her voice. The tone she had used to defy him since their earliest days when she was a tiny nuisance trailing after him and Carn where she was not wanted. Braldt was filled with joy at the sound, for it was the first sign of the old Keri. He squeezed her hand and smiled. "Show me these outer doors."

Leif Arndtson wondered at his good fortune and dared to hope that he might yet survive. Somehow, he had made himself understood by the furry savages who held him and the small remains of his command captive. He had been taken to their leader, an immense, grizzly, gray, furred creature with an angry, glowering countenance. Fortunately, he seemed to defer to an older, more gentle-natured Madrelli who appeared willing to listen to his story.

He was obviously disturbed at the news that the volcano was going to explode, but he did not seem to doubt Leif's word, which was very reassuring. After a moment of deep thought, the old one murmured a set of orders to the large, gruff commander who frowned with displeasure but did as he was ordered. He queried him on all the details of how the charges had been set and where they had been placed. Then, he and two others left the party and trotted off the way they had come.

By this time, many of the others had become aware that something was wrong. Leif and his small party were so obviously frightened and by more than their capture, that it was hard not to realize that something was amiss. The old Madrelli quieted everyone with raised hands, then turned to Leif and urged him to his feet. "You want to return to your world, Scandi. Well, you may have your wish, but know that if you return, you will not go alone. None of us here have any reason to love your people; they have sought to rule our lives and actions for too many generations. If you go back, we go with you, and we will not arrive with peace in our hearts."

Leif Arndtson could do nothing but bow his head at the old one's condemnation, for even he knew enough to know that the other's words were true. He had always accepted the domination of the Madrelli as rightful, for they were slaves and animals, were they not? But somehow, here in this place, they had an aura about them that made it impossible to think of them as either animals or slaves. But still, his allegiance had to be to his own people, didn't it? If he stepped back into his own world bringing a savage enemy down upon them, he would be a traitor to his own people. Yet if he were to live, it was the only way. It wasn't like he had a choice; the whole planet was going to explode any minute now. Surely they would understand!

The old Madrelli was speaking again. "I want you to explain what it is that is happening," he said. "Tell them why you are here, what you have done, and what it is that you are suggesting." Leif could do nothing but comply. He turned and faced the odd crowd, the furred Madrelli and the enraged, captive natives led by the one with the scarred face. He swallowed hard. If he had any hope of living, he would have to use all of his skills to convince them that transmitting to Rototara was their only chance for life. Speaking had never come easy. He gulped and began.

Much to his surprise, they had all been in favor of the plan, some of them openly enthusiastic, others merely stroking their weapons and smiling to themselves. It seemed that many of them had grievances to settle. The primitives had been hardest to convince, but in the end, it was the man with the burned face who had come to his aid. "Down with the false gods!" he had cried, waving his spear in the air. "Death to the priests!"

Leif Arndtson did not know what priests he was speaking of, but they could look out for themselves as far as he was concerned. He was too young to die and a part of him began to get angry that he had been sent to this place. Maybe they had not thought that he would return. Maybe he had a few debts of his own to settle!

He led the odd group of savages and primitives to the transmitter, and after a brief message of instruction, began to send them through two and three at a time, all of them gripping their weapons in eager anticipation of what was to come.

Braldt, Keri, and the lupebeast pup had wandered through the confusing labyrinth of corridors, searching for the outer doors as commanded by Saviq. It was the pup who found them, lifting his head and sniffing, then whimpering and hurrying off down a corridor on his own. Braldt and Keri had followed.

They were huge, double doors with no handles or method of opening, except for the silver plate set into the wall. There was an odd sound coming from the far side of the door, a scratching, scrabbling noise. Braldt stared at the door, undecided, wondering what he would find if he opened the door. What were the true ones? Only one way to find out. He gave Keri a hug of reassurance, then struck the silver door plate with his fist. The door hissed open and there on the other side were multitudes of reptiles, as tall as Braldt and broad, banded with sheaths of muscle, claws and fangs bared, ready for battle.

"Are you the true ones?" asked Braldt, backing up and raising his hands to show that he meant them no harm. Beast growled and showed his own fangs, but was wise enough to remain behind Braldt. Keri, oddly enough, seemed to feel no fear.

"We are the true ones," the reptiles said in unison, bobbing and weaving their horny snouts, their eyes bright and shiny, fixed and unblinking on Braldt. Their scales were washed by the warm, crimson rain, slick and sleek and gleaming. They seemed to revel in its caress. With a start, Braldt realized that they were indeed the true ones, native Rototarans somehow brought forth by the rains, ready to reclaim their world.

"We are not your enemy," Braldt said simply. "We were sent by one named Saviq who commanded us to admit you. We will not stand in your way, but know that there are many inside who were brought here against their will and wish for nothing other than the right to return to their own worlds. Grant them mercy.''

The true ones did not answer, but swept past Braldt, Keri, and Beast without a second glance. Their numbers were endless as they filed through the open doors, slithering and sliding on the wet, red earth, their heavy tails gummed with sediment. They plodded forward in a relentless wave and Braldt felt a moment of fear and pity for the unsuspecting Scandis. It soon passed.

Other doors were found and opened, and more and more masses of true ones trooped through, all fixated with a single-minded purpose, that of reclaiming their world.

There were no more doors left to open. The sounds of alarm and furious battle that had emanated from the center of the arena had diminished. Braldt and Keri wandered from corridor to corridor, searching for the transmission room, wondering if they were too late.

A door opened, one of the hundreds of thousands, all of which looked alike, and Randi appeared, a worried look on her narrow face. She saw Braldt and her eyes lit up. She smiled and gripped him hard, all but ignoring Keri.

''I was afraid I would miss you. Allo and I waited. Septua, he wanted to leave, so we sent him back.'' Her mouth twisted in the familiar, wry grin that had brightened their darkest moments.

''No real loss,'' Braldt replied with an answering grin, gripping Randi as well, knowing somehow that he would never see her again.

''I hope you find everything you search for in this

life," he said, feeling the warmth of her and knowing that her leaving would leave an empty place in his heart. Their eyes met. She raised her hand and held it to his face, then nodded once. "You too," she whispered. "Be happy."

Then she was gone. She looked back at him once, then nodded to the Scandi who manned the controls of the transmitter. He adjusted a dial, punched in some numbers, then touched a single red button and Randi faded from sight and was gone.

Allo had waited as well. Their words were brief, the emotion high. It was hard knowing they would never meet again.

Allo was gone. Randi and Septua were gone. No one remained except the Scandi at the controls. Braldt cleared his throat and blinked back the tears that had suddenly filled his eyes. Now he was able to see that the one at the controls was none other than the man on the dais, the one who had tried to encourage him with silent messages of hope. Braldt opened his mouth to speak, but before he could say a word, there was a flash of light and a group of people, Scandis, Madrelli, and a man, horribly scarred and without hair, tumbled through the transmitter and fell into the room.

Braldt was speechless. He and Keri and the Scandi stared at the jumble of odd companions in astonishment. Keri was the first to recover. "Carn!" she cried, rushing to his side. Braldt realized with a shock the hideously deformed man was indeed Carn, his brother. And there, too, was Uba Mintch. Where had they come from? Before he could ask, there was another flash of light and a fully armed contingent of Scandis came through, all but falling over the Madrelli and Carn. They stumbled forward as another flash lit the small room and more Madrelli, three wounded Scandis and more of Braldt's tribe fell into the room. Voices and weapons were raised in anger, and for a moment it looked as though fighting might break out among the three disparate groups.

Chaos and confusion reigned as more and more transmissions filled the room with seething, yelling, angry beings from different worlds, flinging them at each other's feet, crowding them out of the small room, all of them jockeying for control and none succeeding.

Finally, it seemed that the transmissions were ended. The corridors were filled with the various tribes who had sorted themselves out at last and were glowering at one another and hurling insults. But no actual fighting had begun, for they were evenly matched and no one group knew what to expect if fighting actually began. What if one group allied with another? It was too uncertain. It was easier to throw insults. Nor was it safe to turn and run. It was an intergalactic stand-off.

The man at the controls rose. "Brandtson?" he asked, tentatively. "Then the message did reach you. I—I didn't know if it would."

An old man, taller and bulkier than Braldt, his once blond hair shot with silver and worn long upon his shoulders, stepped forward. "Jorund! That message, it came from you! Is it true? Is he really here, the one they call Braldt?"

Braldt stepped forward, his steps hesitant, feeling at

a loss for the first time in his life. "Sir, I am the one known as Braldt. And you are the father of my father?"

The two men stared at each other, the longing apparent in their eyes. Keri looked from one to the other and saw how much alike they were. There was no mistaking that they were kin.

Braldt started to speak. He took a step forward, and then the transmitter seemed to explode outward, deafening them with the power of the force. A portion of a body flew through the remains of the device and landed on the floor with a bloody thump.

A loud outcry went up among the Madrelli and Braldt's tribe; a sob, screams of rage and deepest despair.

Braldt picked himself up from the floor and looked around him in complete confusion. What had happened?

"Our world is gone," said the thing that had once been his brother. "You have killed our world, you and your kind."

"What is he saying?" Braldt asked, turning to Jorund and Brandtson, refusing to believe that Carn could be speaking the truth.

Brandtson turned to a large display on the wall, studied it for a moment, then turned to Braldt. "There has been a disturbance; it appears that K7 is gone," he said heavily. There was a loud outcry at his words and the Madrelli and Braldt's tribe surged forward, only to be held at bay by Brandtson's men.

"We are not your enemy!" cried Brandtson, holding up his hands and trying to be heard. "We have risked much and lost much in our lives and we are here to aid you. We are allies!"

It was difficult convincing them of the truth of his words, but eventually, since they had nothing to lose and everything to gain, they allowed themselves to be convinced.

"Let us end this fight that has cost us our children and the children of our children," said Brandtson. "There can be no victory based upon defeat."

"What will become of us even if the fighting ends?" asked Keri, her face streaked with tears and her heart aching with the thought of all she had lost. "Our world and all that we love is gone. You and others like you have killed it. How can we ever forget?"

"There is another world," Brandtson replied at last, his voice gruff with emotion and unshed tears glittering in his eyes. "It is our world, that which we have carved out of the universe for those of our kind. It is a beautiful world. It is Valhalla. After all that we have done to you, all that has happened, it is only fitting that it become your world as well."

"But, Brandtson . . . how, there are many who will oppose you," stammered Jorund, staring at Brandtson as though he had lost his mind. "It can never be."

"It must be," Brandtson said firmly as he took Braldt's hand in his own then topped it with the shiny scarred hand of the embittered Carn and the furred hand of the old Madrelli, "there can be no other way."